Love and Other Chances

TRACY BAACK

**LOVE AND OTHER . . .
BOOK TWO**

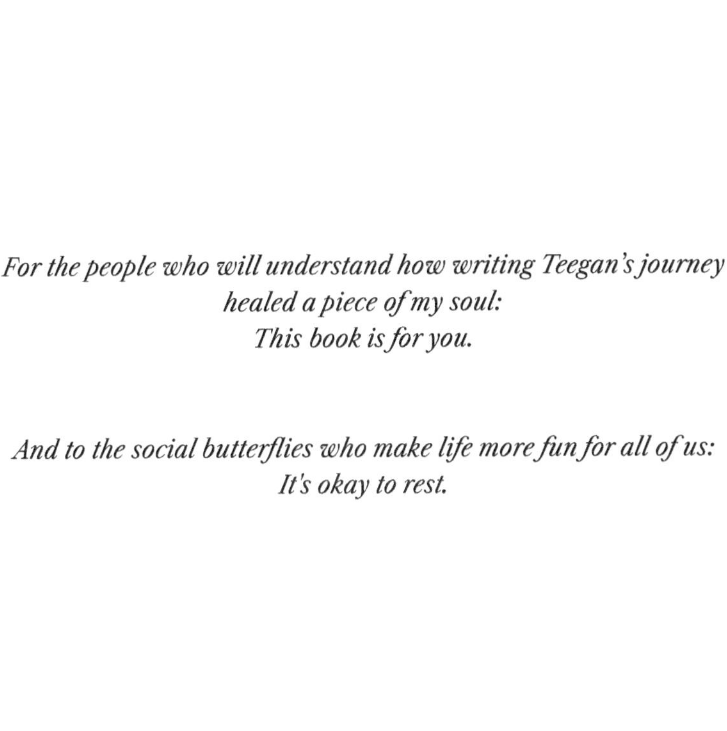

*For the people who will understand how writing Teegan's journey
healed a piece of my soul:
This book is for you.*

*And to the social butterflies who make life more fun for all of us:
It's okay to rest.*

Author's Note

Welcome to Teegan's story! We first met Teegan as one of Lana's best friends in *Love and Other Goals*. If you haven't read that book already, I did my best to write *Love and Other Chances* as a standalone that you will still enjoy. BUT . . . I think you will appreciate this one so much more if you read the books in order. Just my two cents. And Teegan agrees—she's the biggest hype girl ever for her best friends, so she'd want you to dive into Lana's world first. Add in Teegan's two cents, and now you have four cents. If four cents is not enough, you may proceed now. You will still thoroughly enjoy this book.

This novel is a closed-door, kisses-only romance.

If you are a sensitive reader, you can refer to the content considerations below. However, if you don't have particular sensitivities, here's your signal to turn the page and avoid even minor spoilers!

Content Considerations: Divorced parents; present grief over past death of parent

CHAPTER ONE

At the chime of the doorbell, I drop to the floor behind the kitchen counter.

My knee bangs against the tile, but I don't dare cry out.

"Teegan! Are you there?" Loud knocks accompany the voices calling my name through the door.

I sneak a peek around the edge of the cabinet. A cluster of girls' faces peer in the window beside the front door, visible from the kitchen. I opened the curtains this morning to let in the natural light, but now I regret not closing them when I got home a few minutes ago. Gina, my roommate and coworker, isn't home, so I was simply standing in the silence until the doorbell interrupted.

"Teegan! We're leaving to go swing dancing! Are you coming? Are you in there?" the voices clamor. I hold my breath, my body as still as death, afraid that they'll sense I'm home if I move an inch.

"I thought she was coming, but maybe not."

"Maybe she's meeting us there."

"I'll text her."

My eyes widen with panic. I reach a hand up to the counter and feel around until I find my phone. I quickly unlock it and switch it to silent a second before the text comes through. Breathing a sigh of relief, I click the screen off and listen as the girls retreat from the door.

I sit up, leaning my back against the cabinet. Closing my eyes, I breathe slowly, gulping in the silence.

What am I doing?!

My eyes fly open.

Before I can talk myself out of it, I unlock my phone and pull up FaceTime, typing in the names of my two best friends, Amaya and Lana. I hit the green call button and chew on my lip, hoping they'll answer.

Lana's face appears first. Her waist-length brunette hair is pulled up in a high ponytail, and her green eyes are filled with concern. "Teegs? What's up with the impromptu video call?"

Before I can answer, Amaya joins the call. Her forehead is beaded with moisture and furrowed with worry. She's outside, wearing an athletic tank top with her coily hair slicked back in a low bun. *Leave it to Amaya to be out for a run on a Saturday evening.*

"What's going on, Teeg?" Amaya asks, breathing heavily. "We have our regular group call tomorrow afternoon—what made you call now?"

"Can't a girl just want to talk to her Beefs without everyone questioning her motives?" I respond, forcing mirth into my voice.

The three of us have called each other "Beefs" ever since we met freshman year of college. When Amaya didn't like the term "besties," I started calling us "Be Fris" like the first half of a "Be-st Fri-ends" necklace. The nickname quickly got shortened to the single syllable "Beef."

Despite the fact that we're mature adults three years out of college, the term of endearment has stuck with us.

Unfortunately, my Beefs see right through my attempt at levity.

"Uh, no," Lana responds bluntly. "You have way too much going on to video call us out of the blue. Especially on a Saturday night."

A voice calls from the background of her video. "Everything okay, Lana?" Her screen moves as she stands, and a second later I see her husband's face next to her.

"Yeah, babe, I'm going to go talk to Amaya and Teegan in our room for a minute," Lana responds before planting a kiss on Mateo's cheek. They started dating at the beginning of our senior year of college and were married just over a year later. They're so obsessively adorable that I almost forget the reason I called.

"Okay, what gives, Beef?" Amaya asks as Lana closes the door and flops onto her bed.

Lana squints her eyes. "Where even are you?"

"Ummm, sitting on the kitchen floor," I answer.

"Why?" Amaya asks.

"Uhhh, because I'm . . . hiding," I say.

"You're hiding? Are you in trouble?!" Lana's voice rises with the question.

"No, no, nothing like that," I reassure them. "I'm just . . . avoiding the group of sorority girls going swing dancing tonight."

Crickets.

Amaya and Lana both stare at me. I see their eyes move to each other's screens, make virtual eye contact, then move back to mine.

I clear my throat. "So, it dawned on me that something might be wrong. With me. You know, when I ducked out of sight instead of answering the door."

"Yeah, ya think?" Amaya replies with a slight roll of her eyes.

Lana's voice is laden with suspicion. "You love going swing dancing. You love doing everything. There's clearly something wrong if you're hiding in the kitchen instead of socializing. *Why are you hiding?*"

I chew my lip, considering how to answer. *Do I even know why I'm hiding? Why don't I want to go out tonight? Why am I cowering behind the cabinets?*

"I guess the thought of going dancing tonight makes me feel a little . . . explodey?" I explain.

More blank stares.

"Explodey?" Amaya questions.

"You know what, I'm being silly," I say with a wave of my hand. "This week has been packed full of awesome. I was able to hang out in the different sororities after their recruitment activities ended each day, and we had amazing training at our daily Arrow staff meetings. We went over so much content, it was like drinking from a fire hose in the best way possible."

I'm beginning my fourth year as a staff member with Arrow, a Christian group that helps students grow in their faith throughout college. Amaya, Lana, and I were involved when we were students at Townsend University, located in the mid-sized city of Brooklyn, Kansas. We even spent multiple summers together at Arrow's Summer Project, an eight-week program in Florida designed to help college students grow as spiritual leaders.

After graduating, I stayed in Brooklyn to join the Arrow staff team full time while Lana started law school in D.C. and Amaya embarked on a business-world takeover in Kansas City.

I let out a mildly manic laugh. "I don't know what came over me. Temporary insanity. Of course I want to go swing dancing and hear about how all the girls are doing now that recruitment week is over! Sorry to bug you, Beefs!"

"Oh, no you don't," Amaya chides. "Don't you dare hang up, Teeg. So, you spent every day this week in staff meetings and then went straight to a different sorority every evening?"

"Well, yeah, just like every year!" I respond, trying to sound chipper.

"But you also took on a lot more responsibility at the Summer Project this year, right?" Lana asks. When I shrug and nod, she continues. "Did you take any time for yourself to rest or recharge before jumping back into beginning-of-school madness?"

I make a noncommittal *hmmm* sound.

"So that's a no," Amaya states.

"After Summer Project ended, I went on a girls' retreat with our newest staff girl, Gina, who graduated from Townsend in May. You know, my new roommate. We spent a weekend with some of the other Arrow staff girls from the Midwest region so she could get to know more people. After that, I hosted a weekend slumber party for some of the Arrow student leaders who are in sororities. They needed a chance to bond and dream about the upcoming school year before rush week."

"So that's a no to the resting," Lana echoes Amaya.

"But it was fun! I love getting to pour into all these girls and hang out together. It's not like I was locked away at a desk job somewhere with no windows and only florescent lights. My life is awesome!" I chirp, trying to keep that weird panicky feeling locked away in my chest.

Lana and Amaya make more virtual eye contact.

"Teegs, I think you're burning out," Lana observes gently.

"But I can't burn out doing something I enjoy! Socializing is the essence of my being. How could I get tired of that?"

"Yeah, but you've been constantly pouring out into everyone else, Beef," Amaya adds. "Not only this week, but the whole summer."

"More like the past three years," Lana chimes in. "Yes, you love socializing. But you're constantly hanging out with students you're mentoring. Do you have any friends you're socializing with?"

"But I *do* see the girls in my Bible studies as friends. Just because I'm older and the leader doesn't mean I'm their mom," I justify.

"That's not what I mean, and you know it. Do you have any *peers* you're hanging out with regularly?" Lana pushes.

Hmmmm, how do I spin this? Sure, I've gone the past three years without ever hanging out with people outside of the Arrow universe. But it's not like I don't have fun.

"Well, I have you two, obviously. Beefs for life, remember? What more could I need?!" I respond.

"Wrong answer," Amaya says with a frown. "You know that Lana and I both have new friends that we hang out with even though the three of us will always be *best* friends. You need people there with you in person, Teegan. Having *friends* to socialize with purely for the fun of it is different than socializing with students because it's part of your job."

"You can't always be the one pouring out into other people all the time, Teegs," Lana adds. "I know that you love helping people have the best time all the time, but you need people filling up your cup too. Or you wind up hiding in a dark kitchen."

I sigh. As much as I don't want to admit that something really is wrong with me . . . their comments are hitting home. I've thrown myself into my staff role for the past three years, never turning down an opportunity to invest time with students. Always planning epic social events to help everyone enjoy their college experience.

Of course, there are the other members of our staff team who are more like peers. But we're always hanging out in the context of the ministry, not casually as friends. Even when we *try* to hang out casually as friends, we wind up troubleshooting issues with students or coming up with new ideas for Arrow events.

I have coworkers, and I have younger girls I'm investing in. But I guess I don't really have any friends here.

Heat burns behind my eyes, but I don't want to plunge into those sad feelings right now. I talk to distract my thoughts.

"Okay, hypothetically, if you were right, then what would I need to do about it?" I ask.

"You need to meet some peers who aren't wrapped up in the worlds of Townsend or Arrow. Have you met many people at your church?" Lana asks. During my first year on staff, I switched from the church most popular with college students to a different one. I guess I recognized a need for some separation from my full-time ministry job and my personal life. But apparently, I didn't follow through beyond that small effort.

"Not a lot. Well, there's this one woman named Joy who I've talked to several times," I muse. "She and her husband are a few years older than us, but we tend to sit in the same area each week and chat after the service for a few minutes."

"She seems like a good starting point," Amaya says. "Why don't you talk to her tomorrow morning? Ask her to get dinner or coffee sometime?"

"Yeah, I guess I could do that. Hopefully they go to the late service, since I'm sure I won't make it to the early one after swing dancing tonight."

"Absolutely not," Amaya declares, while Lana simultaneously dictates, "Don't you dare."

I huff a laugh in spite of myself.

"No swing dancing. No nothing tonight," Lana says. "Stay home, watch a movie, take a shower, or whatever relaxing thing sounds appealing. Go to bed early. Let your body rest, Beef."

"And that's an order," Amaya concludes with gusto, although they're both smiling warmly at me.

I avert my eyes to the ceiling to try to quell the burning sensation behind them again. *I miss them so much.* The technology of video calls is a blessing I count often, but it's not the same as hugging my Beefs in the flesh. I miss our days of hanging out in the Alpha Omega Pi house—studying, listening to music, discussing boy problems, watching movies, doing Bible studies, attending sorority events together. Everything together.

"I promise I will," I finally say, bringing my eyes back to their faces on my phone screen. "And I'll report back on our regularly-scheduled call tomorrow afternoon, since I know that was your next command, LaLa." Lana's open mouth closes, and she smiles at me.

"I miss you, Teegs," she says. "I miss *both* of you. I have to find a time to make it back to Kansas this fall to see you."

We wrap up the conversation and say our goodbyes.

In the silence of our ended video call, I try to breathe deeply, evenly.

Do I want to keep doing this job? Can *I keep doing this job?*

The thought creeps in like a leech looking for a place to latch on to. I shake my head and stand up, unwilling to dwell on the doubt.

I finally open the text message about swing dancing, feeling guilty for abandoning my plans to join them. Gina is over at the dorms meeting students. *Will she judge me if I stay in tonight instead of spending time with students?*

But I remember my promise to Lana and Amaya, so I send a short text saying I won't make it tonight.

I decide to take a long shower, blasting my "Dancey Taylor Swift" playlist at full volume. Singing along with her greatest upbeat hits distracts me from lingering on the negative thoughts that keep tapping on the door to my mind.

———

"Teegan, I'm so happy to see you!" Joy's face lights up when she turns around after the service ends and spots me in the row behind her. I'd arrived a few minutes late to the church service after sleeping in, and I scanned the backs of everyone's heads, hoping to find Joy's signature pixie cut next to Caleb's crew cut. Thankfully, I spotted them in their usual section and snuck into a seat behind them.

I lean into her hug, already feeling a smidge more peace after seeing her smile. "It's great to see you again!"

"Where have you been all summer? It feels like forever since I last saw you at church," Joy says.

"Yeah, I spent the entire summer at Arrow's Summer Project in Florida. Normally, I would have had a couple of weeks off, but our leaders, Kent and Rachel, had twins over the summer. So I had to stay and keep things running since they couldn't be there," I explain. "And last weekend I had about fifteen sorority girls sleeping all over my duplex, so, needless to say, I didn't make it to church last Sunday."

Joy laughs, crinkling the corners of her brown eyes. "Whew, that sounds like a lot! I'm glad that you're back. Want to go get a donut from the lobby? I'm starving."

I agree, and we make our way out of the church sanctuary. "There's actually something I wanted to talk to you about," Joy says as we pick out donuts. "Caleb and I are starting a new small group with young twenty-somethings this year. I know you're busy leading lots of Bible study groups with students, but I would love it so much if you'd consider joining us. You wouldn't have to do any prep work—just show up and be with us!"

That eye-burning sensation is back, and I seriously need it to stop showing up. I smile widely at Joy, hoping it will distract her from noticing the sheen of moisture in my eyes. "I would really love to be a part of the group, Joy. This is kind of an answer to prayer. Do you know when you'll be meeting?"

"We're thinking Wednesday evenings, although we might do some fun social events on weekends sometimes. Would that work in your schedule? I was hoping that since your Arrow meetings are on Thursdays and the Greek houses have chapter meetings on Wednesdays, you might be more available that evening," Joy says.

"Wow, you remember all that? And you planned the group around my schedule?" I ask, wide-eyed.

Joy laughs. "I told you, I really want you to join us. I know you're a busy woman, so I tried to make it work for you. What do you think?"

The warmth of Joy's smile saturates my heart and gradually spreads through my body. I'm taken aback by her thoughtfulness, her effort to include me. That's usually *my* job.

"Yes. I'll make it work, no matter what. Thanks so much for asking me," I reply.

"Ah! I'm so glad!" Joy exclaims. "We're planning to start next Wednesday evening with a social night for everyone to start getting to know each other. I'll text you our address."

As she walks away to find Caleb, I inhale deeply, feeling my lungs expand more fully than they have all week. With classes starting tomorrow and our first weekly Arrow meeting of the year on Thursday, it's sure to be a hectic week. But I already feel more calm knowing I have this small group social to look forward to.

Find peers who are just friends and not coworkers or mentees—check!

CHAPTER TWO

The first week of class is always a marathon run at sprint speed for our staff team. We're focused on meeting new students by spending extra time on campus, helping freshmen feel welcome at Townsend, and easing their anxiety about starting college.

Throughout the week, the notes app on my phone fills up with dozens of entries like "Samantha, brown hair AOPi, third floor of Boyd Hall, from Wichita, likes skiing and hot tea." It's the only way I can hope to keep track of all the faces and names.

This is typically my week to shine—welcoming people and figuring out how to make their lives more fun is one of my favorite pastimes. Coming into the week on the verge of a burnout breakdown has put a damper on my sparkle, though. But whenever that overwhelmed sensation starts to take over, I let my mind fly away to the church small group social that I'm anticipating.

Thursday night brings our first large-group Arrow meeting. It's pretty much a church service tailored specifically to college students. There's worship music, a message designed to help everyone grow in their faith, and lots of socializing. Ever since my senior year of college, I've been in charge of planning the After Party following the weekly meeting—a fun activity or special location for Arrow students to hang out and have fun.

There are several favorite activities or restaurants around town that we cycle through, but it's been a personal challenge to come up with new and *more* fun ideas for the first After Party each year. Unfortunately, I outdid myself last year planning a massively popular glow paint war at City Park. I'm worried that people will be expecting something even more epic this year—the year that my creative social juices have been running dry. If so, they'll be disappointed when they find out we've rented out the bowling alley in the basement of the student union, exactly like I did my senior year of college.

I'm trying not to fixate on the potential disappointment as I help set up chairs before the meeting begins. The band is rehearsing, and the new Maverick City Music song they're trying out has me singing along and calming down.

I head out to the lobby of the student union to make sure the welcome team is ready to go with name tags, and I see Rachel come in pushing her double stroller. Kent and Rachel have been the directors of Arrow at Townsend for the past decade, even before I was a student here. They had their first baby this summer—surprised to find out they were having not one, but two. The twins were healthy but spent a couple of weeks in the NICU to grow a little bigger before they could go home.

Rachel's lack of consistent sleep has meant I haven't seen much of her the past month, so I'm extra excited to see her here with the twins tonight. I rush over to greet her with a huge hug.

"Oh my goodness, look at their adorable mini headphones!" I exclaim, cooing over the tiny sleeping babies in the stroller.

"They're adorable when they're sleeping. Now if only they'd do more of it!" Rachel sighs. "Speaking of sleep, I wanted to ask you a favor. I know I usually lead the morning leadership book study for the senior girls, but I was hoping you could do it this year, at least for this fall semester? I don't think I'll be functional enough to lead them well."

"Of course I can!" I respond, forcing my usual enthusiasm into my voice. "I'd love to spend time with those girls."

"You're a lifesaver, Teegan. So glad we have you on the team," Rachel says appreciatively. Just then, the first wave of students arrives at the meeting, and all the girls swarm around us to get their first glimpse of the twins. I back away from the group, using the fact that all the attention is on the babies as an opportunity to retreat to the restroom.

I'm alone, so I talk out loud to myself in the mirror. "This is great, Teegan! You love those senior girls! They were your little freshman babies your first year on staff—how special to get to end their college years with them! This is going to be so much fun! Sure, early mornings are hard for you, but you can do anything in the name of having a good time with people!"

The door starts to open, so I quickly clam up and pretend I'm washing my hands. I need to get back out to the lobby anyway because I promised Lana I'd watch out for Sofia tonight. Sofia was one of the English Language Learner students Lana tutored through an after-school program in the Brooklyn school district, starting when Sofia was just a sixth grader. Now, she's starting as a freshman at Townsend, which officially makes me feel old.

I greet students in the lobby while keeping an eye out for Sofia. She's still living at home with her parents, so she may not have had as many opportunities to meet new friends.

A few minutes before the meeting begins, I see Sofia come up the stairs, laughing with a group of six other girls. So much for not meeting new friends yet. Considering how Lana used to describe Sofia's spunky personality, I shouldn't be surprised.

I wave to Sofia, and she runs forward to hug me, despite us only having met a couple of times. "Teegan!" she exclaims. "It's so fun to see you! Have you talked to Lana lately? How's she doing?"

Smiling, I tell Sofia, "It's good to see you too! And Lana's doing great. I mean, she's in the thick of her final year of law school, which is apparently the hardest, but you know Lana. She'll meet the challenge head-on."

"Oh, I do know," Sofia affirms. "And what about that hot husband of hers?" She waggles her eyebrows, causing me to burst out laughing.

"As far as I know, Mateo's doing great too," I say. "He's fully recovered from his injury. But he's focusing on the youth soccer program he started instead of playing soccer professionally. I think he's starting classes towards his master's degree too, but I'll have to ask Lana. Now, how are *you* doing? How was your first week of class?"

Sofia fills me in on her start to college and introduces me to the friends she brought with her. Music streams from the meeting room as the band starts playing the first song, so we make our way into the room.

I take a seat next to a group from AOPi, my old sorority. Although I lead Bible studies with girls from multiple sororities now, old habits die hard. Especially when your sorority pride runs deep, thanks to your best friend being the greatest sorority president ever. No one has been able to live up to Amaya's legacy, but AOPi is still going strong.

As the meeting winds down, the student emcee shares the final announcements. I steel myself for a lackluster response to the After Party activity. The enthusiastic cheer from the crowd causes me to breathe a sigh of relief. I forget that college students can be pretty easy to please when it comes to social activities.

I make my rounds at the bowling alley, taking time to converse with everyone I know and introducing myself to the new faces. Despite the exhaustion I feel, I maintain my flawless social performance—asking interesting questions, telling funny stories, drawing quieter girls into the conversations, and smiling broadly the entire night.

When I fall into bed at 1:00 a.m., knowing I have to meet Rachel and the senior girls in six hours, the suffocating overwhelm creeps its way into my mind. I push the stifling thoughts away, focusing on Joy's smile on Sunday and the possibility of making new friends at next week's social. It's enough to quiet my mind and to fall into a deep sleep, however short it may be.

———

I stand in front of my full-length mirror and consider my reflection. A pile of clothes sits discarded on the bed behind me, the collateral damage of finding just the right outfit for my first small group social.

It's not a church service, so a dress seemed a little too much. But most people my age are working in office buildings, schools, or hospitals. You know, grown-up places of employment. Not hanging out with college students all day. So I'm not quite sure what my *peers* would wear to a casual social gathering.

After cycling through shirt combinations with jean shorts, leggings, and an athletic skirt, I finally settled on a pink sleeveless jumpsuit. It's airy enough that I won't get too hot, even in the Kansas heat, and I'm dressing it down with light makeup and tiny rose gold hoop earrings.

I straighten my blonde hair enough to tame the frizz from the lingering summer humidity. It falls to my shoulder blades now, slightly longer than I used to wear it in college. I consider tying half of it back with a bow but decide against it. I'm not sure if my *peers* embrace the same style as college girls. Amaya and Lana are too busy revolutionizing the world to give me fashion advice.

Rolling my shoulders back, I lift my chin and meet my own gaze in the mirror, staring directly into my blue eyes. "Let's do this, Teegan Jones. It's time to go make friends!"

Ten minutes later, I park in front of the address Joy sent me. There are a few other cars in the driveway and on the street already, assuring me I've found the right place. I make my way up to the porch of the remodeled craftsman house. It's a heck of a lot cuter than the half of a duplex that Gina and I share.

As soon as I set foot on the porch, Joy opens the door and pulls me into a hug.

"Teegan! I'm so glad you're here! Come in and let me introduce you to everyone," she exclaims, guiding me through the entryway. In the living room, Joy introduces me to a young married couple and two single guys. I try to remember names, but I know I'm going to need to write them down before the end of the night.

Joy leads me to the kitchen where the snacks and drinks are located. There are three other women filling plates and talking. One woman looks to have come straight from work, dressed in a perfectly-tailored gray pantsuit. Her microlocs look so immaculate that she should be featured in every advertisement for whatever stylist she sees. A second woman is dressed casually in jean shorts and a top, her brown hair pulled back in a low bun, and the redheaded woman is wearing scrubs.

"Hey there, ladies. I want you to meet Teegan!" Joy says. I reach my hand out to each as they introduce themselves—Catherine, Sarah, and Natalie. "Grab some food and get to know each other a little. I'm going to go check in with Caleb."

I take a Spindrift from the giant bowl filled with ice and various drinks. Sarah, the brunette, hands me a plate, which I begin filling with vegetables, pita bread, and hummus. I start peppering the girls with questions about how long they've lived in Brooklyn and what they do for work.

Natalie, the one wearing scrubs, says she works as a labor and delivery nurse at the local hospital. Sarah is an office assistant at a pediatric practice, and Catherine works at an engineering firm in town. When they ask what I do, I try to concisely sum up my hard-to-describe job.

"I work with college students full time, meeting with them in small group Bible studies or mentoring them one-on-one to help them grow in their faith," I explain.

"So is your schedule consistent?" Sarah asks.

"Oh no, each day is a little different. It's far from a nine-to-five job because everything depends on students' schedules. I fit in my one-on-one meetings with girls between their class schedules on the weekdays. Most of my small group Bible studies happen in the evenings, and sometimes I hang out socially with students on the weekends to reinforce those relationships. But I do have some consistent blocks in my schedule—staff meetings twice a week plus our weekly large group gathering on Thursday nights," I expound.

"Wow, I don't know that I could handle the lack of routine," Catherine admits. "I need a well-ordered calendar to maintain my sanity. But it sure sounds like a rewarding job!"

I swallow a bite of pita before responding. "It definitely is. I thrive off of spontaneity, so it's a good fit—most of the time."

Joy steps up to our group and places a hand on my shoulder. "I'm officially rounding everyone up to the living room. We're expecting one more person, but we're going to go ahead and start getting settled."

We nod and turn to follow her, but Sarah stops me.

"Wait, you have to try one of my chocolate chip oatmeal cookies," Sarah says, handing me a giant cookie. "I've been on a quest to perfect my recipe, and I think this is my best batch yet."

"Well, feel free to make me your test subject. I love dessert!" I smile and take a bite as she watches for my reaction. I make a big show of swooning over the cookie. "*So* good. I think you've achieved cookie perfection, if that's what you were going for."

Sarah grins proudly, and I follow her to the front entryway toward the living room. But not before taking another huge bite. I wasn't overreacting—this cookie really is incredible.

Caleb opens the front door for the final guest, and I'm suddenly choking on that perfect cookie.

Because Brooks Murphy just walked through the door.

Chapter Three

Someday, when I die, they're going to perform an autopsy and find flecks of oatmeal embedded in my lungs. That's how deeply I inhale the bite I'm chewing the moment I lay eyes on Brooks.

My Brooks.

No, *not* my Brooks.

I'd cross my fingers and hope that he hasn't seen me, but there's absolutely no way that anyone in the house could not notice the violent coughing fit wracking my body. By now, crumbs may have made their way into my bloodstream along with oxygen. My respiratory system has become one with the chocolate chip oatmeal cookie.

Nurse Natalie is quickly by my side, patting my back and asking if I'm okay. She hands me a cup of water. I take a sip, trying to settle my diaphragm. My cheeks would be pink just from the sheer exertion of coughing, but they're extra flaming since the first time I'm seeing Brooks in eight years has me hacking up a lung in front of him.

"So sorry! I tripped and choked on that bite of cookie! That's what I get for eating while walking," I joke between coughs. "Everyone should try one of Sarah's cookies—they're to die for!" I add, hoping to divert attention to the baker.

Sarah beams again, announcing that she'll gladly pass along the recipe to anyone interested. She walks forward into the living room, clearing the way for me to make eye contact with Brooks.

The dismay in his eyes confirms that he recognizes me too, and neither of us knows how to react. I'm the proverbial deer in headlights, but at least my Brooks-induced paralysis has quelled my coughing.

Joy doesn't seem to notice and moves between us to make the final introduction. "Teegan, this is Brooks Murphy, the final member of our small group. He recently moved to Brooklyn."

"I know," I say, not extending my hand for the handshake greeting I gave everyone else. Joy looks at me quizzically.

"I mean, I know Brooks," I stammer.

Brooks takes a step forward. "Teegan and I went to the same high school." He fills in my unfinished thought. "I was a year ahead of her, but we . . . knew each other."

The slight pause in his statement was so brief that I'm likely the only one who noticed. Joy smiles widely and says, "Well, what a small world! Glad that you could both be here. Brooks, do you want to grab a plate of food before joining us in the living room?"

"Nah, I'm good. I can get something later," he replies, looking at Joy but darting glances at me. I turn to walk into the living room before I'm forced to say any more words.

Words are gone. Cease to exist.

How am I supposed to find the friends I need in this group when Brooks is here?

I take in the seating arrangement of the space. There are two seats open on a couch and one folding chair in the circle. I rush to claim the folding chair, unable to risk Brooks taking the other seat on the couch instead of Joy.

"Thanks, everyone, for coming tonight," Caleb begins. "Joy and I have been part of a small group at church for the past few years, but we talked all summer about how we wanted to start a new group for some of the young adults at our church. We're excited to connect as friends and grow in our faith together this year."

Joy suggests that we go around the circle to give brief introductions. She and Caleb go first, followed by the other married couple, then Natalie. I try really, really hard to pay attention to what each person says. But that's hard when all my mind can think is: *Brooks* is here. Brooks *is* here. Brooks is *here.*

He's next in the circle to share, and my attention snaps fully into place as he begins speaking.

"Hi, I'm Brooks," he says with a wave. *So he's officially going by Brooks now? In high school, it was always "Murphy" or "Murph." I was the only friend who called him by his first name. I wonder when that changed?*

"I'm twenty-seven, and I moved to Brooklyn a few weeks ago. I grew up in Kansas City and went to a small college in Missouri to play basketball. When I graduated, I started teaching middle school social studies in the KCMO school district. I recently decided to get a master's in educational administration so I can work toward becoming a principal someday. I'm teaching at one of the middle schools here and taking classes in the evenings and online."

"What brought you to Brooklyn, then?" Sarah asks.

"Well, the fact that it's practically my name twin, obviously," he replies with a grin. Everyone laughs. "No, really, I decided to take classes at Townsend because a college buddy of mine teaches here in Brooklyn and told me about a program they have for middle and high schoolers called The Hangout."

I know exactly what he's talking about. Lana volunteered at The Hangout every Tuesday all four years of college. The program is designed to give at-risk students a place to belong and make positive connections with other students and community members. Lana always worked with students like Sofia who were learning English, but many of the kids go to socialize and play games or sports.

"I'm hoping to learn some best practices from the directors and volunteers so I can eventually introduce a similar program in KCMO," Brooks explains.

Natalie interrupts him. "KCMO? Sorry, you've said that twice now, but I didn't grow up in Kansas and need a translation."

Brooks gives an apologetic smile. "Sorry about that—I mean Kansas City, Missouri. The Kansas City metro area stretches across Kansas and Missouri. We shorten to 'KCK' or 'KCMO.' Of course, then you have all of the surrounding suburbs."

"Ahhh, got it," Natalie replies. "Okay, continue on with your Brooklyn migration story."

Brooks mimes tipping his hat to Natalie, drawing more laughs. I huff a belated chuckle so it won't be obvious that I'm too paralyzed to truly laugh at his jokes.

"I showed up at church my first Sunday here, and Caleb introduced himself and invited me to lunch after the service ended. I've missed the past couple of Sundays, but Caleb made it clear I wasn't getting out of joining this group." He says this with a mischievous smirk directed at our group leaders, a smirk I've seen far too many times to ever forget.

Paying attention to Brooks talking has given me an excuse to study him. His hair is the same sandy-blond, but the scruffy mop he sported as a teenager has been cleaned up into a professional quiff cut. The sides are short, but the length on top is perfectly styled to strike a balance between shaped and messy. He was always lanky in high school, but the years have filled out his physique, giving him a fit look without being overly muscular. His eyes are the same captivating sky blue, a shade lighter than mine. He's still clean-shaven, showcasing that cleft chin I used to press my finger against. I blink hard to stop myself from remembering the feel of his jaw.

As Sarah starts sharing, I pull my gaze away from Brooks. But my brain checks out of the conversation. Which is *bad* because this is my chance to get to know new friends, and I'm messing it up. *Brooks* is messing it up for me.

My mind turns over everything he just shared. *Since when did Brooks want to be a teacher? He always pictured himself in sales or marketing. And since when does Brooks believe in God or go to church? High school Brooks certainly didn't.*

After Sarah finishes, one of the other single guys, Jason, begins sharing about himself, and then I'll be next. I use every ounce of willpower to get my cheerful mask in place by the time it's my turn.

"Hi! I'm Teegan Jones," I begin with a bright smile and chipper voice. "I came to Townsend as a freshman, and I got involved with a Christian student ministry called Arrow. During my senior year, the directors of the group invited me to stay and join the staff team after graduating. This is my fourth year on staff, so I've kinda sorta figured out what I'm doing now," I joke, making everyone laugh.

"Can you tell us a little more about what you do, exactly?" Brooks asks, and my heart rate skyrockets at his direct question and eye contact.

"Um, yeah, I guess I mostly . . . well, my job is kind of . . ." I start to stammer. I clear my throat. "You'd think I'd have my elevator pitch down by now." Another group laugh. I give a brief explanation of what I do. "As much as I love the enthusiastic energy of the students, I'm looking forward to getting to know you all better and having some relationships outside of the college world."

Everyone smiles and affirms my statement before we continue around the circle to Catherine. Before I turn my attention to her, I chance a glance at Brooks and catch him studying me with a gleam of curiosity in his eyes. We both quickly look to Catherine, and I don't dare look his way again.

———

"Thanks again for inviting me to the group and having us all over," I tell Joy as I hug her goodbye. All in all, I really did have a fun time this evening. After we finished our mini-introductions, we played a couple of not-lame party games that seemed to start breaking the ice for everyone.

I learned that Natalie knows every word to every ABBA song (complete with a demonstration). Sarah is an avid puzzler in addition to baking. And Catherine founded a STEM club for girls at her high school. Her ambition reminds me of Amaya, automatically endearing her to me.

Jason and the other single guy, Will, met while mountain biking in northwest Arkansas before realizing they lived in the same city. Candace and Brian, who got married last spring, moved to Brooklyn because Brian's family owns Raelynn's coffee shop. They're in the process of opening a second location, and I sacrificially volunteered to frequent their coffee shop with all of my students.

And Brooks. I learned that Brooks is exactly the same and entirely different.

I wonder what he thought about me? No, I don't!

By the time I get home to my duplex, I have twenty-plus missed text messages from various students, plus the start of a group chat from Joy.

JOY

> Respond with your name so everyone can save numbers!

I reply and start saving the contacts as they come through.

816-555-3612

> Brooks Murphy. Great to meet everyone!

My thumbs freeze above my phone screen. Never, ever did I expect to have Brooks Murphy as a contact in my phone again. He must have changed his phone number sometime in the past eight years, because I'm pretty sure I still have his old number blocked.

I exhale the breath I've been holding. *Grow up, Teegan! This is fine. You're a mature adult now with mature adult friends, one of whom just happens to be the boy who broke your heart. But it's fine! It's great, in fact! What better way to prove you've matured than to be friends with your high school ex?*

I'm not sure precisely who I'm proving that to, but I'm going to prove the heck out of it. The gold medal for "Leaving the Past Behind" will hang from my neck. Statues will be erected in my honor: Teegan Jones, The Girl Who Moved On.

BROOKS

> Hey Teegan. I just wanted you to know that it was a pleasant surprise seeing you tonight. I hope we can enjoy the group and be friends!

My mind crashes to the past at lightning speed. Complete with a proverbial boom of thunder reverberating through my bones.

So much for those statues. But I'll never let Brooks or anyone else see how much this has shaken me. I'll figure it out and be back to easy-breezy Teegan in no time. This little hiccup can't keep me down long. Definitely.

> Of course! Looking forward to it!

Chapter Four

"Hiiiiiii!" I sing as I join the video call with Amaya and Lana. I'm only two minutes late to our weekly scheduled call, but my best friends are two of the most punctual people I know. "I didn't miss out on anything important, right?"

"Unless you count recapping a case study analysis as important, no," Lana responds with a smirk.

"Definitely not," I reply. "I mean, *you* are important to me, and I know it's important to you, so it's adjacent to important to me. But I don't need a recap."

Lana laughs as Amaya asks, "So? How was the first small group meeting? You texted and said it was fun, but give us the tea."

I've prepared myself for how I should answer this question, debating whether to mention Brooks or not. But preparation has failed me. My mind goes blank, and I break eye contact with the screen as I pause before answering. "It was . . . great!"

"You hesitated," Lana points out, literally pointing at me.

"Why the pause?" Amaya asks.

I make a *pffft* sound. "No need to overanalyze a little pause. My brain is tired, that's all."

"Liar," Lana instantly assesses. "Your eyes darted to the left before you answered. There's a whole textbook's worth of explanation hiding behind that hesitation."

Having best friends can be so annoying sometimes. Like when they know you well enough to recognize your tells and love you enough to call you out on them.

"Sigh," I say, dropping my chin to rest in my hand.

"Did you just *say* 'sigh,' Teeg?" Amaya asks. "This is more serious than we thought."

"It's not that serious!" I exclaim. "Joy and Caleb rounded up a great group of people my age, and we had such a good time! Got to know each other and ate good food and played some fun party games, and these totally seem like people I will want to hang out with a lot!" I keep my voice chipper and fast-paced as I fly through the sentence.

"But?" Lana asks.

"Well, there was one *tiny* curve ball I wasn't expecting," I reluctantly admit, fiddling with a lock of hair. My best friends stare at me, unspeaking. They know I won't be able to stand the silence.

"So, as it turns out, one of the people Caleb invited to join the group is a guy who moved to town a few weeks ago. And he's someone I knew from high school." I shrug.

"Teegs . . ." Lana prods, no-nonsense tone engaged.

"Fine, it was Brooks. My ex-boyfriend from high school."

They both gasp. And I at least feel validated by their shock.

"You're kidding me," Lana responds.

Amaya is slowly shaking her head. "The *only* guy you dated in high school? That one?"

"Well, if there was only one guy I dated, then by process of elimination, yes, it would have to be him," I say with an eye roll.

"I'm just shocked by the pure odds of this happening," Amaya muses.

"I know, right?!" I reply. "Totally crazy."

Lana is studying me intently, so I smile at her. "I'm fine, Beef."

"Being on a video screen isn't the same as sitting next to you on the bed in our AOPi room," she sighs. "Be honest, Beef. How are you?"

"I'm really fine," I half lie. Although, if it's *going* to be the truth, that makes it not really a lie, right? "It caught me off guard to see him again without warning, but I'm so over him. I mean, that was high school. Forever ago. So much life since then. I'm totally great with it."

Lana eyes me like she's weighing my answer on Lady Justice's scales.

"I really am looking forward to spending more time with the group and getting to know everyone. You were right about me needing some friends my age. I'm feeling better already after one meeting." I lay the positivity on thick. "Now, I want to hear how that big pitch went this week, Amaya. I'm not pretending to understand exactly what it was for, but tell us about it as though I understand every word."

My redirection of the conversation works, at least for now. We talk for another forty minutes before saying goodbye. Every week when we hang up, a wave of despondency floods over me. Some days, I quickly distract myself from the depressing emotions, usually by leaving the house to go hang out with a group of students.

But today, I set a two-minute timer and let myself wallow in the specific sadness brought on by missing the past. Whatever the depressed cousin of nostalgia is—that's what I feel. Loving my current life but also wishing I could go back to those (mostly) carefree college days. Planning AOPi events with Amaya. Learning how to study with Lana. Summer Projects together. Late nights talking. Countless slushie runs.

Wishing we could all be together again.

My timer beeps, and I push myself up off my bed. I picture myself flying up, up, above the clouds. I imagine the rush of the sun on my face, the breeze against my skin.

I'm not sure what Gina has going on today, so I text her to see if she'd want to go over to the dorms together. There are a handful of new sorority freshmen I haven't seen since recruitment week that I need to go visit again.

Some people time is exactly what I need to distract myself from . . . well, everything.

————

When Wednesday rolls around, I'm equal parts exhausted and relieved.

This week was the first time that each of my Bible study groups met. I'm leading groups in AOPi on Monday evenings and one of the other sororities, TriAlpha (short for Alpha Alpha Alpha), on Tuesday nights—which is slightly ironic considering they were our biggest rival when I was a student. This year, I scheduled another group earlier on Tuesday evenings with random girls from the dorms and off-campus. Sofia spearheaded the idea, and I just couldn't say no.

I love the girls in each group and have so much fun in the moment, but as I drive to Joy's house, I feel tension leave my body at the thought of hanging out with my new *peer* friends again. That is, until I think about interacting with Brooks, and then a different tension pops its head out of a new gopher hole.

The song "GOOD DAY" by Forrest Frank starts playing from my "Uplifting Tunes" playlist, and I crank up the volume. Singing along at the top of my lungs, I'm convincing myself of the words.

This is going to be a good day. A good time with good friends. You can be friends with Brooks. No biggie.

I park in front of the house and enter to a hug from Joy and greetings from those who have already arrived. There are light snacks again (and more cookies from Sarah—butterscotch this time). I chat with Will and Natalie as we wait for the rest of the group.

Brooks joins our conversation, and I'm mentally patting myself on the back for how nonchalant I act about it. He shares a little bit about his week of teaching, and I wish our history didn't exist so I could ask a million follow-up questions—why he decided to start teaching, what drew him to it, what he loves about it, what's hard, and what's amazing.

I was so close to stepping into the world of education, and it intrigues me all over again. I was all set to become a special education teacher before I pivoted to join the Arrow staff team after graduating. I want to pick Brooks' brain about his experience teaching, but the last thing I'm going to do is show too much interest in him.

Zero interest over here.

Caleb corrals us to the living room, and he begins by explaining that each week we'll discuss one chapter from the book of John in the Bible. "Everyone can read chapter one for next week, but tonight I thought we could share something about our spiritual journeys. You're welcome to share as much or as little as you're comfortable with, or nothing at all. I'll kick us off, but then we can popcorn around to whoever feels like sharing."

My heart swells with gratitude as Caleb and then Jason share their faith testimonies of how they started believing in God and following Jesus. I never get tired of hearing real-life stories like this.

When there's a lull after Jason, I jump in and share about growing up in church but beginning to take my faith more seriously in high school. I avoid eye contact with Brooks at all costs. "One of the women leading our high school group at church encouraged me to find a college ministry to plug in with so I could continue growing in my relationship with Jesus. I started attending Arrow meetings and wound up deepening my faith *so* much throughout college. It was the greatest blessing to be involved with such a great group, especially alongside my two best friends."

Catherine shares next, followed by Candace. Brian seems more shy than Candace, so I'm not surprised when he doesn't jump in after her.

"I can share," Brooks says, and I try to prepare my heart. Is there any way to prepare myself for the missing puzzle pieces to be filled in? To find out what got him from *there* to *here*?

"My family didn't really go to church growing up, and neither did most of my friends." His eyes dart ever-so-briefly to me. "But when I went to college, a couple of my teammates were really involved with Fellowship of Christian Athletes. I wasn't interested at first, but there was something about those guys that drew me in. I eventually went with them to an FCA event and met other athletes who were also Christians. Over time, I learned about the Bible and Jesus. One day, I realized I wanted him in my life, to *be* my life. I recognized bad choices I had made in my past and selfish patterns of living that I wanted to change."

Another fleeting look in my direction, one that paralyzes my lungs.

"I kept growing in my faith throughout college, and the difference my family saw in me caused them to start going to church too. Now, I'm excited to continue growing along with all of you," Brooks concludes with a smile.

Natalie speaks up next, and I will myself to listen to her instead of ruminating on Brooks' story. Ruminating on how things could have been different if only . . .

Don't think about it. Don't think about it. Don't think about it. Listen to Natalie.

As the hour grows later, Caleb closes our time in prayer. Before everyone leaves, I pull a page from Social Chair Teegan's book. "It's only eight-thirty, so if anyone wants to hang a little longer, we could head over to Creamiery to get gelato!"

Sarah, Will, and Brooks chime in positively, but I'm otherwise met with a chorus of apologies. I forget that not everyone socializes until nine or ten o'clock every night as part of their job. Or maybe everyone else isn't as spontaneous as I am?

Creamiery is in the heart of Center Square, the hub of the city. All of Brooklyn's major retail and social businesses line the streets. Local restaurants, coffee shops, gift stores, bars, and bookstores draw crowds from the community and the university every day. I pull up to Creamiery and parallel park like a boss. Unlike Lana, who'd drive circles around the streets until she found an angled parking spot, my impatience won out, and I learned to master parallel parking.

I take an extra few seconds in the car to ground myself. *You are going to have a good time. Sarah and Will are so nice. They are your friends now. Brooks is also your* friend *now. This is just four friends eating frozen dessert together.*

After choosing our gelato flavors, we find a table. I take a bite of the new coffee cheesecake flavor I decided to try this time. "Oh, this is so good. You all should have ordered this flavor!"

"I think even the trace amounts of caffeine in that would keep me awake all night!" Sarah laughs. "I can tell I'm not a college student anymore—I need my beauty sleep, and caffeine after lunch does not jive with that! How do you keep up with the perpetually young students all the time, Teegan?"

I huff a laugh. "Copious amounts of caffeine and sugar, I suppose," I tease with a wry smile. "I'm sure the day will come when I can't hang with the night owls anymore, but it's my natural bent. Well, being around people *any* time of day is my natural bent."

In my peripheral vision, I notice the corner of Brooks' lips twitch before he takes a bite of his gelato.

"So, in addition to caffeine and sugar, extreme extroversion required," Sarah recaps. "Count me out for college ministry then! I'll stick with my day job."

Will speaks up next. "I was recently in the Kansas City area for a work conference." He motions toward me with his spoon. "What part of the city are you from?"

"I grew up in Lee's Summit, a suburb on the Missouri side of the metro. I doubt that's where you would have been for a conference," I respond, dreading the next question he might ask. And who he might ask.

"Yeah, we were downtown somewhere. What about you, Brooks? You said you're from KC too," Wills pivots.

"Actually, I'm also from Lee's Summit," Brooks answers. He clears his throat, as though clearing away a bite of gelato. I recognize it as a stall tactic, though. "Believe it or not, Teegan and I went to the same high school."

"No way!" Sarah exclaims.

"I know! Small world, right?" I say as breezily as possible.

"Did you know each other?" Will asks.

My blood pressure skyrockets. Pretty sure it would blow the cuff right off my arm if I were at the doctor's office. *How should I respond? What do I say?*

"Yeah, I was a year older, so we didn't have any classes together," Brooks answers. "But Teegan was on the dance team, so we'd always see each other at basketball games and stuff before I graduated."

It's a half-truth, but that's still the truth, right? It's not like Will and Sarah need to know my entire history with Brooks. It's not like they'd *want* to know every detail about how our souls were so enmeshed that we were practically one person instead of two individuals.

Right up until he ripped our souls apart and shredded mine.

Don't think about it. Don't think about it. Don't think about it. Think about this delish gelato. Ask a new question.

"What was your work conference about?" I ask Will, praying he'll take the bait and get this conversation going on a different track. Luckily for me (and Brooks), Will launches into a lengthy explanation of the intricacies of a cyber security conference. He's surprisingly hilarious, totally bursting all of my preconceived notions about tech guys.

Sarah asks Brooks what made him get into teaching, and I want to hug her for giving me this chance to hear his answer without having to be the one showing interest.

"Before I answer, you have to promise not to think less of me," Brooks starts with a wry grin. I can't help but laugh along with Sarah and Will. "I started college thinking I'd wind up in some sort of PR or sales role, something with lots of relational time built into my responsibilities. But shortly after I began reading my Bible and going to church, I started rethinking how I could have an impact on people with my career."

"No judgment so far," Sarah says.

"Well, here's where the story takes a turn," Brooks replies. "I was scrolling social media and saw a viral video." He pauses for our laughter again. "It was a group of high schoolers celebrating their teacher's birthday. It had a compilation of clips they had taken of him teaching, mixed with their comments about how much he had changed their lives by caring about them. It blew me away to see a teacher be so engaging with the kids and especially the impact it had. One of my teammates who was a year older than me was an education major—I think because he wanted to become a coach someday. I asked him lots of questions about the classroom experience he'd had so far, and it intrigued me even more. I changed my major to secondary education the next semester. I've always been interested in history, so I chose social studies as my emphasis."

I think about all the historical documentaries Brooks used to watch in high school that I teased him relentlessly about. I fell dead asleep the one time I attempted to watch a World War I docuseries with him. Although, I do remember not being mad when I woke up snuggled against his chest with his arm around me.

Don't think about it. Don't think about it, Teegan. Think about the squirrels dropping acorns on students' heads every year on campus. Think about the AOPi girls pranking the Omega Gamma frat house's letters last night. Think about slushies with Lana and Amaya.

"I suppose if social media can inspire such a noble career choice, then it can't be all bad," Sarah muses.

"Oh, it's definitely still mostly bad," Brooks says with an exaggerated grimace. "The very thing that inspired me to become a teacher is now the bane of my existence as an educator. But despite the challenges, I've never regretted my decision to pursue education. I love being in the classroom, love making learning fun for moody teenagers."

Conversation comfortably popcorns between the four of us for the next hour. Lots of belly laughs later, we start to wind down. Aside from those few tense moments when we skirted past Brooks' and my relationship history, I had a fabulous time tonight. My cup is full, and I'm silently thanking Amaya and Lana for prodding me to pursue some new friendships.

Also, I proved to the whole world that I *can* hang out with Brooks Murphy without acting like a psycho. Today absolutely goes in the win bucket.

Chapter Five

Look where I am! <photo of kayaks on lake>

LANA

I love that you send me a variation of the same photo every year

Have to celebrate where the love of your lifetime started

LANA

Thank goodness you and Amaya ditched me for Lake Games that year so Mateo had the chance to swoop in and rescue me <heart eyes emoji>

Let's not forget me talking some sense into you to get back together. I deserve an award

LANA

I hereby dub thee Queen of Accidental Matchmaking. Please appreciate the time I took to capitalize

<queen emoji>

LANA

Now go have fun supervising the fun!

I slide my phone into my skort pocket, smiling to myself. Each year, Arrow hosts a big social at a nearby lake over Labor Day weekend. It's a chance for students to participate in games and relays, plus get free dinner. Mateo stepped in to patch up Lana's heart when the guy she'd crushed on all of college led her on one too many times at the Lake Games senior year. It was the initial spark of their ridiculously lovable relationship, so I can't resist an annual text to Lana about it.

Today has largely been planned by Lucas, one of the single guys who joined the staff team the year after I did. He asked me out, and we went on one date last year. But I immediately knew we weren't compatible as a couple. Thankfully, he was cool about it, and things have been mostly not awkward between us. Which is good, since we can't avoid seeing each other an average of four times a week. I'm secretly hoping that he and Gina might hit it off this year.

One of the perks of being a staff member is that I can assign myself to oversee various events as opposed to participating. Dirty lake water is low on my list of pleasurable experiences. I'd much rather spend the day socializing on land than steeping in the fish pee.

Hours later, I'm driving a car full of TriAlphas back to their sorority house. Normally, I'd blare music to encourage car dancing, but the girls are all chattering so enthusiastically that I leave the volume low. Hearing them talk about the fun they had today, the connections they made, and their excitement for the year hits me in my feels.

I really do love this job.

But lately, little flickers of doubt about my future on staff have started popping up. This year will finish out my initial commitment, so I'll have to decide by spring break if I'm going to recommit or not. Twelve months ago, I wouldn't have even dreamed that I'd be considering other possibilities.

Although this job provides ample variety to spice up my daily schedule, lately, I've been feeling a restlessness I can't explain. It started last spring when an AOPi I was mentoring was in the middle of student teaching. Processing life with her each week brought back all the memories of my time spent in schools doing practicums and my final semester of being in the classroom full time. Although I felt confident in my decision to accept the offer to come on staff with Arrow, a part of me has always felt a little bit sad about not using my special education degree.

My near-breakdown last month probably didn't help matters. But I'm feeling more balanced and level-headed after just two Wednesdays with my church small group. However, hearing Brooks' passion for teaching at small group gave a dose of caffeine to that niggling career restlessness.

After parking in front of the TriAlpha house, I hop out to go inside with the girls I'm dropping off. I'd love nothing more than to take a shower and relax after a long day, but I want to say a quick hello to anyone hanging out in the common areas.

I manage to keep my time short but sweet, reconnecting with several sophomores I already know and meeting two new girls. I'm heading through the foyer to the front door when I hear my name.

Nothing could have prepared me for the moment I swivel on my heel and end up face-to-face with Bailey Williams.

Amaya and Lana are not going to believe this. What's with all these blasts from the past?

Like a tiny pebble in your shoe, Bailey was a constant irritant to our time in college. She was the president of TriAlpha at the same time Amaya was the president of AOPi, but Bailey's condescending remarks about our sorority started our freshman year.

Of the three of us, I had the most cordial relationship with Bailey, possibly because I worked with her on social activities for Arrow a handful of times. Or maybe because I'm the least ambitious of our squad. Her snooty attitude toward us and AOPi didn't rub me quite as raw, but it drove Lana and Amaya crazy. And I'll defend my Beefs to the death, so I stayed distant from Bailey throughout college.

A half-second assessment reveals that nothing has changed about Bailey. At least, not outwardly. Her hair, makeup, and outfit are styled to perfection, just like always. Even her eyebrow raise at the sight of me evokes intense déjà vu. *Of course, I would run into her after spending six hours in the blazing sun having my hair blown apart by the Kansas wind. Fantastic.*

"Bailey?" I recover quickly. "I can't believe it's you! What are you doing here? I thought you moved to Texas?"

A look flashes through Bailey's eyes that I can't quite decipher. She responds, "I was in Texas, but I moved back here to Brooklyn a couple of weeks ago. I'm the new assistant nutritionist for the athletic department at Townsend. Since I'm back in town, I signed up to be one of the chapter advisors for TriAlpha. Are you still on staff with Arrow?"

"Yeah, I am!" I reply, covering up my mixed feelings about seeing her again with an extra chipper voice. "We just finished Lake Games—I'm sure you remember that."

Bailey huffs a laugh. "Paddling around the lake collecting giant rubber ducks isn't exactly a forgettable experience. It was fun the first couple of years, but I can't say I've missed that particular event. Good for you to keep it going." She says this with a smile, but I can't read if she's being sincere or patronizing.

"Well, it was nice seeing you again. I have a Bible study with some TriAlphas, so I'll probably see you around." I say this with a smile, but I'm not sure if I'm being sincere or forced.

I arrive home to an empty house. Before I can make my way to the bathroom for a shower, a calendar reminder dings on my phone.

Call Mom.

Flopping onto my bed, I debate ignoring the alert. My mom and I have a good relationship, but I tend to be a bit of an "out of sight, out of mind" type of person. Consequently, I forget to stay in touch with people (the Beefs are my one exception to this natural tendency). I set alerts in my calendar every couple of weeks reminding myself to call my family members, staggering them so I don't get too overwhelmed. Which means I shouldn't ignore this one.

It's a little after 9:00 p.m., but I inherited my night owl disposition from my mom. I know she'll be awake and kicking. I hit the call icon next to her name.

She answers after a few rings. "Well, hi there! Phone calls from both my babies in one day—this must be my lucky Saturday!"

"Hey, Mom! So you talked to Logan today too? What's he up to?" I ask. My brother is two years older than me and lives in St. Louis. He's an engineer who does . . . engineery things. I've never quite understood his job.

"Oh, same old, same old," Mom replies. "Nothing too exciting on the St. Louis front. What about the Brooklyn front? How are you? Anything new?"

"I'm great! A little tired, but that's only because it was Lake Games day," I say. A half-second debate about whether or not to mention Brooks to my mom takes place in my mind. But my brain quickly squashes the notion of talking about Brooks any more than necessary. "A little something new—I joined a small group with some other twenty-somethings at my church this year! That's been a nice change of pace to be around peers without having to lead anything."

"That's fantastic, Teegan. I'm so glad you're making time for that. Have you met some nice people?"

I fill Mom in on the small group members, leaving Brooks' name out of the mix. Flipping the focus, I ask how her job is going.

"It's wonderful. I think I'm getting into the groove, and I really enjoy putting my skills to use," she responds. A few months ago, Mom started working as an executive assistant to the CEO of a small company in Kansas City. She never worked a job outside the home when I was growing up. My dad's career as a contract lawyer provided well for our family, so when Logan was born, she became a stay-at-home mom.

She was the class mom, the PTA president, the head of the booster club, and every other supportive parental role you can think of. And she was *incredible* at all of it. Everything she touched turned into a well-oiled machine. Mom never met a mess she couldn't organize. It makes perfect sense that she'd kill it as an executive assistant.

After my parents got divorced my sophomore year of college, Mom struggled with depression for the next year. With help from a therapist and taking medication for a season, her mood improved drastically my senior year. But she still struggled to find a career path after so many years of being disconnected from the workforce. I'm grateful that she's finally found the right professional niche.

We chat for a few more minutes before hanging up. Before I head to the shower, I decide to text Logan.

Just talked to mom. She said you called today too

LOGAN

Yep. She seems to be happy with her new job. Don't you think?

"You're kidding me," Lana says.

"What's with all these people from the past showing back up in your life?" Amaya adds, face looking as shocked as Lana's on our weekly video call.

"Thank you! I've been asking God the same question!" I exclaim. I've just filled them in on running into Bailey last night. They're responding with exactly the dismay that I expected from them. Which is the perfect diversion from having to talk about Brooks again.

We briefly reminisce about the AOPi glory days—Lana and I are careful to steer clear of mentioning our homecoming loss to TriAlpha senior year. It's one of Amaya's biggest sore spots, despite the fact that she's killing it in the real world.

"Oh, Lana! I forgot to mention this—you'd be proud to know that Sofia is following in your footsteps," I say. "She told me at Bible study this week that she's volunteering at The Hangout like you did with her. We're switching our group to Monday nights so that she can be at The Hangout on Tuesdays!"

Lana grins. "I love that girl so much! Please give her an extra squeezy hug from me next time you see her!"

I scout's honor promise, and then Lana has to sign off to study for a big test. Her window closes from the video call, but Amaya stops me from hanging up. "I know you're enjoying making friends at your church small group, but it doesn't sound like you've cut back on your work schedule at all."

Winding a strand of hair around my finger, I shrug and avoid eye contact.

"Teeg . . ."

"I don't know what to cut back on, though!" I exclaim. "I can't exactly cut out the Thursday nights or staff meetings. And the four Bible study groups I'm leading are already set in stone for the semester. If I'm going to get one-on-one mentoring time with girls, it has to be during the weekdays. And I won't have close relationships with any of the girls if I don't spend social time hanging out with them in the sororities or wherever. What do you expect me to do?"

"At least start taking your weekends off!" Amaya chides. "You've temporarily avoided the flaming burnout you were headed toward at the start of the semester. But you still need to find more ways to fill up your cup if you're going to keep pouring out so much."

"Right, like you take all your weekends off," I retort with an exaggerated glare.

"I *like* working," Amaya huffs.

"Well, maybe I like working too," I scoff.

"I wasn't the one hiding in the kitchen a few weeks ago," Amaya replies, eyebrow raised.

"Touché," I concede. "I promise I'll take time to myself on the weekends. I'll try to find a hobby that I get excited about that doesn't involve Arrow students."

Amaya gives a nod of approval. "Speaking of weekends to yourself, I wanted to tell you about an event going on here in KC next weekend that I think you'd enjoy," she says. "There's going to be a silent disco in the Power and Light District downtown."

"You have my full attention," I say, sitting up straighter.

Amaya laughs. "I knew you'd be intrigued. I thought of you as soon as I saw the info. It's Saturday night—I'm going to be in Wichita for my mom's birthday, but maybe you could convince some of your new church friends to come with you. It sounds exactly up your alley."

"It sounds like an alley that I would create. In fact, maybe I should look into planning a similar event for an Arrow social sometime!" I say.

"Don't turn this into a work thing," Amaya chides with an eye roll. "Just come and have *fun*, Teeg."

"You're right. Not that you ever need to be told that you're right." Amaya raises a smug eyebrow. "Text me the info for Saturday!"

As soon as we hang up, Amaya sends me the event page, which I promptly forward to my small group chat.

> Hey everyone! One of my best friends who lives in KC told me about this silent disco happening next weekend. You can click the link to see all the info. Would anyone be up for a road trip?? It would be so fun to go together!

I wait, staring at my phone, hoping that other people will want to join.

BROOKS

> I'm totally in. Sounds like a blast!

My heart skips a beat at Brooks being the first to respond. And so enthusiastically. *Don't make a big deal out of it, Teegan. That's simply Brooks' personality.*

NATALIE

> I work that night or I totally would!

SARAH

> Count me in!

The rest of the group sends regrets and reasons they can't go, which is fine. We'll have the perfect number of people to carpool and have a good time socializing.

CHAPTER SIX

By the time Saturday morning rolls around, our perfectly-sized carpool has dwindled down to two. Sarah has a sinus infection, and Jason's brother came to town unexpectedly. Will's company spent six hours fighting off hackers overnight Friday, so he's not up for another late night.

I'm sulking on the couch about my exciting plans going down the drain when my phone dings with an individual text from Brooks.

BROOKS

> I'm still game to go tonight if you are. I could honestly use a fun break from adulting for a night

Staring at his text, I weigh my options. If I stay home, I can avoid all of the memories and confusion that would inevitably come from being alone with Brooks. But I've been looking forward to this all week. Amaya wasn't wrong when she said this was right up my alley—this event was *made* for me. Not to mention, I'd get a mini break from Brooklyn and get to see my mom.

I chew my lip. *Is avoiding Brooks worth giving all that up?*

> Same—let's do it!

BROOKS

> Amazing. I'll pick you up around 4:30?

> Sounds good!

This is fine. This is going to be loads of fun. Sitting in the car alone with Brooks for three hours will be the perfect opportunity to prove that all the water is under the bridge.

The part of my brain that doses out adrenaline doesn't listen to my calming self-talk, though. I'm jittery all day. I have no choice but to channel all that restless energy into combing through my closet for the perfect outfit.

I settle on a jean skirt and a white tank top to maximize the effect of the black lights I assume will be there. After showering, I spend more time on my hair and makeup than usual. But not because I'm going to be with Brooks. Only because I need something to do with all this nervous energy.

At 4:35 p.m., Brooks' car pulls up in front of my duplex. I've been watching out the front window for him, but I stop myself from opening the door to walk out and meet him. *You can't look like you've been standing here waiting for him! Show some chill, Teegan!*

I scamper down the hallway out of sight from the windows before he can see me. *Will he text me that he's here, or will he come up and ring the—*

My thought is cut off by the sound of the doorbell. I give myself an extra three seconds in the hallway to take a deep breath before walking out to answer the door.

"Brooks! Hey! Thanks so much for picking me up! And for still being willing to go," I say with a bright smile. My eyes race to drink in his appearance in split seconds. Perfectly styled hair. Blue eyes twinkling at me. Looking like my twin in jeans and a white t-shirt.

"Of course—I wouldn't miss it. Even if you hadn't wanted to go, I might have still driven up by myself," he responds with an equally bright smile. "I've always wanted to go to a silent disco. It's gonna be a blast."

I punch the code to lock my front door and pocket my phone. Brooks leads the way to his car and opens the passenger door for me. Just like he used to.

"Oh, thanks," I tell him as I slide into the seat. My heart picks up speed. *He's allowed to be a gentleman without it meaning this is a date, Teegan. Stop making a big deal of things.*

Once settled in the driver's seat, Brooks reaches behind him to grab a grocery bag. "It's possible that your tastes have matured more than mine," he says, grin teasing. "But if not, help yourself to some car snacks."

Setting the bag on his lap, he pulls out a giant package of Sour Patch Kids and a can of Pringles. Panic prickles my skin, making the hairs on my arms rise.

He's allowed to remember your favorite snacks. It's not like you've forgotten how much he loved Reese's Pieces. Which is the next bag he pulls out of the grocery sack.

I shake off the panic with a laugh. "I definitely haven't matured that much," I say, accepting the Sour Patch Kids from him. I rip open the bag and pop a couple in my mouth, saving myself from having to say anything else for a moment.

Brooks props the Reese's Pieces bag on the seat next to him before starting the car. We pull away from my duplex and begin the drive away from Brooklyn.

"How was teaching this week?" I ask, desperate to get him talking. I need time to calm my fluttery heart. Also, my desire to learn more about teaching is craving a fix.

"Pretty normal," Brooks responds.

I lean forward slightly, forcing him to look at me. "That hardly counts as an answer," I say, raising an eyebrow. "I assume you wouldn't let that pass from one of your students."

Brooks' head falls back in a laugh. The same laugh that was once my favorite sound in the world. It's deepened a bit with age, but the cadence is the same. My heart both expands and aches a little.

"You're right—I wouldn't let a student get away with that kind of answer," he says. His eyes return to the road as we merge onto the highway out of town, but the shadow of his laugh remains in them. "'Normal' for a middle school teacher pretty much means part of the week was infuriating and part was exhilarating."

"Do tell," I prod, chewing on another candy.

"We're far enough into the semester that I've got a decent read on most of my students—who's going to struggle with the content, who might have a harder time socially, who's going to naturally take charge in class, and who's going to want an extra challenge." He pauses, glancing at me with a smirk. "Who's going to be the class clown."

I burst out laughing. "Oh, you mean who's going to give you a taste of your own medicine?"

Brooks shrugs and momentarily holds his hands up off the steering wheel. "No idea what you're implying there, Teegan." I can't help but giggle again. Brooks continues, "I have a couple of students who have lots of potential but not much support at home. So I'm always trying to think of out-of-the-box ways to keep them engaged. I did manage to rework the lyrics of 'Bad Blood' to help the kids review for our American Revolution test. That paid off on their scores."

I snort. "Oh my gosh—you did not!"

"What? You doubt my skills?" Brooks teases.

"You have to sing it for me right now," I demand. Brooks tries to wave me off, but I know that he secretly wants to perform it for me. I know because that's exactly how I'd act if I was him. It was never hard for Brooks and I to read each other. All we had to do was picture what we'd be thinking at any given moment, and we'd know what the other person was thinking.

My gentle prodding is all it takes for Brooks to start singing his revamped version of Taylor's masterpiece. He manages to stay seriously in character, while I'm laughing so hard by the end that I think I might be literally hyperventilating.

"I'll never be able to hear 'You forgive, you forget, but you never let it go' without thinking of the battles of Lexington and Concord again," I say, tears of laughter streaming down my cheeks.

Brooks laughs along with me until we manage to calm down. He clears his throat and asks, "So, how's the Gan Clan?"

The Gan Clan. It was Brooks' nickname for my family back when we were together. My dad, Morgan, married my mom, Reagan, and they thought it would be really neat for all of us to have names ending with "G-A-N." Hence, Logan and Teegan. Brooks always thought it was the funniest, cleverest idea.

"Ah, um, good!" I say, stumbling over my response. "I mean, we're all doing good as individuals. No complaints. Just . . . not so much of a clan anymore."

Brooks glances over at me, concerned confusion in his eyes.

"My parents got divorced during my sophomore year of college," I explain. "So, you know, my parents are doing fine. Just not fine together."

Keeping his eyes on the road, Brooks quietly remarks, "I'm really sorry, Teegan. I'm sure that sucked. What happened?"

I exhale slowly and look out my window. "Nothing major. It was the most cliché split ever—once both of their kids were out of the house, they felt like they had nothing in common anymore. Had grown apart, or whatever. My mom tried to keep fighting for them for a while, but my dad eventually filed for divorce."

The air around me is starting to feel heavy, pressing down on me uncomfortably. I abruptly change the subject. "So, when did you officially start going by Brooks instead of Murphy?" I ask. "Did you drop the last name nickname as soon as you left high school or not until you started teaching?"

"Oh, um . . ." Brooks looks caught off guard, face falling slightly. "It wasn't until three years ago." He pauses again, like he's struggling to answer. I suddenly wish I hadn't asked this question.

"You know my parents named me Brooks after my mom's maiden name," he says. I do remember. His older brother was named Steven Jr. after their dad, and then his mom wanted her maiden name to be carried on by their second son. Brooks clears his throat again. "Ah, three years ago, my mom passed away."

I physically flinch. His mom was one of my favorite people. She was always so spunky and carefree. So generous with her love. "Brooks. I am so, so sorry. I didn't know, or I wouldn't have brought it up," I say, voice barely above a whisper.

He shrugs one shoulder. "Of course, you didn't know. She had a brain aneurysm that ruptured, and she died instantly. Didn't suffer at all." Brooks pauses, and I see him fighting to stuff down his emotions. "After that happened, it felt like going by my first name—her maiden name—was a way to remember her. Honor her. Keep a piece of her alive with me."

The heavy air I was attempting to alleviate by asking that question is now one hundred times heavier. I'm suffocating, and I know that

Brooks must be too. I close my eyes and picture a sunny meadow, pretending I'm running through it. Mentally escaping from uncomfortable feelings has become a well-rehearsed habit. This time, I even allow myself to include Brooks in the daydream, holding hands and smiling as we run through the grass. Running far away from the heavy air.

Brooks breaks the silence. "No one warns you that growing up means a lot more sucky life moments coming at ya, huh?"

I huff a small laugh and continue the attempt to lighten the mood. "For real. Where is that class in high school—'Preparing for Life's Suckiest Moments 101?'"

"I'll include it as a suggestion on my end-of-the-year staff survey," Brooks jokes. And with mutual understanding, we move back to light-hearted conversation.

"How did you know Joy and Caleb to get plugged into the small group?" Brooks asks.

"I've slowly gotten to know Joy a little bit over the past few years. Mostly short conversations after church on Sunday mornings, but she always made me feel so welcome and asked lots of questions. So I was always drawn to her, but I never made time to get to know her better," I respond. "But at the beginning of the school year, I was having a mini meltdown, feeling overloaded with my responsibilities and relationships on campus. My two best friends, Lana and Amaya, suggested that I try to meet some friends who aren't connected to my Arrow world. So, I jumped at the chance when Joy invited me to the group."

"Your best friends don't live in Brooklyn?" he asks. I shake my head.

"They used to. We went to college together. Met freshman year and were in the same sorority," I explain.

"You must have become really close if they're still your best friends now, long distance even. What are they like?" Brooks questions, glancing over at me.

"You want the CliffsNotes or unabridged version?"

He smiles. "Unabridged. Definitely."

I spend the next thirty minutes filling Brooks in on my friendship with Amaya and Lana. Our AOPi and Arrow shenanigans. Amaya's lofty business ambitions. Lana's laser-focused goal of changing the world as an immigration lawyer. Mateo's disruption of her plans that led to even *better* plans. Our weekly video calls and daily text messages. Brooks doesn't even tease me when I explain our "Beefs" nickname. He sincerely smiles.

"Wow," he replies. "It sounds like you three really have something unique. I still keep in touch with some of my buddies from college, and we hang out when we can. But what you have is next level."

I sigh. "Yeah, it *is* really special. Which makes it that much harder to be so far apart from each other. Thank goodness for technology keeping us in touch because I don't know what I would have done without them." I stare out the window for a few seconds, feeling the melancholy nostalgia that washes over me whenever I think too long about the distance between me and my best friends.

"How was it playing basketball in college?" I ask. It seems we have an unspoken agreement to avoid talking about high school. Or anything related to when we were "us." But I'm dying to know about his life since then. I'd purposely avoided all of Brooks' social media accounts, all of his friends' accounts, even his college team's account in an attempt to wipe him from my memory. For eight years, I systematically starved myself of knowing any information about him. But now, I've had a tiny taste, and my mind is frantically scrambling for more scraps.

Brooks tells me about his college experience, including more details about the guys on his team who sparked his interest in FCA. The antics he describes sound exactly like the playful, easygoing guy I knew in high school. Although, he also seems to have matured and changed a lot after he started growing in his faith. No more sneaking out after curfew at tournaments or scraping by with the bare minimum in class. I'm quietly impressed to see the way years of growth and maturity have amplified Brooks' best qualities while chiseling the rough edges down.

That impressed feeling is suddenly mixed with emotions adjacent to sadness, disappointment, and bitterness. Emotions that I am *not* rolling out the welcome mat for right now.

"We're on our way to a silent disco—we'd better get in the zone before we get there," I abruptly announce. "Let me have your phone to pull up some dance music."

Brooks hands his phone to me, and I hold it in front of his face momentarily to unlock it. The wallpaper on his phone is a photo of him with his mom. From the looks of his jersey and sweaty hair, it must have been taken after one of his college games. Another wave of sadness slams me in the chest, and I quickly open his music app. I find my favorite EDM remix playlist and turn up the sound dial.

Soon, we're car dancing and singing along to a lively version of "Sky Full of Stars." I shake off all the negativity and lose myself in the moment.

CHAPTER SEVEN

After eating a quick dinner at a taco truck, Brooks and I pay our admission fees to the silent disco. We secure the LED bracelets and loop the headphones around our necks, then scout out the area.

The Power and Light District has a variety of local shops, restaurants, bars, and clubs. But the disco is being held in the KC Live! space, which hosts sports watch parties and other large events. The high-energy DJ is set up on stage, and black lights illuminate the dancing crowd. The "silent" part of the silent disco makes the scene somewhat comical to observe without the headphones on. But it only takes a few seconds before our headphones are in place and we weave our way to the middle of the dancing crowd.

Song after song plays, and my body absorbs the energy of the upbeat music. All the tension from the past couple of months fades away as I throw myself into dancing and reveling in the fun. Brooks and I stay within eyesight of each other but also join in with strangers dancing around us.

I'm going to send Amaya a giant thank you card for suggesting this, I think as I scream sing along to the EDM remix of "Love Story."

I laugh at Brooks passionately mouthing every word. He grins at the sight of my laughter, and my heart skips a beat. The edges of his smile soften to a more contemplative expression, and my heart skips *several* beats.

We both turn away from each other, dancing and singing, when the lyrics reach the crescendo of kneeling to the ground to pull out a ring. I get extra into the song with the circle of girls I've joined, ineffectively distracting my thoughts away from Brooks behind me.

Two songs later, Brooks yells something at me, but I can't hear him. We both take off our headphones as he yells again, "I need some—"

He breaks off as our ears adjust to the quieter noise level without music pumping through the headphones. We laugh. "Forgot I wouldn't need to yell," he says. "I need water. Do you want some?"

"Yes! I could use a hydration break," I reply, and Brooks gestures for me to follow him. We weave our way through the crowd to the handful of standing tables set up around the perimeter. I snag a table right as a group is leaving, and Brooks heads off to buy some water bottles.

I'm catching my breath and watching the DJ when I sense someone looming over me. I turn to see a tall, broad-shouldered man standing far too close for comfort. I might think he was good-looking if he wasn't invading my personal space and reeking of alcohol.

"Sorry. I couldn't help but come say hellooo. I was watching you out on the dance floor, and your boyfriend issa lucky man," he says, slurring some of his words.

I take a step away from him before answering. "He's not my boyfriend. We're just friends." *Shoot! Teegan, why did you say that?! Just because you're reminding yourself that you and Brooks are just friends doesn't mean you need to confess it to creepy men!*

At my clarification, Drunk Guy leans impossibly closer and places a hand on my waist. "Well, that's good news for me, then. Care to head back out to the dance floor and show me more of those moves?" His eyes unabashedly rake over me, making my stomach lurch.

"No, thanks. I'm going to wait for my friend," I say firmly, trying to back away from his touch. His hand only moves further around my back, tightening his grip as he steps forward to close the space I've put between us. Up close, his sweat-mixed-with-alcohol scent makes me nauseous, and his hand traveling south of my waistline makes me sick.

"Leave me alone," I say, voice wobbling with panic. I place a hand on his chest to push him away when there's suddenly another body between me and Creepy Man.

"You need to step away. She did not give you permission to touch her, and she asked you to leave her alone." Brooks' voice is firm, authoritative.

This guy apparently doesn't know when to stop, though, because he tries to take another step forward.

Despite the fact that he has a good four inches on Brooks' 5'10" stature, Brooks grabs a fistful of the guy's shirt and bumps him back.

"Let go of me," he says to Brooks, eyes narrowed. "She already told me that you're not her boyfriend."

There's ice in Brooks' voice as he replies, "Yeah, but that doesn't mean I won't yeet your gyatt right outta here if you don't leave her alone." He punctuates his statement with a hard shove, sending Drunk Creep stumbling backward. He glares once more at Brooks but, thankfully, turns and stalks away.

Brooks immediately swivels to me, gently clasping a hand around each of my elbows. There are shots of fear, panic, and concern mixed in with the residual anger filling his eyes. "Teegan, are you okay? I'm sorry for leaving you alone. I shouldn't have done that."

Painful emotions start snapping into place like cage bars around me. Panic at feeling trapped by the unwanted advances. Disgust at the guy's hands on me. Fear of not being able to escape. Longing to bury myself in Brooks' arms. Frustration with myself that I'm longing for Brooks.

I'm suffocating.

"Brooks . . . did you just say 'yeet your gyatt?'" I enunciate slowly, trying to magic away the cage bars by ignoring them.

Brooks gives me an incredulous look, then groans and throws up his hands. "I'm around middle schoolers all day, every day, Teegan. Their ridiculous vocabulary seeps into my brain against my will, okay?"

"Bet," I deadpan.

We both laugh before Brooks' face reverts back to concern. Concern and . . . maybe something else? He asks quietly, "Do you want to get out of here? I can take you to your mom's."

I don't even pause before answering. "No. I refuse to let the last memory of this fun night be some gross drunk guy. Let's get back out there and dance some more."

I lead the way back to the middle of the dance floor, radiating confidence with every step. But I don't miss that Brooks stays extra close to me. I'm determined to wipe away every trace of ickiness left behind by that encounter, so I dance with even more abandon than before.

I start pulling out every viral social media dance I've ever learned, and Brooks matches me move for move, beat for beat. We egg one another on, building off of each other's energy as the music pulses. Laughing, lip-syncing, and dancing take up every ounce of my brain space. I need it to consume every ounce, leaving no room to dwell on the growing melancholy of wishing Brooks was still mine.

Chapter Eight

I'm slow to wake the next morning. Through heavy eyelids, I check the time on the clock.

10:36 a.m. But considering I didn't fall into bed until 2:30 a.m., that's not exactly *that* late. Especially when you add in the extra hour I spent tossing and turning in my childhood bed, unable to turn off my racing mind.

The tangle of thoughts comes back full force, effectively waking me up.

How good it felt to get out and spend an evening dancing, just for the sake of having a good time.

How fun it was to be there with Brooks, our parallel energies synthesizing exactly like they used to.

The fun being dampened by my encounter with Sketchy Guy.

Being rescued by a very protective Brooks. His commanding voice as he ordered the guy to leave me alone. *I bet that's the voice he uses when he's scolding students who cross the line. It was kinda sexy.*

No! Stop it, Teegan! No associating anything about Brooks with the word sexy. Get a grip!

I roll out of bed before my thoughts can sidetrack any further. Wrapping my throw blanket around myself, I lumber down the stairs, feet moving on autopilot.

Although my parents may not be together anymore, they've done their best to keep things amicable. That included my dad signing our house over to my mom in the settlement, giving Logan and me a small semblance of "normal" to return home to when we visit. I'm grateful again for that fact as I walk the familiar path from my room to the kitchen without consciously thinking about where I'm going.

"Morning, honey!" my mom says in a chipper but soft voice. She knows I'm not naturally a morning person. I see a plate of pumpkin streusel muffins on the counter, and my mouth immediately starts watering. "There's caramel macchiato creamer in the fridge," she says as she pours me a cup of coffee.

"Thanks, Mom," I reply, swallowing a yawn. I grab the creamer from the fridge, along with the jar of Mom's homemade cinnamon butter. Mom heats up one of the muffins in the microwave for me while I doctor up my coffee.

"How was last night?" Mom asks.

"It was really fun," I reply, smearing butter on the steaming muffin. Taking a large bite, I moan with pleasure. "I've missed your baking," I add. The compliment is sincere, although it's also a diversion to buy time before the inevitable. I can't avoid telling my mom that Brooks is back. Not after last night.

"Where did everyone wind up staying?" Mom had generously offered to house anyone who needed a place to sleep after our outing, so it's a valid question. But the answer is the point of no return for the Brooks conversation.

I take another bite of muffin.

"Actually, most everyone had to cancel," I begin. "Only one other person was able to come, and he stayed at his dad's house."

"Oh, really? What's his name?"

Another completely valid, non-intrusive question. It's simply one I wish I could avoid.

I clear my throat. "Ummm, well, ironically enough, as it turns out, when the small group formed, it just so happened that one of the guys who joined was . . ." I trail off, avoiding eye contact with what I know is my mom's piercing stare. "It was Brooks."

Silence. I dare a quick peek at my mom's facial expression. Her very shocked facial expression.

"Brooks as in . . . ?" she questions.

"*Brooks*, Brooks."

"Brooks Murphy?" she clarifies. But it doesn't really sound like a question.

I nod.

"Oh, boy." Mom blows out a breath.

"But it's fine!" I say. "It caught me off guard at first because, I mean, what in the small world are the chances? But we're both mature adults. We've grown and changed. We can handle being friends! We *are* handling being friends."

"Okay." Her tone of voice says the word as a statement, but her eyes clue me in that it was more of a question.

"It's really okay," I reassure her. "I can handle it." She raises an eyebrow. "I'm not seventeen anymore. We had fun last night without it being awkward at all."

I completely leave out all irrelevant information, such as Brooks' pensive expression while singing "Love Story." Or him rescuing me from a drunk man. Or the brush of his fingers against my elbows. Or the melancholy heartache in my chest that won't dissipate.

"If you say so," she remarks. "Wait—you said that he was staying at his dad's house. What about Angela? Are she and Steven not together anymore?"

My expression falls at her question, and I can see on my mom's face that she senses the answer before I even explain Brooks' loss.

"Their poor family. Oh, that's so heartbreaking," Mom says, dabbing tears from her eyes. "Angela always was a special soul." I nod my agreement, unable to say anything more.

"Well, how's the rest of life going?" my mom asks.

Appreciating the opportunity to move on from the sadness in the room, I tell my mom about all of the different groups and individuals I'm leading with Arrow this year. We discuss my job extensively before pivoting to hers. I love the way her demeanor lights up when she talks about her executive assistant role.

"Of course, you're killing it, Mom," I praise her. "I'm not surprised at all that your boss gave you a raise already." She blushes at my compliment, but I can tell how much it genuinely means to her.

"When's the next time Logan will be home?" I ask.

"Probably not until Christmas," Mom replies with a sigh. "He's taking some big guys' fishing trip over Thanksgiving week. Something about better rates. But he promised he'd be here for a week at Christmas. I'll go visit him in St. Louis sometime before then."

I drain the rest of my lukewarm coffee before announcing, "Okay, I desperately need a shower."

"Well, I wasn't going to be the one to tell you that you smell, but . . ." Mom trails off with a cheeky grin. I roll my eyes at her before retreating to my room to shower and get dressed. I have about four hours before Brooks will pick me up to drive back to Brooklyn, and I'll need every possible minute to prepare myself to spend another three hours alone with him.

"Let me get this straight. You spent every summer during college *at the beach*?" Brooks glances over at me as he asks the question, a teasing grin on his face.

I slap him on the arm, light enough he won't swerve the steering wheel but hard enough to express my displeasure at his prodding. "We were not lying out on the beach all day! Yes, we were in Florida, but Summer Projects were a lot of hard work. Especially as a leader. You're working a full-time job plus doing all the meetings and group Bible studies in the evenings and on the weekends. I barely slept. I swear it wasn't all fun and games."

"But there were still fun and games. At the beach for eight weeks." His lighthearted tone and taunting smirk reveal that he's still having too much fun messing with me.

I cross my arms with a huff. "You're impossible."

Brooks' head falls back as he laughs. "You know I'm just teasing you. In all seriousness, that sounds amazing. I wish I could have done something like that during college. And it's awesome that, as a staff member, you're able to create that experience to help more students grow spiritually. Is Summer Project your favorite part of the job?"

"*Hmmm*, it's one of my favorite parts for sure," I reply. "I love anything where I get to be with people and help them feel included. The nice thing is that even though I have consistent meetings on my weekly schedule, there's wiggle room each day for spontaneity. If I have a deep conversation with a girl and she's interested in talking more, we can grab lunch or coffee the next day. Or I can spur of the moment go hang out at one of the sorority houses after a meeting."

"Sounds like a great job description for you. Fun. Flexible. People-oriented. Checks all the Teegan boxes," Brooks observes.

"Yeah, I guess so. I'm just not sure if . . ." I trail off, not sure where I was taking that thought. Surely my brain wasn't planning to admit to Brooks that I'm contemplating moving on from my job. It's a thought I've hardly allowed myself to dwell on, much less announce to anyone else. But every time he talks about his job, it makes me more and more interested in pursuing education again. It beckons my mind to dwell on the possibility. But that doesn't mean that I should be looping other people into my confusion yet. *Especially* not Brooks.

Do your job, Brain, and keep a tighter rein on my tongue! I can't go around confessing personal things like that to Brooks!

"You're not sure if . . . what?" Brooks prods.

"I don't know. It's nothing," I evade, staring at the Kansas plains rolling past my window.

"Didn't sound like nothing."

There's silence, aside from the music playing from the stereo in the background. Brooks doesn't say anything else, clearly waiting for me to fill in my thoughts.

"I'm not sure if I want to keep doing it. If I want to recommit to staying on staff or not," I say after the long pause.

"Okay," Brooks states.

"Okay?"

"Yeah. Okay," he says again. He looks over at me briefly. "You don't have to keep doing the same thing if you don't want to. Try something different. Nothing's stopping you."

"But it's hard to argue with a job that fits my personality so well *and* makes a huge difference in people's lives," I contend.

"It's not the *only* job that would fit your personality, Teegan. Or the only job that makes a huge difference in people's lives. There's nothing to say you can't change it up," Brooks doubles down.

"Have you ever thought about doing something other than teaching?" I ask, shifting the focus off of me.

Brooks huffs a laugh. "Only every single April since I started teaching. But even though I'm exhausted at that point in the school year and start questioning every life choice I've ever made, in the end, I never feel like God is calling me away from teaching. I've only ever felt confident in staying. At least, so far. But if that ever changes, I won't back away from giving something else a shot," he finishes with a shrug.

I hum, considering his thoughts. *I changed course once to come on staff in the first place, even though I enjoyed all my hands-on classroom experiences in college. Maybe it wouldn't be a terrible thing to change course again?*

The serious tone of the conversation (and my internal monologue) is making my insides feel itchy. "I still can't believe that you're a teacher," I comment with a light tone. "Never ever would I have guessed that in high school."

Brooks smiles. "I've changed in a lot of ways from who I was in high school." His smile tightens, and the itchy feeling gets worse. He continues, "Teegan, I really need to tell you how sorry I am. I need to explain—"

"It's fine! Let's not rehash the past!" I interrupt with a shrill voice. *We can't go there. I can't go there. It hurt too much. I can't feel that again. Can't think about it.* "I forgive past you. We've both grown up now. Let's just keep moving forward."

I don't look directly at Brooks, but I see him swallow hard in my peripheral vision.

"Tell me more about The Hangout," I quickly redirect. "I mean, I know about the program in general since Lana used to volunteer there. But tell me about what you do specifically."

Brooks takes the bait, thank goodness. "Some weeks, I float around and chat with students who seem less included in the groups. A lot of times, I'm in the rec area playing basketball or other sports with the students in there. I recently coordinated with the Townsend basketball team to organize a tournament over the course of several weeks, before their season begins. I think that will help draw even more guys to come, and then hopefully they'll continue to stick around."

"That's amazing, Brooks," I say, impressed. "A girl in one of my Bible studies, Sofia, used to be an English Language Learner student at The Hangout. Lana was her tutor. Now Sofia is at Townsend as a student and volunteering as a tutor at The Hangout. I should go visit her there sometime."

"You should definitely come check it out," Brooks says with enthusiasm. He grins. "It would be fun to show you around."

Heat flushes my cheeks. "So you're hoping to start a similar program in KCMO eventually?" I ask.

Brooks nods. "Yes, I hope I can. So many students in the district would benefit from having a place to go after school, a place to belong. A way to make positive connections in the community. Ideally, I'd love to offer the program more than once a week if we could pull it off. Anything to give more students access to productive community."

Hearing Brooks talk about his vision for the KCMO district intrigues me. We both grew up extremely privileged—in financially stable, two-parent households; received good educations from our school district; graduated from college with no student debt (thanks to my parents and to Brooks' athletic scholarship). My experience working with college students from all different backgrounds and upbringings has made me appreciate the upper hand I had in life. It's inspiring and compelling to see the ways that Brooks is leveraging his advantages to pull others up as well.

"Tell me more about the Bible studies you do at Townsend." Brooks' question pulls me out of my thoughts. He continues, "I confess I still feel a little foggy about what exactly your day-to-day job looks like."

I laugh in response. "I know. It doesn't really make sense unless you've experienced it firsthand. I lead four different small groups in addition to our large group events, plus I meet one-on-one with girls who want to deepen their faith and grow their leadership skills."

Brooks' eyebrows raise, though his eyes stay on the road. "That sounds like a *lot*."

"I guess so. It's exhausting sometimes, but I really do love it." I give an overview of the Bible studies I lead, highlighting the irony that TriAlpha was our rival house in my college days.

"Ooo, building bridges with the enemy, huh?" Brooks teases.

"Something like that," I say with a giggle. I can't help myself. "This semester, I took over meeting with a group of seniors on Friday mornings because Rachel, our head staff woman, recently had twins. They don't like to sleep much, so she asked if I could cover the early morning group this fall."

"Oof, early mornings plus Teegan. What an explosive combination," Brooks says with a quick smirk in my direction.

"Har har," I scoff. "It might not be my favorite time of day, but I'm managing. And exactly when did you turn into an early bird?"

Brooks shrugs a shoulder. "College plus basketball equaled a pretty demanding schedule, so the only time I could read my Bible was early in the mornings. I slept through my alarm a lot at first, but eventually it grew into a habit to wake up early. Which helped prepare me for teaching."

We pull into the Brooklyn city limits, and my heart deflates a little, knowing our time together is coming to an end.

"Would you want to grab some dinner before I drop you off? I heard there was going to be a pop-up restaurant event in Center Square this evening," Brooks says.

I want to say "yes" so badly. Too badly.

You cannot get sucked back into Brooks' gravity, Teegan. You can't do this again.

"I can't," I respond quickly, before my impulsive heart overpowers my mind. "Uh, my weekly video call with Amaya and Lana. I have to do that. So, no time for dinner, even though the pop-up restaurant sounds super cool."

Never mind the fact that I still have another two hours before our rescheduled time.

Brooks' hopeful expression falls for a split second before he smiles again. "The Beefs, right. Can't keep them waiting. It was nice of them to bump back the time of your call by a few hours today."

"Yes, it was. They're the best!" I say it with enthusiasm, but then trail off to silence again.

A few minutes later, Brooks pulls up in front of my duplex. "I'll carry your duffel bag inside for you," he says, moving to open his car door.

"No, no! I'm fine. I got it!" I reply, quickly getting out of the car. Grabbing my bag out of the back seat, I shut the door a little too hard, wincing at the sound.

"Teegan, wait!" Brooks calls out the open passenger window. "Take the rest of the Sour Patch Kids. You know I won't eat them." He holds the bag up, and I accept it from his hand.

"Thanks for the ride. And for going with me this weekend," I say.

"I had a lot of fun." There's sincerity and something slightly sad lacing Brooks' voice as he says it.

"Me too." There's sincerity and something *very* sad lacing my voice. I rush up to my front door, giving only a brief wave over my shoulder before shutting myself inside.

CHAPTER NINE

"**O**h my goodness, I wish I could have seen that!" I exclaim. "A one-two punch from Mateo to Lana for the game-winning shot? Epic."

"You need to have someone video these games for us, Beef," Amaya adds. Lana grins at our enthusiasm. She and Mateo have been playing on a recreational soccer team together ever since Mateo rehabbed from his ankle injury but retired from professional soccer. In college, Lana never told us that she was a closet soccer connoisseur until she started dating Mateo. Amaya and I teased her about that for a long time, but she quickly converted us into casual soccer fans. Even if I still don't understand all the rules, despite her repeated attempts to explain.

"How was the silent disco?" Amaya asks me. My heart beats wildly, then jumps up into my throat, making breathing a challenge.

"Super fun!" I squeak.

Amaya narrows her eyes at me. "Why are you being weird about it?"

I huff. "I'm *not* being weird."

"Yes, you are," Lana agrees.

Phooey.

"It *was* super fun! There's nothing weird about that!" Both faces stare me down through the screen. "Fine, there was one minor snafu, but it turned out to not be a huge deal at all. And I had a great time."

"What snafu?" Amaya asks, eyebrow raised.

"Well, originally, five of us from small group were supposed to go, but several people had to cancel the day of the event. So it wound up being only two of us," I say, eyes darting around the screen but not maintaining eye contact.

"And that was you and . . . your ex?" Lana deduces.

"Wait, you spent the weekend alone with your ex and didn't think to lead the call with that information?" Amaya exclaims. Lana hums her agreement.

"I didn't lead with that information because it wasn't a big deal. We had a good time *as friends* at the disco, and nothing was awkward at all. We're being total grown-ups about it."

"Sure," Amaya states.

I roll my eyes. "Maybe *this* is why I didn't lead with this information! Because you're making it a bigger deal than it is."

Lana looks locked and loaded with more commentary. I need a diversion.

"Now, would you two like to hear about the actual life crisis I'm dealing with?" I ask. *I may not have been ready to discuss my doubts about my future yet, but sacrifices must be made in the name of diverting attention from Brooks.*

"What do you mean, life crisis?" Lana bursts out.

Here goes nothing. "Well, you know this is the final year of my initial commitment on Arrow staff and that I'd been planning on signing on for another two years," I begin. They nod. "This might seem kind of out of the blue, probably because it *is* a little out of the blue, but I've been having some . . . doubts about if I want to recommit or not."

Their eyebrows shoot up in unison, as though they had choreographed their reactions ahead of time. I clarify, "Doubt is maybe too strong of a word. Questions? Hesitation? Minor uncertainty?"

"It's okay to change your mind, Teeg," Amaya says. "There's nothing wrong with deciding to do something different. But what's making you question things?"

"Is it because you were feeling burned out at the start of the school year?" Lana asks.

I blow a breath through the hair on my face. "Not exactly. I'm actively trying to head off the job burnout because I know that's not a good mental state for making huge life decisions. I've been feeling better since I joined the church small group. You were right that I needed some friendships with peers outside of the students in Arrow. Plus, I had so much fun dancing this weekend that just a little bit ago I looked up a gym in town that offers a dance exercise class a couple of times a week. I'm going to try to go at least once a week so I have a hobby that's not related to Arrow."

"You're welcome for that advice," Amaya teases.

"A million thanks," I say with a smile. "I've been thinking a lot about teaching lately, about being around younger kids and making a difference in their lives. I really enjoyed my student teaching experience, even though, by that point, I already knew I'd be joining Arrow's staff instead of becoming a teacher. It's like this 'road not taken' that keeps beckoning, making me curious about what could have been."

"Do you regret staying on staff at Townsend?" Lana asks, head cocked to one side.

"No! Not at all!" I emphasize. "I've loved loved *loved* these years on staff. It's been a dream job. I guess I'm trying to figure out if it's *still* the dream for the next phase of my life or not. But is it bad that I'd consider doing something else when helping college students grow spiritually is so impactful? Am I wrong to even think about quitting when something so meaningful is something I enjoy, something I'm good at?"

"Teegs, no!" Lana asserts. "It's not bad to consider doing something else! It's not like working with college students is the only meaningful thing you can do with your life. You'd make an incredible impact as a special ed teacher. Or any other path you might choose to pursue. You'd make an impact because of who you are as a person, not because of your paid vocation."

"Not to mention, it wouldn't be quitting, Beef," Amaya jumps in. "You're coming to the end of your commitment, so choosing not to recommit isn't quitting. You can extend your commitment, or you can move on. Either choice is valid. Pray about it, process the options, let us know how we can help you—but don't beat yourself up for considering a change."

"Ahhh, thanks, Beefs," I say. "I've been afraid to vocalize this to anyone. But I know I should never be afraid to tell you two anything. I'm not even close to making a decision, but I'm grateful to have you as a sounding board."

"We're here any time you need us," Lana says. "Except right this minute. Because I have to leave to go to a study group session for a giant test tomorrow. I can't wait to be done with law school," she concludes with a sigh.

"Good luck, LaLa! I'll be praying for your test!" I respond. "And hope you have a killer week at work, Amaya!" I blow kisses into the screen before signing off.

Clutching my phone to my chest, I exhale a sigh of relief. *Dodged the bullet. Wait, no I didn't. There's no bullet to dodge! They can side-eye me all they want, but there's nothing to worry about with Brooks.*

Nothing to worry about at all.

———

I bolt upright in bed, cheeks moist, chest heaving.

No. No, no, no. I haven't had that dream in years.

Looking at the clock, I see it's a little past 6:00 a.m., long before my alarm was set to go off at 7:00 to get ready for our Monday morning staff meeting. My heart is racing, and I know I won't be able to fall back asleep.

I quickly dress in leggings and a t-shirt, sweeping my hair up into a ponytail. The shower is running in the bathroom, which means Gina must be awake already. Slipping my phone into my pocket, I sneak out the front door to avoid having to talk with her yet.

The sun is barely beginning to cast light into the darkness, leaving the early morning draped in charcoal gray. I turn down the sidewalk, my feet moving on autopilot as they carry me toward my regular prayer walk path. When my mind is most muddled, I need movement to help me get my thoughts out.

I'm so confused, God. Why did Brooks have to come back into my life? Why now? Was this just your way of pointing me back to teaching? Couldn't you have found some other *arrow to point me in that direction? Why did it have to be the one person I can't afford to get close to again? The one person I have such a hard time resisting?*

Why would you be this cruel?

A single tear slips down my cheek. I wipe it away and quicken my pace, determined to outrun the pain.

Okay, I'm listening to your plans for my future. Please help me figure out what I'm supposed to do. What you want me to do. Whether it's continuing on Arrow staff for a few more years, or if it's teaching, or something completely different. Maybe you want me to be a flight attendant? Except I really don't know if I could handle stressed-out people yelling at me all day. Could it not be that, please?

I'm suddenly role-playing imaginary conversations with angry passengers who didn't want to check their overly-large carry-on bags when my elbow bumps into someone running in the opposite direction.

"Whoa there, Teegan!" Bailey says, slowing to a stop and pulling out her earbud. "I know it's still a little dark, but watch out." She says this with a smile, so I don't think she's upset with me. *Interesting.*

"I'm so sorry, Bailey! I don't think I'm fully awake yet," I apologize.

She gives a slight laugh. "It's okay. I get lost in my thoughts sometimes too."

We stand there, awkwardly smiling at each other for a beat.

"Hey, I'd still love to hang out sometime," Bailey says.

"Yeah, for sure!" I respond, channeling cheer into my voice. "Maybe we could grab dinner sometime after you're off work? Or lunch on a weekend?"

"I'll text you about it," Bailey replies with a nod. "See you soon, hopefully!"

She puts her earbud back in right as I call out, "Enjoy the rest of your run!"

Running into my other blast from the past sends my thoughts to Brooks again. To him still going to the disco with me after everyone else bailed. To him bringing my favorite snacks and our easy conversation. To the pure enjoyment of dancing our cares away together. To the look on his face when he stepped in to rescue me.

To the look on his face on the drive home, right before he was about to apologize for our past.

I can't risk that again. Please, God, help me to keep my distance emotionally. I want to be friendly at small group, but I can't handle more.

Help me.

CHAPTER TEN

September flies by now that students have settled into their routines. I'm enjoying each of the Bible studies I'm leading (even the earlier-than-preferred Friday morning senior group). I'm on my way out the door for church when a text comes through.

BAILEY

> Hey Teegan. Would you have time for dinner this week? I'm usually available after 6:30. Or I'm even open tonight if you're free.

I'm busy practically every weeknight, so I decide to jump right in and get this awkward first hangout over with.

> My evenings are pretty packed M-Th, but I could do dinner tonight! Taco Lucha ok?

BAILEY

> Sure, sounds good. 6:00 work?

> Yep! I'll meet you there!

I arrive at church a couple of minutes late and slip into a seat next to Sarah and Catherine. It's been fun sitting with different people each week, especially when I'm running late and don't want to walk all the way up to the front where Joy and Caleb typically sit.

A minute after I've gotten settled, Brooks slips into the row in front of us and sits next to Will.

Fantastic.

I do my best to stay focused on the worship songs and the sermon, but I'm only halfway successful. As soon as the service ends, Will and Brooks turn around to talk to us. We're casually chatting about life when Brooks throws out an idea.

"I saw an advertisement that the pumpkin patch is doing spooky corn mazes every Saturday night in October," he says. "Our group should go together sometime."

"That's a great idea!" Catherine pipes up. "Can we go this Saturday? I'll be out of town the next weekend, and Joy is hosting that game night for our group the third Friday of October."

Will and Sarah murmur agreement, and Brooks looks to me. "Yes, totally!" I chirp. "That will be totally fun." *It will be totally fun, minus the bonus torture time with Brooks.* "You should send that over the group chat," I add.

We all mingle a while longer in the church lobby before parting ways. Of course, Brooks falls into step beside me on the walk out to my car. Apparently, God's idea of helping me keep my distance from Brooks is by forcing me to *practice* distancing myself whenever he's nearby.

"How's everything going on campus?" he asks.

"Oh, it's great!" I reply. "The Greek houses are already gearing up for homecoming, so some of the girls are getting busier. But it's a contagious energy."

"Are you still thinking of coming to visit Sofia at The Hangout sometime?" Brooks inquires as we reach our cars. Parked right next to each other.

"Umm, yes, I'm hoping to," I respond aloud. *Could you let me know a week you* won't *be there so I can choose that week to visit?* I add internally.

"Any exciting plans for the day?" he asks. My usual knack for easy conversation is failing me right now. That's the third question in a row that Brooks has asked without me asking anything in return. *Pull it together, Teegan. Don't be obvious about how much his presence throws you off.*

"I'm getting dinner tonight with an old acquaintance from college who moved back to Brooklyn," I say.

"Oh, cool—was she in your sorority?" Brooks asks.

I shrug one shoulder. "No. She was in our rival sorority that I told you about. We . . . weren't exactly close in college. But it will be good to catch up. What about you? Anything revolutionary on your schedule?"

"Unless you count grading tests as revolutionary, not quite," he responds with a wry grin.

"I don't know, a chance to sing through your remix of 'Bad Blood' could be pretty exciting," I tease, even though I know I shouldn't be teasing Brooks.

Brooks laughs. "Unfortunately, we've moved beyond the Revolutionary War now, but maybe I'll pull out the song to keep grading interesting."

We smile at each other softly until I abruptly open my car door. "See you on Wednesday!" I exclaim as I move into my car.

"Yep, see you then," Brooks responds, before singing a line from his song while opening his car door.

I can't stop the smile that springs to my face, but I'm quick to banish it as I drive away.

———

"What made you decide to come back to Brooklyn?" I ask Bailey before stuffing a queso-laden chip into my mouth.

Bailey is slow to answer. Her hesitation catches me off guard. "Sorry if that was somehow an intrusive question!" I quickly add. "You don't have to answer that." Even though I don't know how that could be an uncomfortable question.

"No, it's fine," Bailey begins, setting a taco down on her plate. "I tried working alongside an independent nutritionist and health coach in Texas. It was fine. But I didn't really love working with her. And I never really felt like I found good community there."

I nod, hoping that gives her enough encouragement to continue sharing.

"Brooklyn was the one place that felt the most like home. Or the closest thing I've ever felt to home, I guess," Bailey says, dropping eye contact.

Swallowing my bite, I clear my throat. "You didn't want to move back to California, where you grew up?"

"Oh, heck no," Bailey retorts. Based on her widened eyes, I think she surprised herself with her strong reaction.

All of my best-developed social skills have not prepared me for this conversation. I stare dumbly at Bailey, completely lost as to what to ask next.

"Look, Teegan, I probably should have kicked off this conversation with an apology," Bailey says, finally looking me in the eyes.

I was not prepared for that either. "Okay?" I question.

"I know that I wasn't kind to you, Lana, and Amaya when we were students," Bailey starts again. "I was rude and condescending, and that's something I deeply regret."

Ummm, where's the guidebook for discussions like this? Because I'm lost. She was *condescending and rude. But is it rude of me to agree with her?*

Thankfully, Bailey continues talking before I need to formulate a response. "The truth is, I was really jealous of you three."

I laugh out loud but then clap a hand to my mouth.

"Bailey, I'm so sorry. I shouldn't have laughed," I apologize. "That was so rude of me. I'm genuinely a little . . . perplexed as to how you could be jealous of us? You were the Queen Bee of TriAlpha. The Queen Bee of Townsend, really. You always oozed confidence and were surrounded by people."

Bailey sighs. "I know I projected that image, that I came across as 'popular.'" She accentuates the word with air quotes. "But I always wanted the closeness the three of you had. I never really found those deep relationships with anyone in TriAlpha. Everything was always surface level. And, well . . . I had a lot of insecurities coming into college."

She's fiddling with her napkin, and I silently give her space to continue.

"I grew up really wealthy. Ever since I was a baby, there's been a trust fund with my name on it. And my parents just always assumed I would live off of those funds. They never expected anything of me. Never thought that I would make a career for myself." Bailey pauses again. "I chose to come to Townsend as my petty way to get back at them for their lack of belief in me. Found a small, no-big-deal university in the middle of Kansas instead of choosing one of the posh private universities they wanted me to attend. Because, really, they only thought my degree would be a trophy, not something I'd actually use.

"When I met you three our freshman year, Amaya had all these lofty career goals and the charisma to achieve them. Lana was ridiculously driven, with her life path all mapped out and supportive parents cheering her on. And you were always the social sun that everyone revolved around in Arrow. People genuinely wanted to be around you because you made everyone feel so special. You created so much joy, like it was your sole mission to make people have fun. The three of you had these clear ambitions and people in your corners."

Bailey's eyes well up with tears as she continues. "And you had each other. This special connection—even your own made-up group nickname. I just wished that I could have a fraction of the friendship and vision and support that you all had. But I let that jealousy and insecurity drive me to act like I was better than you, that I had everything together. I covered it up because I didn't want anyone knowing how lonely I was."

There's a lull as Bailey stops talking and wipes her eyes. I know I should respond, but I still feel too stunned to know what to say. Reaching a hand across the table, I place it lightly on Bailey's arm to buy my brain time to formulate thoughts.

"I wish you would have said something in college, Bailey," I finally say. "I'm sorry that you were going through that without anyone knowing. And I'm sorry that I didn't make more of an effort to get to know you or include you in our friend group."

Bailey waves me off. "No, it wasn't your fault, Teegan. The way I treated you all didn't exactly invite deeper friendship. I was completely immature and snooty. I know I was."

"Even so—we could have done more to build a friendship with you. We were immature too, not making an effort to see beyond the surface of your actions. Will you forgive me for that, Bailey?" I ask.

"Even though I don't think you really even owe me an apology, I absolutely forgive you," she responds, earnestness in her eyes. "Will you forgive me as well?"

"Of course!" I assure her. "With you being back in Brooklyn now, maybe we can have a fresh start."

"I'd like that." Bailey smiles, but then the corners of her mouth fall again. "Do you think that Amaya and Lana would be open to hearing an apology? Or are the bridges totally burned? I wouldn't blame them at all if they didn't want to give me a second thought."

I'll make sure they give it thought. "I think you could absolutely reach out to them. Maybe let me give them a tiny heads-up first?"

Bailey nods, then picks up her taco. "Thanks for giving me another chance, Teegan."

———

After leaving dinner with Bailey, I immediately send a long voice memo to the Beef group chat. We already had our weekly video call earlier this afternoon, and I know they're both busy this evening, but I couldn't delay filling them in on what Bailey shared.

AMAYA

> Wow. I never ever would have guessed that she acted that way because she was jealous of us. I mean, it always seemed like she had a whole posse from TriAlpha following her every move

LANA

> You know what—Mateo tried to tell me once that Bailey was jealous of me. Right after she confronted me at that Arrow meeting after Mateo and I had started dating.

> At the time, I blew off the suggestion, but turns out my insightful man was right all along

She's planning to contact you both to apologize, so prepare yourselves. Please respond well to her!

LANA

I can respond well!

LaLaaaa—we all know you have zero poker face

LANA

Rude

AMAYA

She's right

LANA

Double rude

This is why I told Bailey to let me give you a heads-up first. Now your reaction won't be so raw

LANA

Fine <eye roll emoji>

And you too Madame President. We all know how much you wanted a repeat homecoming win senior year just to rub it in Bailey's face

AMAYA

Hey! I wanted to win to prove that AOPi was the best

AMAYA

Fine. Maybe also to stick it to Bailey just a little. ok, I promise I'll be nice

Good. I think she's genuinely sorry and needs some friends

LANA

You're right, Teegs—we all could have done a better job at trying to befriend Bailey instead of letting her get under our skin so much

AMAYA

I'm willing to wipe the slate clean. We all made immature mistakes, and we can all do better

Well said. This is why I love you both so much. One of so many reasons <heart hands emoji>

CHAPTER ELEVEN

October sweeps in, carrying a breath of anticipation. Crisp mornings promise hope of hoodie season. The first changing leaves whisper of the vibrant colors that will soon paint the town. Campfire scent lingering in the evening air assures the return of all things cozy.

Every year on the first Friday of October, the city of Brooklyn hosts a fall festival in Center Square. College students and town residents alike flood the retail-area-turned-autumn-wonderland for a festive evening of pumpkins, photo ops, local shopping, and apple everything.

This year, I'm attending the festival along with the freshman Bible study group that Sofia is part of. Parking is always sparse, so I planned to pick up Sofia and three other girls to carpool.

I spend extra time curling gentle waves into my hair before assembling my perfect fall outfit: cream sweater, plaid skirt, and sheer black tights. I debate for a while between wedge booties or knee-high boots, finally settling on the latter.

Checking my reflection in the mirror, I instantly feel happier. "Welcome back, fall fashion," I say out loud. "I've missed you."

Making the carpool rounds, my car gets louder and more enthusiastic with each passenger added. We arrive at Center Square, where I quickly find a tight parallel parking spot that everyone else was apparently too intimidated to take. Sofia applauds as I whip into the space.

"Lana would never," Sofia jokes.

I laugh. "We all have our different strengths."

We make our way through the festival, stopping for apple cider donuts and hot cocoa right away. My heart feels light as we make easy conversation in between taking pictures and shopping at the local booths set up around the perimeter.

I'm taking a photo for a random couple that stopped me when I hear my name.

"Teegan? Hey!" Brooks calls, stepping into my peripheral vision.

The couple thanks me as I hand back the phone. I take a moment to compose myself before turning to Brooks, who's looking much too attractive for my own good. He's wearing those black jeans and gray button-up like it's his job.

I shake all thoughts of attraction to Brooks from my mind. "Hi! Enjoying your first Brooklyn fall festival?" He didn't mention any plans to be here when we were all chatting about the weekend at small group on Wednesday. Otherwise, I would have prepared myself.

"Absolutely! This is the kind of small-ish town experience you don't necessarily get up in KC," he says. "You would know that already, of course."

"Are you here by yourself?" I inquire.

"No, I'm here with the other teachers on my team at school. We teach the core subjects to half of the eighth-grade class. We thought it would be fun to come and freak out our students by proving that we exist outside of school. I saw you and thought I'd come say hello," Brooks replies, giving me a one-sided smile.

"And who is this?" Sofia's enthusiastic voice asks behind me.

Oh great. Sofia loved to openly tease Lana about Mateo when she found out they were dating. The last thing I need is Sofia's mischievous meddling with Brooks.

"Wait a second—aren't you one of the teachers who's always at The Hangout on Tuesdays?" Sofia says, head cocked and eyes narrowed. "Mr. Murphy?"

"Yep, that's me. You're Sofia, right?" Brooks asks.

Sofia nods before looking between us. "How do you two know each other?"

"We're in church small group together!" I blurt at the same time that Brooks says, "We went to high school together."

Sofia's eyebrow raises at me. I huff a laugh. "Brooks and I first knew each other in high school, but we lost touch. Now we're in the same small group at church."

"*Mmmhmm*," Sofia hums. "How serendipitous."

"Lana would be impressed by that five-dollar word," I tell Sofia, scrambling for a way to end this interaction with Brooks. "We'd better go find the other girls."

"They're right over there," Sofia says with a smirk, angling her head over my shoulder.

I glance back. "They sure are!" I turn to Brooks. "Great to see you. Enjoy the rest of the festival—don't skip the donuts!"

"See you tomorrow, Teegan," Brooks says with a smile. "And see you on Tuesday, Sofia."

He walks away with a final glance over his shoulder.

"What's tomorrow?" Sofia asks, a sly grin taking over her face.

"Our small group is going to the pumpkin patch tomorrow night," I tell her.

"To the spooky corn maze? Sounds like a perfect date," she says.

I roll my eyes, probably with too much gusto. "It's not a date, Sof. Our entire group is going."

"But you wish it could be a date," Sofia adds, mischief increasing.

"I did not say that! No!"

"Teegan Murphy—has a nice ring to it," she says.

"Quit it, Sofia. We're just friends. More like members of the same friend group," I chide, pulling her arm toward the other girls.

"I'm just saying, the way his eyes sparkled at you looked more than friendly," Sofia concludes. She mercifully turns her attention to the other girls.

This is not helping my heart keep its distance! Ugh, why do freshman girls have to be so boy crazy!

I pull up to the pumpkin patch on the outskirts of Brooklyn at 5:30 p.m., parking right next to Natalie as she's getting out of her car.

"This is going to be so fun!" she says. "I haven't been to the pumpkin patch in ages."

"Yeah, I don't think I've ever been here," I reply. We begin walking to the big barn entrance to pay the fee. "I always go to the fall festival in Center Square, but I've never made it out here before."

"I've definitely never done the spooky corn maze—I'm a bit of a scaredy cat," Natalie says sheepishly. "I looked it up online, though, and it looks like it's not a full-fledged haunted corn maze. Nothing jumps out at you. At least, I hope that's true!"

I laugh. "It will be fun. Safety in numbers!"

As we join the rest of our small group members, I try to avoid eye contact with Brooks outside of our initial greeting.

Everyone disperses to food trucks to get some dinner before we play the festival games, and we plan to walk through the corn maze in smaller groups once darkness falls.

Catherine wins the pumpkin ring toss game, but Brooks annihilates us all at basketball. I rally everyone to race on the adult tricycles, garnering hysterical laughter as we take over the small track and basically turn it into a bumper cars experience. We take turns riding tubes down the mega slide, cackling at our shenanigans (and possibly earning some glares from the employees).

My heart is filled to the brim. *This is exactly what I needed in my life. Peers who encourage me in my faith but are also friends I enjoy spending time with.*

As if sensing my thoughts, Joy walks beside me on our way to the corn maze. We slow to an ambling pace. "I'm really glad you joined the group, Teegan. You bring such a special dose of energy. I always enjoyed talking to you after church, but I've really enjoyed getting to know you better."

"It's been a lifesaver for me this semester," I respond. "This group is exactly what I needed. Thank you for including me. I know I'm not the only one who's grateful that you and Caleb formed this group."

By the time Joy and I catch up, Natalie has already started through the corn maze along with Candace and Brian. Sarah, Catherine, Jason, and Will are making their way through the entrance right as we arrive.

Leaving Brooks and me to join Caleb and Joy. *Of course.*

Brooks' smile is all mischief as he turns to us. "Ready to be spooked out of your mind?"

Joy laughs. "I don't think it's quite that scary. More moody than anything."

"The experience is what you make it," Brooks replies.

We walk through the arched entrance to the pitch-black maze. After allowing our eyes to adjust, there's enough light from interspersed lanterns to make out the corn walls but not much else. There's fog being pumped in by machines and spooky music playing quietly over speakers buried in the stalks of corn.

I stick close to Joy in order to avoid proximity to Brooks as we make our way through the maze, frequently turning around at dead ends. Caleb and Brooks occasionally try to scare us by pointing out spooky shadows or making eerie noises. However, Joy and I laugh at their attempts, enjoying the experience.

We must be nearing the end of the maze, given how long we've been exploring, when one of the LED lanterns flickers off. I don't know if that's an accident or a planned part of the experience, but it's creepy either way. We're in near total darkness, and I can't help but inch slightly closer to Brooks' presence next to me as we cautiously make our way forward.

"BOO!" Caleb jumps out of the darkness in front of Joy and me. Both of us scream, and I reflexively reach out to grab on to Brooks. His arm quickly wraps around me, pulling me against his chest.

And now my heart has two reasons to beat wildly.

The perfection of Brooks' accidental embrace is too much. I jump back from him as Joy vigorously scolds Caleb for scaring us. Caleb apologizes and takes Joy's hand to continue through the maze, although she continues giving him an earful.

"You okay?" Brooks whispers in the dark.

"*Mmhmm*," I reply, abruptly turning away from him. He's quiet the rest of the way through the maze, his light-hearted banter missing from the otherwise serious ambiance. Thankfully, we make it to the exit in a few minutes.

Now, I just need to escape from Brooks' presence altogether, because my attempts at emotional distance are coming up short.

Chapter Twelve

I'm grateful for a break from seeing Brooks the Wednesday following our pumpkin patch excursion, due to his parent-teacher conferences. My heart initially misses his presence at small group, until I scold it for disobeying instructions.

I throw my focus into work on campus, spending more time than usual in the sorority houses, hoping to distract my attention from Brooks' troubling existence. Luckily for me, it's peak homecoming season, so the sororities are eager to have extra hands painting yard displays and pomping floats. It's the perfect opportunity to have meaningful conversations with the girls while working alongside them in their world.

Bailey and I get dinner together on another Sunday evening, and she confirms that she had encouraging conversations with both Lana and Amaya. She seems to be enjoying working for the athletic department, and she asks lots of questions about my experience on staff. I find it helpful to talk to someone who understands my Arrow ministry world without being directly *in* it.

I miss our third small group meeting of the month because two Arrow students are performing in a musical on campus. But this week is our group game night on Friday, so I'm not too sad about missing.

I *love* game nights. They are one of my favorite pastimes ever. My hidden competitive side comes out full force, and I'm fueled with enough social energy to last several days.

So when I wake up feeling sluggish for my early Bible study on Friday morning, I'm concerned. But I write off the worry that it's been a busy week, resulting in a lack of sleep. Tomorrow morning is commitment-free, so I can sleep in and recover.

Unfortunately, as the day goes on, my body objects more and more. I'm barely capable of contributing to the discussion during our staff meeting, frequently spacing out and missing chunks of the conversation.

"Teegan? Can you handle planning that?" Kent's voice cuts in.

"I'm sorry, what?" I ask, my cheeks flushing with embarrassment.

"We were talking about doing a costume dance party this year for the After Party the week of Halloween. Are you up for taking the reins on that?" Kent repeats.

"Oh, yes! Of course, I can!" I answer with more enthusiasm than I feel. I don't feel much of any kind of energy right now.

"Okay, great," Kent replies. "Lucas offered to pitch in with setup, and I'm sure you can talk with Gina about helping you when she gets back to town."

By the time the staff meeting has ended, I'm barely functioning. I cancel the lunch I had scheduled and head home, hoping that a little down time will help me bounce back.

Gina is out of town for a week at her cousin's debut celebration. Gina's mom's family is Filipino, and they've continued the cultural tradition of a coming-of-age celebration for their eighteenth birthdays. Gina won't get back until Monday, giving me a chance to relax in a quiet house.

Locking the front door behind me, I fling myself down on the couch. *Maybe a quick nap will help me feel better for tonight.*

———

I'm slow to come back to full consciousness. I click my phone on and see that it's after 5:00 p.m., which means I passed out for three hours. And I'm supposed to be at Joy's house at 5:30.

Groaning, I sit up but promptly lay back down.

Is this what dying feels like? I think this must be what dying feels like.

Slowly attempting to sit up again, I steady myself enough to use the bathroom. Next stop is my bedroom, where I swap my jeans for flared leggings and my scratchy sweater for a soft, oversized sweatshirt to ward off the goosebumps. I know that I should stop in the kitchen and get some water, but the couch is calling out to me. Easing back onto the cushions, tears fill my eyes as I plunge into a pool of self-pity.

Of course, I get sick on small group game night. So unfair.

I shoot off a text message to Joy letting her know that I won't be able to make it.

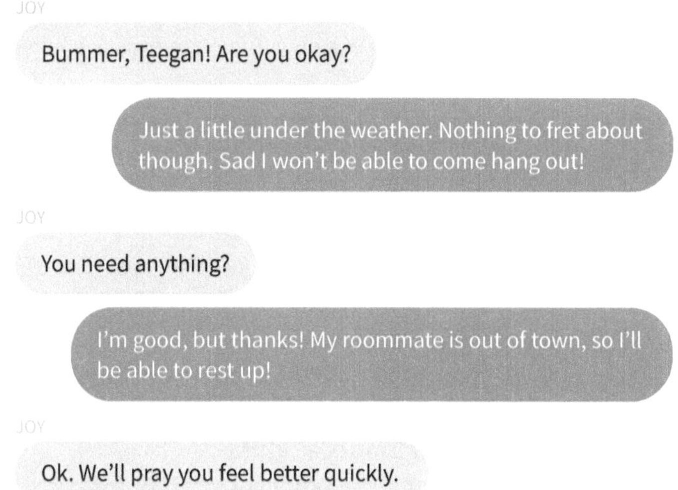

I click off my phone and turn on the television, hoping to distract my mind from the depressing FOMO.

Half an episode of *The Voice* later, there's a loud knock on my door. Assuming that it must be some solicitor with no sense of appropriate calling times, I ignore it.

There's another knock, and a familiar voice calls out, "Teegan? Can you hear me? I know you're there."

No. No, no, no. Brooks doesn't need to be here right now. Not when my defenses are down. Not when I look like Death's daughter.

I decide to ignore him and feign absence, but, next thing I know, my phone lights up and rings loudly with a phone call from him. *So much for feigning absence.*

Slowly rising to my feet, I smooth my hair down as best I can before opening the door a crack. Brooks is standing outside, arms laden with grocery bags.

"What are you doing here?" I ask. Whatever germs have taken up residence in my body apparently shut down my manners. I don't even open the door fully.

"You're sick," Brooks responds, as though that's enough of an explanation.

"Only a little. I told Joy I'd be fine," I say.

"Yes, Joy said you told her that," Brooks replies. "But you forget that I know you, Teegan. You'd never miss a game night unless you were at Death's door."

A chill runs through me. Brooks-induced or fever-induced? Jury's out.

I'm still staring, which is likely unnerving, given the less-than-human state of my eyes.

Brooks raises his arms, holding up the grocery bags. "Let me take care of you, Teegan," he says, voice quiet and eyes pleading.

"But I'm probably contagious. You'll get sick too if you come in here," I reason, even though that's not the *real* reason I don't want to let him in. I don't trust the decision-making skills of my fever-addled brain under the influence of Brooks' nearness.

"I'm a teacher. I have an immune system of steel," Brooks says, voice firm and commanding. "I'm coming in, and I'm taking care of you."

He pushes his way in the door, and I step back to let him enter. Which might be the beginning of the end for me.

"I didn't know what your symptoms were, so I got pretty much every medicine and remedy I could think of at the store," Brooks says, spreading the grocery bags out on the table. "What hurts?"

"What doesn't hurt?" I quip back, trying to make light of the situation. Brooks gives me a scolding look. "My stomach is fine. But a hammer has taken up residence in my head, and every muscle in my body has joined a picket line. Moving hurts so much."

Brooks puts the back of his hand to my forehead and swears under his breath. "Sorry, old habits die hard. Especially when I'm stressed. You're burning up," he says. "We need to get your fever down."

He places his hands on my shoulders, and, despite his gentleness, the touch causes pinpricks of pain under my skin. I flinch, and he lightens his touch even more as he guides me back to the couch.

"I'm going to give you ibuprofen first to help with the muscle aches and fever. When's the last time you ate something?" he asks.

I give an indiscriminate shrug.

"Food first. Or your stomach will join your muscles on the picket line," he states. "Toast or potato soup?"

"Soup, please," I answer as I sit down on the couch. Closing my eyes, I lean my head back on the cushion. I hear microwave beeps, and Brooks brings over a small bowl of soup, an electrolyte drink, and two pills. He takes the TV remote and sits down on the love seat perpendicular to the couch.

"You eat. I'll find something to watch," he commands. I can't help the whisper of a smile that crosses my lips before I take a bite.

Brooks confidently navigates the television menus as I eat more of the potato soup. A minute later, he hits play on *Trolls*.

The spoon in my hand pauses midway to my mouth. I look over at him.

He meets my eyes. "What? You don't like this movie anymore?"

I was secretly obsessed with *Trolls* in high school. Except, it wasn't a secret from Brooks since we had no secrets. I identified with Poppy on a soul level. Her inclination to find the bright side of any circumstance. To turn any situation into an adventure. Her impossible-to-dampen spirit.

That is, until reality smacked her in the face and she temporarily lost her color. Relatable.

I pause for a beat to tamp down the swell in my chest before answering. "No, I still love *Trolls*. But no one is supposed to know that a kid movie is my favorite."

Brooks tilts his head, considering me. "Well, it's only you and me here. So you don't have to hide."

My eyes drop from his. He clears his throat. "You should be okay to take the medicine now as long as you finish the soup."

I nod, appreciating the excuse to focus on something other than him. I swallow the pills and several gulps of the sports drink before returning to the soup. Brooks takes the bowl from me when I'm done, and I hear water running in the sink followed by the clank of the bowl in the dishwasher.

My energy is drained from sitting up and eating. Propping my head on a throw pillow, I pull my legs up onto the couch, shivering. Brooks returns to the living room, and I motion to the love seat.

"Will you hand me that throw blanket?" I ask.

"No," he answers.

"What? Rude."

"I know you're cold, but your fever is super high, Teegan. You can't trap your body heat in with a blanket," he states, firm yet gentle. "Do you have an extra bed sheet somewhere?"

"Yeah, in the hall linen closet," I say. "But I'd rather have the blanket. I'm freezing."

"Sorry, can't do that. But I'll get a sheet if you sit up and drink the rest of that energy drink."

"You're so bossy," I grumble, but I sit up to grab the drink. Brooks walks down the hallway and returns with a flat sheet. He makes good on his threat and doesn't hand it over to me until I've chugged the rest of the bottle.

I dramatically flop back down on my pillow and hold out my hand. "There! I drank it. Now give me the sheet."

Brooks spreads the sheet over me, making sure it covers my feet. His nearness makes my heart flutter, and I wish with every fiber of my achy being that I did not look like the plague right now. When he leans in to tuck the sheet around my shoulders, I get an inhale of his mountain spring body wash scent. *Why does he have to smell so good?* I mentally whine. I close my eyes, willing myself not to whimper out loud.

He settles back into the love seat, and we watch *Trolls* in silence, apart from an occasional laugh from Brooks. I fight the heaviness in my eyes to stay awake, but I lose the battle by the time Poppy and Branch reach Bergen Town.

As I slowly regain consciousness, I recognize the sounds of the second *Trolls* movie before I drag my eyes halfway open. I'm disoriented but notice two things.

One: I am blazing hot. Apparently while I was asleep, my blood morphed into lava and is incinerating me from the inside out.

Two: My arm under my head is stretched the short distance between the corner of the couch and the loveseat, my fingers wrapped around Brooks' hand propped on the cushion.

And it's the smallest, biggest comfort.

No. No, Teegan!

I combine the withdrawal of my hand from his with a full-body stretch, avoiding any acknowledgment of the contact. The loss of his comforting touch focuses my senses on the lava flowing beneath my skin.

Kicking the sheet off of me, I abruptly sit up—too abruptly. The hammer inside my skull protests the movement, and I fall back to the pillow. "I'm so hot," I sputter.

The feather-light touch of Brooks' fingers returns to my forehead. "Yeah, your fever is back in full force," he says, concern deepening in his voice. "It's been three hours—you need more medicine."

Brooks moves from the love seat, and I hear the rustling of grocery bags. I manage to slowly ease myself to a sitting position. My sweatshirt feels like a heating blanket now, so I pull it off over my head.

The air hits the skin around my tank top with cool relief. I hear Brooks' sharp intake of breath in front of me. Looking up, I see him shake his head briefly before closing the gap between us. He holds out two green capsules to me, along with a glass of water.

"Nighttime cold and flu medicine to bring down the fever and pain. Hopefully it will knock you out too, once it kicks in," he says.

I accept the medicine and quickly swallow it. Even the couch is making me feel hot, so I slip to the floor, plastering my face to the cool surface of the coffee table. My hair is stringy and sweaty, sticking to my neck and shoulders.

"I want to take a cold shower," I mumble. My brain tells my limbs to crawl to the bathroom, but my muscles are still on strike.

"That's not a good idea," Brooks says gently. "Having wet hair when the chills come back would only make you feel colder."

"I'm never going to feel cold again in my life," I say, eyes closed. "I've turned into the lava monster from *Moana*."

Brooks huffs a laugh. "I'll remind you of that declaration next time you beg me for a blanket. Hold on."

He retreats down the hallway, and I hear water running in the bathroom. When he returns, he takes my hand briefly to slip off the hair tie perpetually available on my wrist. I sense his presence behind me on the couch before he asks, "Can you hold your head up for just a minute?"

I raise my head, a "why?" poised on my tongue. His fingers slide across my scalp, gathering up sections of my hair one by one.

"You know how to braid hair?" I ask, voice shaky.

"Well, I'm not going to win any cosmetology awards," Brooks responds, a tease in his voice. "But I watched you braid enough hair to remember the basics."

"Oh my goodness, I forgot about that," I murmur. One of the girls on dance team with me had thick, lush locks that were perfect for intricate braiding styles. She was kind enough to humor my obsession with braiding her hair at every party or social event we ever attended. "Kelly had the best hair ever."

"She had *long* hair," Brooks corrects.

"Right. Same, same," I say.

"Not same. Having waist-length hair doesn't make it the *best* hair," he states.

"Tell that to Rapunzel," I quip.

"Pretty sure she liked the non-cursed short style that Flynn gave her better," Brooks quips back. He twists the hair tie back and forth around the end of my braid, silencing me. When he's done, I feel a cold, wet washcloth press against my neck.

"*Mmm*, that's perfect," I murmur, returning my head to my arms on the coffee table.

Brooks tucks a missed strand of hair behind my ear. Even though my eyes are closed, I feel his tangle of emotions in the slightly lingering touch of his fingers against my skin.

This is not good. This is not distance.

"You really need to hydrate. Can you drink some more water?" Brooks asks, voice thick with those muddled emotions.

I nod my head but keep my eyes closed as long as possible. Sitting up, I accept the glass of water from him, draining it. I immediately shut my eyes again. The lava in my veins is slowly cooling, although there's a different kind of heat competing with the fever.

"It would probably be a good idea for you to lie down in your bed now. You'll sleep better if you're more comfortable," Brooks says. "Can you stand if I help you up?"

"I can stand on my own," I respond, pushing up onto my knees. The movement offends my muscles and my brain, so I pause to brace myself on the coffee table.

"Just let me help you, Teeg," Brooks says, reaching down to take one of my elbows and holding his other hand out to me. I reluctantly place my hand in his and allow him to pull me up to stand. He intuitively waits a moment for my balance to calibrate before leading me down the hallway to my room.

"How'd you know which room was mine?" I jest, trying to alleviate the intimacy of this moment.

"The pink comforter gave you away," Brooks replies, laughter in his tone. "The comforter I'm taking away."

"Fine. I don't want it," I say with a small toss of my head. *Oof. Bad idea.*

Brooks steers me toward the hallway bathroom and removes the washcloth from my neck. "I'm going to take the comforter off and get the throw blanket from the couch to put next to you if you get cold. No burrowing under layers, though."

I use the bathroom and trudge to my room, falling onto my comforterless bed. A moment later, Brooks is beside me, pulling the flat sheet over me and placing the throw blanket near my feet. "Get some sleep," he whispers. That medicine must be doing its job because I don't even remember him leaving the room before I'm asleep.

The sound of an alarm disturbs my very vivid, very odd dreams. I've nearly fallen back asleep when I feel a hand gently shaking my shoulder.

"Teegan? It's been three hours—you can have more ibuprofen now to keep the fever down. But you need to eat this toast first so your stomach doesn't get upset."

My bedside lamp clicks on, interrupting the darkness. I roll onto my back and cover my face with the crook of my elbow. "I don't want toast."

"But I sprinkled cinnamon and sugar on it."

I crack one eye and see Brooks holding a plate and another sports drink. "Okay then."

He helps me prop up against my headboard and hands me the plate. I manage to eat one piece of toast, but I'm too tired to eat the second. "Can one be enough?" I plead.

Brooks clucks his tongue but takes the plate from me. "I knew you'd negotiate. But half a piece of toast isn't enough. One piece will do."

A smile turns up the corners of my mouth. I quickly take the medicine and drink several swigs of the electrolyte drink before settling back into my pillows. Brooks' hand finds my forehead again, and I hear him murmur, "Still hot, but not as bad as before."

The lamp clicks off, and his footsteps retreat from the room.

For the first time in a very, very long time, I close my eyes *hoping* to dream about Brooks.

———

Muted morning light barely filters through the blinds when my eyes flutter open. My body and head still hurt, but it's a dull pain compared to last night. Throat scratchy, I roll to the side and take a drink from the glass of water left on my nightstand. As much as I don't want to leave the cocoon of my bed, I need to use the bathroom.

Wrapping the throw blanket around my shoulders, I pad across the room with sleepy eyes, not fully awake. As I exit my door into the hallway, my foot trips on something. Yelping, I nearly fall over.

It's Brooks. Lying on the floor of the hallway outside my room with a couch throw pillow and my pink comforter.

Between me accidentally kicking him and loudly yelping, he jerks up, startled awake.

"I'm sorry!" we both cry out. Brooks quickly stands up, and now we're inches away from each other in the tight hallway.

"I didn't mean to trip you. I had an alarm set to hopefully wake up before you did," Brooks says, hair disheveled and eyes blinking awake. The day's worth of stubble on his face adds to the sexy, sleepy vibe.

NO! Not sexy. Stop thinking that word about Brooks!

"I'm sorry I kicked you," I say, voice shrill. "What were you doing lying on the floor?"

"Um, ah," Brooks fumbles a response. "I just . . . I felt like it might be an intrusion to sleep in your room, but I wanted to be close by in case you needed anything. I didn't want to miss it if you called out—I'm a heavy sleeper."

"I know you are," I whisper. We stare at each other in the near-darkness, conflicting emotions weighing down the air between us.

"I was just on my way to the bathroom," I say suddenly, voice too loud for the quiet hour. Pushing past Brooks, I close myself in the bathroom, breathing deeply.

Looking in the mirror, I wince. I resemble an apocalypse zombie. Hair is sticking out everywhere from my braid; my skin is pale, and my eyes are glassy. Even my lips managed to become grossly chapped, even though they were perfectly moisturized this time yesterday. *Fantastic. There's a sure-fire way to make sure Brooks keeps his distance.*

Despite the need for that distance, I still take an extra moment to splash water on my face, brush my teeth, and quickly rebraid my hair. By the time I walk out into the living room, Brooks is armed with more water, medication, and cinnamon toast.

I take a seat at the dining table, pulling one foot up to prop my chin on my knee. Brooks sits down next to me. "Feeling any better?" he asks.

Nodding slightly, I swallow a bite of toast before answering. "Still achy, but not as bad."

Brooks reaches over and places the backs of his fingers against my forehead. "Still warm, but not on fire like you were yesterday," he murmurs. His eyes find mine as his fingers trace down the side of my forehead, brushing a strand of hair away in one smooth movement. "You had me scared for a little bit there, Sneaks."

Blood freezes in my veins at the sound of his old nickname for me on his lips.

I stare in shock for a moment before finally whispering, "Don't call me that."

Brooks flinches. "I'm . . . I'm sorry, Teegan," he says.

Despite my recent challenges with balance and movement, I spring to my feet. "Thank you for coming over, for bringing medicine, and for staying with me until I felt better. I'm feeling fine now, so you can head home and get on with your weekend." I'm speed talking as I move toward the front door, hoping he follows me.

"Teegan, hang on," Brooks begins, standing to his feet. "Please just let me—"

"I'm fine, Brooks," I assert, voice too loud again. "Thank you for the help, but you really can go now."

He's looking at me with so much of *everything* in his eyes. I'm trapped by the weight of us.

"I can still—"

"Brooks, please!" My voice cracks. "*Please* go so I can . . . so I can go back to sleep. I'll be fine. I'm fine now." There's a pleading in my voice that I can't control, can't stop from begging him to leave and let me escape this moment.

"Okay." His voice is quiet, resigned. He slips his arms into his jacket and his feet into his shoes. When he stands, he looks into my eyes, but I can't hold his gaze. "Set an alarm to take more meds in three hours. Please text me if you need anything, Teegan."

My voice is a traitor, so I nod instead of speaking. I manage to squeak out a small "thanks" before I close the door behind him.

I stare at the space he occupied, sobs building in my chest but refusing to escape.

It's been just long enough that I forgot why I needed to forget him.

CHAPTER THIRTEEN

I spend the rest of Saturday in a daze, blaming it on the lingering fever. I'm dutiful about taking medicine every three hours, trying to dull the pain, but there's a deeper pain that the meds don't touch.

There's leftover potato soup in the fridge, so after eating a bowl I lie in bed, hoping to nap.

Sleep eludes me as my mind replays the affection in Brooks' care. The tenderness in his touches. My chest suffocates with the weight of tears that won't spill out of my eyes. I open Spotify on my phone, thumb hovering over the search bar.

No. No, no, no. Don't go there, Teegan.

Sighing, I click it off instead. The silence is oppressive, so I begin talking out loud to fill it.

"Why, God? Why?! I've moved forward. I've lived my life. I've grown and matured as a person. Why would you make me go back there?"

Silence.

It's only 4:00 p.m., but I eat a banana and then take more of the nighttime medicine, hoping and praying that sleep will overtake me, quiet my thoughts, and shut down the memories.

My comforter is folded at the foot of my bed, so I shake it open to spread it out. Brooks' scent lingers on the fabric, flooding my nostrils. Groaning, I yank it off onto the floor. Curling up under the throw blanket, I clamp my eyes shut, begging for sleep.

After tossing and turning most of the night, I give up on sleep and roll out of bed at 7:00 a.m. My taste buds are craving more cinnamon toast.

I pour a bowl of cereal.

Sitting at the dining table, slowly taking bites, my mind whirls. Physically, I'm feeling much better than two days ago. But my heart is paralyzed. It stuttered to a stop, and I don't know how to get it back to beating normally.

There's no escape hatch from the bars trapping me. I'm captive to the past. The now. The what-ifs. The if-onlys. They're locking me in, clamping down tighter and tighter.

I fail at every attempt to fly my mind away from my feelings. No amount of envisioning sunsets, oceans, or sunny meadows takes the edge off the pain my heart feels.

Unlocking my phone, I send a text to our Beefs chat before I can talk myself out of it.

> I'm not ok. Force me to talk about it on our video call this afternoon. Don't let me wriggle my way out, or I don't know how I'll find myself again

Thirty seconds later, my phone starts ringing with a call from Lana. I silence it. Her second call is overlapped by a call from Amaya. Sighing, I text them again.

> I need a little time. I promise we'll talk this afternoon. Make me

AMAYA

> ok, but I don't like this, Teeg

LANA

> Praying for you till then, Beef

I take a long, hot shower, blaring upbeat music that doesn't match my mood. Leaving my hair to air dry, I start a load of laundry to wash my sheets and clothes. I throw my comforter in for good measure, just to erase all traces of Brooks.

Pulling out our cleaning caddy, I meticulously wipe down every surface, if only to give my mind something to do other than *think*.

I'm loading the dishwasher when I hear the doorbell ring. *No. Please don't be Brooks. I can't take it.*

"Teegan? It's Amaya!" my best friend's voice calls.

Rushing to the foyer, I fling open the front door. Amaya is standing there holding two giant slushies from Brooklyn's finest gas station slushie machine. The answer to every angsty situation we ever encountered in college.

I burst into deep, wracking sobs.

Amaya wraps her arms around me, despite the slushie cups, and I realize she's also holding her phone with Lana's face on video call.

I gesture for Amaya to come inside and close the door behind her, still shaking with sobs. "Wait, Amaya, I've been sick. I don't want to get you sick."

She spears me with a look. "Like that's what I care about right now? You could spit your germs in my slushie, and I still wouldn't leave you."

Her devotion brings a fresh wave of tears pouring down my cheeks. We sit down on the couch, propping her phone up on the coffee table so we can see Lana. I wave at the phone. "Hi, Beef."

Lana's face is stricken. "Ugh, I hate that I'm not there in person. I looked into flights but there was nothing leaving until late this afternoon. I wouldn't even make it to Brooklyn until tomorrow."

I burst into tears again. "You're the best. You're both the best. I have the best friends. Why am I being this way when I have you two?"

By now, I'm almost hyperventilating. Amaya lightly rubs my back and hands me a slushie cup. "Here. Take a few sips."

I obey orders, and somehow the slushie works its magic. I hum appreciation. "There's nothing a slushie can't fix, right?" I joke. Our college motto makes me feel a tiny bit more like my normal self.

"I'm totally jealous," Lana says with an exaggerated sigh.

"Not gonna lie—it's been way too long since I've had one of these," Amaya says, offering me a smile before she takes a sip from her cup. She pretends to tip her cup over. "Don't worry, we'll pour one out for you, Lana."

"Don't you dare!" Lana says. "Don't waste a single drop of that precious frozen liquid."

Lana's video screen is interrupted by Mateo walking in behind her. She swivels to look at him, and I hear her gasp. She turns back to the screen with a Styrofoam cup in hand.

"He brought me a slushie," Lana says, stars in her eyes.

"I couldn't let you miss out on the central feature of a good slushie chat," Mateo says, grinning at her. "Even if it's nowhere near as good as a Brooklyn original."

"True, but it's absolutely the thought that counts," Lana says, kissing him on the cheek. I smile at them, feeling genuinely delighted by their love.

Mateo turns to look at me in the screen. "Teegan, do you need me to fly out there and rough someone up for you?"

A laugh bursts out of my throat. Mateo is the sweetest, gooiest cinnamon roll of a guy there ever was. He was always the one pulling his teammates away from fights on the soccer field, not the one participating in them. "I have a hard time picturing you roughing anyone up, Mateo."

He smiles in response, but then his face takes on a serious tone. "Maybe so, but I'd do anything for the Beefs."

Lana looks at him like he's the embodiment of every fantasy. She reaches up to turn his face toward her and kisses him on the lips, for a not-short amount of time.

"Okay, okay, Lana, that's enough! Focus!" Amaya huffs next to me, rolling her eyes. I smile. Even my present broken heart could never begrudge Lana and Mateo their connection.

"I can't help it if him being protective of my people is irresistibly attractive," Lana says after breaking off their kiss. She whispers in Mateo's ear, making him smile, before giving him another quick peck on the cheek.

Mateo looks back at me and says, "Don't forget about my offer. I'm on call if you need me."

I chuckle, amazed that anything resembling a laugh could come out of me right now. "Thanks, Mateo. I'll keep that in mind." He salutes and then walks away.

After watching him leave, Lana turns back to the screen and cuts to the chase. "Okay, Beef, you've had time to calm down. Explain."

I blow out a breath through the hair on my cheek. "It's Brooks."

"Yeah, we guessed that much," Amaya says next to me. "But you've made it sound like he wasn't a big deal. This reaction feels like something is a big deal."

"I may have under-exaggerated our relationship a tiny bit," I admit but fall quiet again, lost in memories that I don't want to remember. Everything I packaged up so tightly and left to rot in the recesses of my subconscious is being yanked back to the light again, and I'm afraid of what will come crawling out.

Lana's voice is gentle. "Just tell us when you're ready, Teegs."

There's no way around this. I take a deep breath.

"Brooks and I met my freshman year and started dating at the beginning of my sophomore year of high school. He was a junior at the time. He was on the basketball team, and I was on the dance team. We were the stereotypical high school 'it' couple, but our love was so genuine. So real."

I pause, emotion clogging my vocal cords. "I know it sounds so cliché, so dumb considering we were only teenagers, but he was my soulmate. His energy clicked with mine in this flawless way that I don't even know how to explain. Brooks was my best, best friend. And the sweetest boyfriend. We were perfect together, brought out the best in each other. We had so much fun together every day. I know I was young, and probably starry-eyed and immature, but I was positive that he was my person. My forever. And he felt that way too. Or, at least, it seemed like he did."

A tear trickles down my cheek as I reach the painful part of the explanation.

"From a physical standpoint, we'd never done anything more than kiss because we agreed we didn't want to go any further than that. Over Christmas break of my junior year, Brooks started acting weird. He began pushing the boundaries a little bit, and when I called him out on it, he didn't react well."

My cheeks flush remembering the embarrassment I felt. I take comfort in the pressure of Amaya's arm around my shoulders. "I mean, we loved each other, so the temptation to go further physically was always there. I had friends from my church youth group who shared my personal convictions about physical boundaries, but Brooks had the opposite. I think the other basketball guys were giving him grief about it. But I told him that I hadn't changed my mind. Brooks said that if I wouldn't be physically intimate with him, our relationship was done."

Lana interrupts as she flips open her laptop next to her. "One second. I'm buying Mateo a plane ticket right now."

I exhale a breath through my tears. "Unless you also have a time machine, that won't do much good."

"I'm very resourceful when it comes to issues of justice. I bet I could will one into existence," Lana says. I can practically see steam spouting from her ears.

"I never want to be on your bad side, LaLa," I try to joke, but everything falls flat right now.

Amaya squeezes my shoulder. "I'm really sorry, Teegan. I'm sorry you were treated that way."

I look down at my hands in my lap. "I know it sounds ridiculous, but I was crushed. Beyond crushed. I was pulverized. Vaporized. I was only seventeen, but I felt like I'd lost the love of my entire life. But you know me—I couldn't let anyone know that I was that sad. So I acted like it was no big deal," I explain. Amaya nods, and Lana makes an affirmative sound.

"During the day, I put on the mask of my usual upbeat self. I acknowledged my disappointment that the relationship ended, but never told anyone how destroyed I was. By the time spring semester rolled around, Brooks was going out with a senior girl on the cheer squad. They only dated for about a month, but she openly flaunted their physical relationship. It was crystal clear that she did not have any of the boundaries that I did with him. Nor did the next girl he very publicly dated after her. He moved on like we'd never meant anything, even though I *know* we meant everything."

I sniff as a new wave of sobs gathers in my throat. "Nothing was okay. Because as much as I faked it, as much as Brooks acted like we never mattered, I knew I wasn't crazy. That I wasn't exaggerating or misremembering the depth of what we'd been to each other. I hid the truth from everyone, but at night, I would shut myself in my room and listen to 'All Too Well' on repeat. Every night for months, I'd cry alone, with Taylor as my only witness."

"Oh my gosh—that's why you wouldn't ever watch the ten-minute version music video with us," Lana says.

I nod. "Yeah, I listened to the ten-minute version one time the day the album came out, then swore I'd never listen again. Because every aching moment of those lonely nights flooded back. In excruciating detail."

Amaya moves her arm from my shoulders to place her hand on mine. "You could have told us, Beef," she says quietly.

My eyes fill again. "I know I could have. I just wanted to pretend he didn't exist." I close my eyes. "But he *does* exist. And he shared his faith testimony at small group, so I know he's not the same person he was in high school. I can see the ways that his relationship with Jesus has changed him. Still, I was determined to keep some distance between us, you know, because of our history. But he came here Friday night and took care of me when I was sick." I fill them in on the extent of Brooks' tender attention.

I take a long drink of my slushie, trying to calm down my flight instinct.

"Yesterday morning, he called me 'Sneaks.' It was his nickname for me in high school," I say. Amaya and Lana both look confused. "I used to be a huge Sneakerhead," I say sheepishly. Their jaws drop in surprise.

"Wait a second," Amaya interrupts. "So, Lana was secretly a soccer star in high school, and you were secretly a Sneakerhead. Am I the only one who didn't hide some essential part of my identity when we became friends?!"

Lana rolls her eyes.

"It's like we don't even know you," Amaya jokes, bumping my shoulder.

"I know, I know, that doesn't jive with the version of me that you know. But I used to ask for different Nikes every year for any birthday or holiday gift. Brooks and I both collected them. We'd spend hours together scouring websites for good deals on Dunks, Jordans, and Air Force 1s. But when he broke up with me, I sold every pair I owned and never bought another one again. It felt too much like a part of *us.*"

We're all silent for a beat. "I'm sorry I never told you about all this. But talking about it makes me feel it." My voice breaks off, and Amaya rubs a hand across my back again. "I don't want to feel it," I whisper.

Amaya pulls me into a hug, unleashing a new wave of silent tears.

"We're here for you, Teegs," Lana says. "I know you don't want to feel the painful things. But when you can't avoid feeling them, you don't have to feel them alone."

"That's right," Amaya adds. "We've got your back, always."

"Thanks, Beefs," I say, wiping my cheeks.

"How do you need us to be here right now?" Lana asks. She smirks before adding, "I do have flights pulled up for Mateo and me if necessary."

I huff a laugh. "No roughing up required. Honestly, I don't know what to do at this point. There's a part of me that wants to avoid Brooks at all costs. Like, I would catch a flight to D.C. and move in with you and Mateo rather than risk ever seeing him again."

"Done and done," Lana says with a tender smile.

I give a weak smile back. "But there's another piece of my heart that feels like Teegan is missing. I was okay all these years that Brooks was behind me. But now that he's back . . . I'm lost all over again. And *that* slice of my heart never wants to be apart from him again. But I don't know if that's actually a good idea." I groan and bury my head in my hands.

"I know you're not going to figure it all out right now," Amaya says. "But we're in your corner no matter what. However the pieces come together, we're with you. You don't have to hide from us, okay?"

I give a grateful nod. "If I'd had you two back in high school, maybe I wouldn't have floundered so much. Maybe I would have had a better way to cope. But I'm glad I have you now."

"You have us always, Teegs," Lana says. "Beefs for life."

Chapter Fourteen

Homecoming week gives me the perfect excuse to skip small group and avoid seeing Brooks the Wednesday after my sick weekend. I throw myself into the contagious energy of the events, attempting to brush off the weight of last weekend's emotions.

Lana and Amaya text me often, checking in and offering encouragement. Each time, I'm grateful all over again that God led me to them our freshman year. Their constant friendship stops me from shutting down inside myself.

On Saturday, I send a triumphant text message to our Beefs chat.

> AOPi came out on top! Homecoming winners!

LANA

> Even though I know you're supposed to be neutral now, I hope you're inwardly celebrating

> Like I could hide my enthusiasm

AMAYA

> YES. It was a crap week at work, and this is exactly the good news I needed

LANA

> Aw, I'm sorry, Beef. The real world sucks sometimes

AMAYA

> Truth

Need anything? I've heard we have some muscle available to rough people up as needed

LANA

<laughing GIF>

AMAYA

Nah, I'm fine. Just an annoying coworker not pulling their weight

Not everyone can be as amazing as you

I'm smiling down at my phone when I hear Bailey's voice. She's talking to a group of TriAlphas, so I head over to say hi.

"Hey, Bailey! I should have figured you would be here!" I say.

She smiles at me. "Congrats to AOPi! They did a great job this week." Her praise seems genuine. *I guess that goes to show that anyone can change their ways.*

"Are you going to the soccer game?" I ask.

"Nah, I don't think so," Bailey responds as the TriAlphas leave to join their group. "You?"

"I was thinking about it, but I'm worn out. Want to go grab an early dinner?" I ask.

Bailey's eyes momentarily widen with surprise. "Yeah, I would. Thanks, Teegan."

———

After an entirely pleasant dinner with Bailey, I head home. Gina texts me an update from the soccer game—the Townsend Bobcats are winning 1-0 to start the second half. In the past, I never would have passed up a social opportunity with students, but lately, I've been better at occasionally saying no so I can refill my own tank.

I plop down on the couch to watch a show. Halfway through, my calendar reminds me to call my dad. Dialing his number, I turn down the volume on the TV.

"Hey, Teegan," my dad's booming voice answers. "How are ya?"

"Hi, Dad! I'm good. Had a busy homecoming week, but I'm watching TV and relaxing at home tonight. How's work going?" I ask.

"Oh, nothing too interesting," he responds. "What show are you watching? Have you seen that conspiracy theory dance show on Netflix?"

"Yes!" I exclaim, and we spend the next fifteen minutes dissecting our reactions. "Are you still going to come over for Thanksgiving dinner?" My parents' amicable divorce has meant joint holiday celebrations some years, at least when my dad isn't traveling to visit his extended family.

"Um, probably so," he replies, sounding hesitant.

"Did you decide to travel this year?" I ask, unable to hide the disappointment from my voice. I was really looking forward to being with both my parents together this year, especially since Logan won't be there.

"No, I just hadn't fully ironed out my plans yet," Dad says, still sounding flighty. I'm silent.

He clears his throat. "You know what—I'll make sure I'm there."

"Yay! Good," I respond before changing the subject.

By the time I hang up with my dad, I have a long string of text messages on our small group thread.

BROOKS

> Are we dressing in costumes since small group falls the night before Halloween?

SARAH

> Lol—I couldn't tell you the last time I dressed up in a costume!

WILL

> I'm game as long as everyone dresses up. I'm not going to be the only one showing up in costume.

BROOKS

I promise not to leave you hanging

JOY

That could be fun! I'll plan some festive Halloween snacks

CATHERINE

Nothing creepy though. I don't like gory costumes

NATALIE

Agree. I see enough blood at work

JASON

Gross, Natalie

NATALIE

Realities of life. Particularly of bringing new life into the world

JASON

Someone change the subject please

Jason's latest text comes through as I'm catching up, and I take it upon myself to jump in and save this conversation.

Idea! Let's dress up as each other! I can draw names for everyone like a Secret Santa, then we can try to guess who is who

BROOKS

Best idea ever

SARAH

Oh I love that

WILL

Deal

I smile, congratulating myself on an excellent idea. Also, since I'm in charge, I can make extra certain that Brooks and I do not get each other's names.

———

I arrive at Joy and Caleb's house, dressed up as Will. My borrowed khaki pants and dress shirt scream "tech guy" to me, even though I have no idea if this is how he actually dresses for work.

We have a riot of a time laughing at each other's outfits and guessing identities. Natalie nailed her impersonation of me with a dress, matching hair bow, and color-coordinated nail polish. Brooks has on an apron and carries around a tray of cookies the entire evening, a perfect Sarah depiction. Will makes a big fuss about tech guy stereotypes, but everyone instantly guesses who I'm dressed as.

When the night is wrapping up, I'm talking with Catherine, Candace, and Sarah in the foyer. "Hey, Sarah, I have a request. Next Wednesday is my birthday, so would you pleeease bring a batch of those oatmeal chocolate chip cookies to small group? Pretty pretty please?"

Sarah's face brightens, and she says, "Oh yeah, I kno—"

Her statement is cut off by Catherine falling into a loud coughing fit, and I notice Candace giving Sarah an evil eye. *Weird.*

"I know you love those cookies!" Sarah says, cheeks red. "I promise I'll bring some."

I hear Brooks' voice approaching, and I'd like to avoid any further conversation with him. I think I've done a fine job tonight of acting like my normal, energetic self. I could win an Academy Award in the "Don't Let Anyone Know Your True Feelings" category. But let's not push the limits.

"See you Sunday!" I say, heading outside to my car. I notice Brooks on the sidewalk, watching me drive away.

Physical distance might be my only weapon until I figure out how to handle him.

Chapter Fifteen

I smile to myself, excited about a birthday dinner.

I love my birthday. I'm one of those annoying, over-the-top people who wants the whole day to be a giant party. Even the whole week, if I could pull it off. My mom always went overboard celebrating when we were growing up, and college was the perfect atmosphere for celebrations.

But ever since I graduated, I haven't done anything major for my birthday. One year, it fell on a weekend, so I was able to go back to KC and hang out with Amaya. As an Arrow staff member, I'm typically the person planning the fun for students, so it felt weird trying to plan something to celebrate myself.

Of course, I have gushing messages from Amaya, Lana, and my family today. But the prospect of dinner with a friend and then cookies with my small group has me giddy all day. *Maybe they'll even sing "Happy Birthday" to me tonight!*

Catherine pulls up to my duplex at 5:45 on the dot. I practically float down the steps to her, bubbling with excitement.

"Thanks for doing this! It's going to be great!" I tell her as I buckle my seatbelt.

"I have the perfect place in mind," she replies with a grin. Catherine tells me about her day at work as we drive toward Center Square. She finds a parking spot, but when we get out of the car, she comes around to my side.

Catherine holds up a handkerchief. "I'm sorry, Teegan, but I'm going to have to blindfold you."

My heart lurches with excitement. *What?! A surprise?! Yes!*

I submit myself to the blindfold and let her lead me down the sidewalk. Music grows louder as she leads me through a door. Even though I'm blindfolded, I can still sense the darkness of wherever we are, interrupted by flashes of light.

I love this so much. My smile might permanently burst my cheeks, I'm grinning so widely.

Catherine leads me through another door and then pulls me to a stop. She takes off the blindfold, and I open my eyes to see a crowd of people wearing party hats. There's a loud jumble of "Happy Birthday!" and "Surprise!" screams. I take in the room filled with everyone from my small group, Gina and Lucas from staff, Bailey, and a handful of seniors from Arrow.

Yep, my cheeks are goners. They'll never recover from the happy grin splitting my face.

"You guys! This is amazing!" I exclaim, turning to hug Catherine. "Thank you!"

She laughs. "Don't thank me—I was only the decoy, not the mastermind."

Glancing around, I see a table full of food and drinks. A heaping platter of Sarah's cookies caps the table, alongside a huge cake with "Happy Birthday Teegan" iced on top. The next thing I notice is a small stage with microphones at the front of the room.

"Oh my gosh! We're doing karaoke?!" I can't stop myself from jumping up and down.

Gina and a couple of the senior sorority girls kick things off with a karaoke classic, "Party in the USA," as I take a few moments to walk around to thank everyone for coming. Bailey is standing with my church small group, and I gush my enthusiasm for the party.

"This is absolutely the best," I exclaim. "I love surprises. And parties. And karaoke! Gah, I couldn't be happier!"

"Hold on, you have one more surprise still," Bailey says with a smile, then nods over my shoulder.

I swivel around to find not only Amaya, but Amaya *and* Lana grinning behind me.

I scream.

They scream back and envelop me in a tight hug. I would cry if I wasn't so impossibly happy to be back together with both of my Beefs in the flesh. I haven't hugged Lana since spring break.

"What are you doing here?! Oh my gosh! I can't believe you flew all the way here, Lana! Don't you have class?" I'm squeezing her so hard she probably can't breathe, but she manages to laugh anyway.

"I got my work done ahead of time, so I could be gone for a couple of days," she says. "I'll fly back to D.C. tomorrow evening, but I couldn't miss an epic birthday party for my Beef!"

"You're the best ever! And you too, Amaya! This is two trips to Brooklyn on my behalf now," I say, transferring my squeeze hug to her.

"And I'd make a hundred more," she declares.

"How did you even know to come?" I ask, mind still reeling with delight.

Lana and Amaya glance at each other, the look laden with unspoken communication. Amaya shrugs a shoulder, and Lana turns back to me. "Brooks planned this whole thing," she says in a low voice. "He got Bailey to contact us to see if we could come and surprise you."

That information is possibly the only thing that could still my hyperactive energy.

Brooks planned this whole thing?

Of course, he would remember how much I loved celebrating my birthday. But why would he go to this much effort?

My mind is overloaded with puzzling thoughts and emotions. The kind I don't want to sort out right now. Or ever, maybe. Besides, I can't waste this perfect night with all of my people in one room. A *karaoke* room, no less!

"I'm just going to table that bombshell for later," I tell Amaya and Lana. "Let's party!"

My time is divided between killing it in karaoke and conversing with each person in attendance tonight. Lana and Amaya take the stage with me for a flawless rendition of "22," even though I rolled past that age a few years ago. Hey, if Taylor can sing it on tour at age thirty-four, then I'm allowed to sing it at twenty-six.

Brooks rallies Will and Jason to sing with him. He carries the group through a performance of "Bye, Bye, Bye," surprising no one when he dances all the choreography. Will and Jason are a half step behind, but they mimic his moves, being good sports for my party even if it may not be their jam.

Bailey even appears to be having a good time, joining in a group song with Catherine and Sarah. I notice that Amaya and Lana both make it a point to include her. Having all of these people here to celebrate me, to celebrate *life*, makes me all kinds of grateful and elated. I just have to avoid the one person responsible for it all.

By the time our reservation ends at 10:00 p.m., my vocal cords are shot, but my heart is full.

Best night ever.

"This is just like the old days! I could cry!" I exclaim. Lana and Amaya are staying at my place tonight, and we're currently camped out on my double bed with slushies. I'm sitting cross-legged in the middle of the bed, facing them as they lean against my headboard.

"Thank you so, so much for coming. I still can't believe you're here," I say. "I'm so HAPPY!" I throw my hands up and fall back on the bed. Amaya has the presence of mind to remove the slushie cup from my hand before I risk dropping it on the floor.

Lana laughs, but then her voice takes on a curious tone when she comments, "Seems like Brooks planned your dream birthday party."

I fold my arms to cover my face. "Yes. Yes, he did. Why did he plan my dream party?"

"That question might be secondary," Amaya states. I peek out from behind my arms. "The real question is: how do you *feel* about him planning your dream party?"

I groan, staring up at the ceiling as I process out loud. "I don't know. I mean, of course, it makes me feel special that someone went to so much effort. That someone knew what I would want and made it happen, right down to getting you two in attendance."

Lana pats my leg that's stretched out next to her. "But how do you feel about *Brooks* being the someone who did that?"

I don't want to admit the truth out loud. Because the truth is that far down in the deepest recesses of my heart, I love it. I *love* that it was Brooks who did this for me. But the fact that I love it makes me recoil. I want to run away from my reaction to him. Run away from *him*. I'm the kid who got burned and is now skittish around the fireplace. Every instinct screams to stay far away, yet the mysterious beauty of the flames entices me.

"I don't know," is all I manage to say. "What do you think?"

"This isn't something we can think for you, Teegs," Lana says softly.

"That's not fair though—I told you that you should get back together with Mateo, and look at you now! You owe me decisive advice," I whine. Lana rolls her eyes.

"Well, if that's the card you're going to pull, then I'll remind you of what you said to me," Lana chides.

I yell out, "Don't remind me!" as Lana talks over me saying, "*You don't have to limp through life knowing you've been cut off from your person.*"

I'm silenced.

"You were thinking about Brooks when you said that, weren't you, Teeg?" Amaya asks.

My continued silence is enough of an answer.

Lana plops down next to me, leaning the side of her head against mine. "We're not going to tell you what to do, Beef. You obviously have some tough history with Brooks. *And* he's clearly changed a lot since high school. But this is your heart we're talking about here. Amaya and I can't tell you how you should hold your heart in this situation."

Amaya flops down on my other side, making me the middle of a Beef sandwich. My happiness would be complete in this moment if not for these lingering questions.

"No matter what you decide to do, we're with you," Amaya adds.

I chew my lip. "So, if I decide to fly to Italy tomorrow to start a new, exciting life, you'll come with?"

Lana slaps my arm. "Be serious. You know what she means."

"I'm always serious," I deadpan.

"Always," Amaya says, and I can hear the eye roll in her tone.

"No more serious talk. Time to reminisce about all of our favorite college memories," I announce. The great thing about best friends is that they know you as well as you know yourself. So they know I need to move on to light-hearted conversation. And that's exactly what we do.

I barely sleep, but it's not because of my conflicting thoughts. It's because we stay awake most of the night talking and laughing, swapping memories and current updates. And draining our slushies, of course. This night with my Beefs is the balm for my soul I didn't know I needed so desperately.

The balm that Brooks made possible.

Chapter Sixteen

I ride the adrenaline high from my birthday for the next two days. I'm indefinitely putting off any serious thoughts about Brooks until I feel confident about what I should do. Hence, the "indefinite" putting off.

Friday evening, I get home from having dinner at one of the sorority houses to find Gina stretched out on the couch. She's watching TV with a bowl of popcorn in her lap, which looks like a marvelous way to end the day. I'm about to sit down next to her when she gestures to the table.

"A package came for you earlier," she says.

I detour to the table, thinking my mom must have sent me a belated birthday gift. Ripping open the cardboard box, I find a Nike shoe box inside.

My breath dies.

I slowly pull out the box and open the top, revealing a pair of white Dunk Low sneakers with pink accents. There's a gift receipt that simply reads:

Happy Birthday, Teegan.
- Brooks

My lungs are choking in the absence of fresh oxygen, but I can't remember how to inhale.

Slamming the lid shut, I tuck the box under my arm and clomp toward the door. "I'll be back later," I call over my shoulder to Gina.

Shutting myself in my car, I search our small group text thread to find Brooks' address he sent several weeks ago. Minutes later, I arrive at his apartment complex, not remembering anything about the drive here.

I stomp up the stairs to his top-floor apartment number and bang my fist on the door. When there's no answer after two seconds, I bang again, harder and unrelenting, until the door opens away from my fist.

"What are you doing sending me these?" I blurt, holding up the shoe box like an accusation.

Brooks' eyes widen and then furrow. "They're a birthday gift."

"I know. The message inside communicated that much," I say, chest heaving. "You didn't need to get me a gift. I don't want these." I hold the box out toward him.

Maintaining eye contact with me, Brooks raises his hands slightly. "They're a gift, Teegan. Keep them."

"I don't collect Nikes anymore, Brooks," I explain, voice bitter. "I haven't worn Nikes since—" I cut myself off, unwilling to confess more. I shove the shoe box hard against Brooks' chest and turn away.

He grabs my wrist before I can escape, pulling me into his apartment. "Teegan, stop. Come in and talk to me."

"No!" I yell. He drops my wrist but blocks the door with his arm. I huff. "I want to leave, Brooks."

"We need to talk, Teegan," he says, easing the door closed behind me and setting the shoe box down. My eyes are burning, my chest bursting from the shallow breaths I'm panting.

"There's nothing to say." My voice shakes. "There's nothing I can say to you, Brooks," I whisper.

"There's everything I want to say to you, Teegan," he responds, voice calm even as his eyes flash with fire. "I want us to talk through this. Because I want *us*."

The dam behind my eyes fractures, flooding my tear ducts. I press my palms against my eyes, spinning on a heel to hide my face from him.

Brooks wraps an arm around me, pulling my back against his chest. "Teeg," he whispers. My knees surrender as I sob, and Brooks drops to the floor with me. His knee props up beside me, his arm still cradling me firmly against him as he leans against the wall.

"I can't, Brooks," I gasp between sobs.

"You can't what?" he asks, voice quiet beside my ear.

It takes a minute before I can get another word out through my tears. "You," I whisper. "All of you. I can't do it again."

I focus on Brooks' right foot extended beside me, noticing the no-show athletic socks he must have worn with his own pair of Dunk Lows. He holds me tight but doesn't say anything.

"You don't understand, Brooks. When you ended things in high school, I . . ." I trail off, tamping down another sob. Talking to the wall instead of his face makes it easier to speak, bit by bit. "I wasn't fine. I completely lost myself for a long time. You were . . . I couldn't . . ."

He squeezes me tighter against him, notching his face against my shoulder, still silent.

"For months I had a dream. Every night, the same dream. You were back. You loved me again. We were together." I take a shuddering breath. "But I didn't even get that tiny moment of happiness, not even while I was asleep. Because, even in the middle of the dream, I was aware that it wasn't real. I would cry *in* the dream because I knew you weren't really there. That you didn't really love me. Even Dream Teegan knew it wasn't reality. I'd wake up crying, feeling the pain fresh. All over again, every night. Every day."

I feel moisture trickle down my neck where Brooks' face is pressed. The sensation uncorks a new bottle of my own tears.

"I can't go back. I can't survive that again, Brooks. Not from you. You ripped our souls apart once and made me feel like I made it all up, and I just . . . I can't." I break down again, covering my face with my hands.

Brooks' other arm wraps around my waist, clutching me against him. I feel his shudders all around me. We just sit there, silently mourning together.

"I'm sorry, Teeg. I'm so sorry." His voice is scratchy, broken as he speaks. "What I did to you is the worst thing I've ever done. The dumbest, most immature decision I've ever made in my life. I'd give anything to have the chance to go back in time and stop myself."

He pauses to take a breath, and my head falls back against his shoulder. His voice is barely above a whisper as he continues speaking against my ear.

"I never should have let the guys on the team convince me that you were anything less than everything. I was young, and I was an idiot. I cared too much about what the guys thought of me and not nearly enough about you. I was selfish and cruel and disgusting. The amount of shame and hatred that I've felt toward myself isn't something I can quantify. But regret can't change that I did it." He takes a deep inhale and exhale, my head rising and falling with the movement of his chest.

"Never, ever was I over you, Teeg. I know I acted like I was, that I started dating and sleeping with other girls right away. I know it looked like I was flaunting it in your face. But those relationships were so fleeting they don't qualify as relationships. They were all empty. *I* was empty. I used being with those girls as a way to dull the self-inflicted pain of not being with you. Which is a whole other set of behaviors and attitudes toward those girls that I've had to work through and repent of over time."

Brooks pauses again. Releasing his arms from holding me, he leans around my shoulder. "Please, can I look you in the eye when I say this?"

Blowing out a shaky breath, I shift on the floor to face him, and he immediately pulls my hands into his. "I loved you, Teegan. That was real. The most real thing I'd ever experienced until I found Jesus. After I became a Christian, I dated a girl from FCA for a couple of months. It was the closest thing to a relationship I've had aside from you. It was different in every way from the flings I kept throwing myself into after we broke up. But I ended it when I realized I couldn't stop comparing her to you. And that wasn't fair to her.

"I told you our relationship was over, but you've never been over for me. So many times, I thought about trying to reach out and reconcile with you, to beg you to forgive me. Even if we couldn't be together, to at least give you the apology you deserved." Brooks squeezes his eyes shut. "But I convinced myself that you would have moved on by then, that it would only hurt you more by bringing it back up."

He reaches a hand up to brush the tears off my cheek, cupping my jaw. "And then I walked through the door of Caleb's house, and there you were. Standing right there, back in my life again. Looking devastatingly gorgeous in that pink jumpsuit. Choking on a cookie," he says with a hint of a smile.

"And my heart remembered everything. I wanted to grab your hand and leave with you right then. To tell you I was sorry, to tell you about all the ways I've changed, to ask you about every detail of your life since I ruined it. To ignore everyone else in that house and beg to know everything about you again."

Brooks shakes his head softly as he closes his eyes. His hand drops back to mine. "But I didn't deserve that from you. I *don't* deserve that from you. I stopped myself, told myself I should give you distance from me.

"But getting to know you all over again ate away at my resolve. Seeing the same Teegan I once loved but also the new ways you've blossomed as a woman. Especially now that we share the same faith, I'm seeing you through this whole different lens. Appreciating the nuances of your character, your care for other people. Sitting in small group, listening to you share insights from the Bible, hearing the ways it shapes your life. Hearing your heart for the students you're guiding spiritually. It was sexy in a way I didn't realize was possible."

"Brooks!" I gasp, cheeks burning. He looks at me with a wry smirk for a moment before his face falls serious again.

"And then at the disco, when I saw that guy all over you, all I could see was red." Brooks' jaw hardens, his grip tensing around my hands. "I've never been filled with that kind of rage in my life. But then I stepped in, and he said you told him I wasn't your boyfriend. And all that anger instantly shifted to my own shoulders. I was furious with myself that I wasn't yours. Angry that I ever let you go."

A new tear trickles down my cheek, falling onto my arm. But I don't move.

Brooks takes another breath. "I spent that entire night, the entire drive home the next day, trying to think about what I could possibly do to earn my way back to you again. To prove to you that I'm different, that I'm not the same Brooks who was dumb enough to ruin us. I'm still desperate to figure that out. Desperate to have a chance."

I close my eyes, trying to breathe as thinking and feeling drain all of my energy. *What do I do? What do I want? What can I risk? I don't know. I don't know. I don't know.*

"I'm so overwhelmed, Brooks," I finally say, eyes still closed. "I don't know how to sort through what I'm feeling. I don't even understand what I'm feeling. It's so much." I open my eyes to meet his, still seeing the same pleading in his eyes. But there's understanding, patience there too.

Inhaling a deep breath, I slowly blow it out. "I need some time to think."

Brooks reaches up to tuck my hair behind my ear, his fingers lingering on my neck. I shiver. My heart may be undecided regarding Brooks, but there's nothing undecided about my body's reaction to his touch. "I'll give you however much time you want, Teegan. And if you reach the conclusion that I've lost my chance with you forever, I'll be heartbroken, but I'll back off."

Brooks swallows hard and glances down, then looks up at me with a gleam in his eyes. His fingers grip more possessively behind my head. "But until then, you need to know that I'm bringing the full-court press. Because I know what I want. And it's you. It's us."

His face is inches from mine, so even his whisper cuts straight through me as he adds, "It's everything."

We're frozen in place for what feels like hours, though it's probably only seconds. I'm confident that Brooks is fighting the urge to kiss me because *I'm* fighting the urge to kiss him, and I haven't decided if I want us or not. He eventually stands and pulls me up to my feet. I wipe my cheeks with the back of my hand, unsure how to transition out of this moment. At least my puffy eyes are matched by the red rims of Brooks' eyes.

I motion toward the shoe box on the floor. "I need you to keep those. At least for now." A pair of shoes shouldn't be such a big deal, but they carry the weight of the past. I don't think I can handle having them under the same roof as me.

Brooks nods. "They'll be here." He looks meaningfully at me. "I'll be here."

I'm starting to feel jittery, like I need to climb out of my skin. I pull open the front door, grateful for the rush of cold November air. On my way out, Brooks grabs my hand again. I look back at him.

"Full-court press—I'm warning you. Unless you shut me down, I'm coming for you, Teegan Jones." His tone is slightly teasing, but his eyes are impassioned.

I rein myself in from sprinting down the stairs to my car. Once inside, I clutch the steering wheel, trying to calm the tremble in my fingers.

Brooks' whisper fills my mind. *"It's everything."*

I know it is. But could I ever recover from losing everything a second time?

Chapter Seventeen

After driving aimlessly around town for a while, I eventually send a voice memo recap of my conversation with Brooks to the Beefs group chat. Lana and Amaya send back their supportive but non-directive thoughts, refusing to solve the "what should I do?" dilemma for me.

My sleep is restless, so I get up early and hop in my car, deciding to break out of town for a day. I send a text to Amaya asking if we can hang out in KC and start driving that direction before she even responds. She's probably sleeping in on this Saturday morning, but my flight instinct can't wait for her to wake up.

I have my "Forget Everything and Dance" playlist pumping while I drive, helping me escape the thousands of thoughts piling up in my mind. An hour into the trip, I get a text back from Amaya.

Girl, you're crazy. But yes, let's hang. Meet me in Westport and we'll find somewhere to go

A couple of hours later, I hug Amaya like I haven't seen her in a year. "Thank you, thank you, thank you, Beef!" I tell her, and she only laughs in response. She pulls back from me and raises her eyebrows in silent communication.

"I need distraction. No serious talk," I state, and Amaya nods.

We spend the day jaunting around Kansas City, eating lunch, shopping, exploring a park, picking up dinner, and talking about anything other than Brooks. Aside from appreciating the distraction from my thoughts, I love seeing Amaya in her new element here. Not sure how

I managed to snag such a powerhouse of a businesswoman as my best friend, but I'll proudly ride on her coattails forever.

I spend the night at Amaya's apartment. I can't risk in-person conversation with my mom just yet, knowing she'll sense my dodginess and pull the Brooks angst out of me.

Right when I've gotten comfy on the couch, a text dings on my phone. I can't handle the suspense of what I might be missing out on, so I check it.

BROOKS

> Gina told me you weren't home this morning, so your kind but confused roommate got to enjoy your cinnamon dolce latte. Please enjoy this video instead. #fullcourtpress

A video comes through a second later. It's Brooks dancing and lip-syncing to NSYNC's "I Want You Back," hitting every move flawlessly.

I giggle softly, and watch the video on loop. It's everything my viral dance-loving heart can't resist. But maybe he's everything I *should* be resisting.

BROOKS

> And now you know how I spent my Saturday. Hope you've had a good day

> <clapping emoji>

I don't say anything else, and Brooks doesn't respond further. Switching my phone to silent, I close my eyes to resist rewatching the video.

———

Brooks is fully committed to his "full-court press" approach. The Monday morning after my impromptu trip to KC, there's a bakery bag with fresh double-chocolate muffins waiting on the porch. The attached card reads:

I asked them for the sweetest muffins they had for the sweetest girl I know. Please read that with the cheesiest tone of voice you can imagine.
- Brooks
#fullcourtpress

I sigh, the breath full of delight or exasperation. Unclear which. Or maybe both. Because every emotion under the sun seems to be constantly bickering inside my head lately. Driving to our staff meeting, I don't bother resisting the muffins. Sugar is certainly one of the ways to my heart.

Tuesday arrives, and I'd promised Sofia that I would visit her at The Hangout this week. I want to support her and see what it's all about, but knowing Brooks will likely be there has me hesitating in the parking lot.

"You can fake it, Teegan," I tell my reflection in the rearview mirror. "Walk in there, support your friend, and pretend Brooks doesn't affect you. Easy peasy."

I confidently walk into the community center with my head held high. After checking in at the front and getting a visitor badge, I look around for Sofia. She waves me over to where she's standing and introduces me to a group of four girls. We're chatting animatedly when I spot Brooks across the room.

We make eye contact, and the joy in his eyes flips into bright mode. There's no other way to describe his actions than to say he positively *bounds* over to me, beaming.

He chills out by the time he reaches us, but not before Sofia saw his initial reaction. Her eyes glimmer with mischief as Brooks approaches our group. "Teegan, welcome to The Hangout!" Brooks says.

The group of teenage boys that was standing with him trails behind, merging into one large mob of middle school hormones and body odor. There are several whispered speculations about who I am, and I stifle a laugh at the unsuccessful attempts to be inconspicuous.

"Teegan is my Bible study leader at Townsend, and she came to see everything that we do here at The Hangout," Sofia claims with authority. "I'm always telling her about what a cool program it is, and how it's been even better since Mr. Murphy came this year." She adds that last bit with a not-at-all-subtle tone of voice and facial expression as she glares meaningfully at the students gathered around.

"Oh, yeah, Mr. Murphy is the GOAT," one of the boys announces, catching Sofia's drift. "He cares about us, no cap."

"Bet. He's always bussin in the classroom. It's the first year I've been interested in social studies," another student chimes in.

"We're all Mr. Murphy stans," one of the girls gushes.

Stifling my laughter is growing harder and harder as the students lay it on thick with their absurd Gen Alpha slang. Brooks, for his part, rolls his eyes with a smirk. "Besties, you're delulu. Stop acting so sus."

I burst into laughter, unable to keep it contained any longer. Brooks grins at me but rallies the guys to head to the rec area for their basketball tournament. I follow Sofia and the girls she's tutoring to their table, stopping to grab pizza on the way.

Sofia abandons their ELL workbook for the evening, choosing instead to make tonight a conversational lesson. I ask the girls lots of questions, giving them space to mentally translate their answers into English. Sofia is able to fill in the blanks for me when they revert to Spanish to give their full thoughts.

By the end of the night, my emotional tank is filled to the brim. These middle schoolers have so much energy and enthusiasm, a different variety than what I see with college students. Sofia thanks me for coming, adding a sly, "Feel free to come back to visit me—or Mr. Murphy—any time."

Back at my car, I'm choosing a playlist for the ride home when there's a tap at my window. My heart rate spikes when I see that it's Brooks. I roll down the window.

He leans an arm on the car door. "It was nice to see you here, Teegan. I know that meant a lot to Sofia. She talks about you all the time. And not just in an ornery, trying-to-make-me-like-you way. Not that I need any assistance on that front," he says, his smile contagious.

"You genuinely mean a lot to her," he adds. His smile takes on a wry twist. "That doesn't mean they're not all in there conspiring to get you to like me."

I laugh. "I'm glad I could come and see The Hangout for myself. For as much as Lana used to talk about it, I never visited when I was in college. This really is a unique program. I hope you're able to start something like this in KCMO someday."

Brooks nods, then taps my car door like he's about to stand up and leave. "And Brooks?" I add, stopping him. "It was fun to see you here too. Witness your middle school teacher rizz firsthand."

He laughs, but I can see a blush on his cheeks, even in the dark. "I'll take whatever rizz points I can get," he says, face turning serious as his eyes hold mine.

"Goodnight, Brooks."

"Night, Snea—" Brooks visibly catches himself mid-word. "Teegan. I'm sorry, it just slipped."

I realize the sting—the panic—that felt so all-consuming the first time he used my old nickname has completely dissipated. It feels . . . almost comforting again. "It's okay. You can say it now. It . . . it doesn't bother me so much."

The look of gratification that spreads across his face makes me feel fuzzy and fulfilled inside, like I've curled up on the couch in a sherpa blanket after a Christmas feast. His smile is tender as he whispers, "See you soon, Sneaks."

———

Two days later, I receive a midday text from Brooks. It must be his lunch break or planning period. Or he's texting during class just like high school Brooks.

BROOKS

> I thought about surprising you but decided against it. I'm coming to your Arrow meeting tonight because I want to experience what you do on campus for myself. But I didn't want you to feel awkward trying to explain who I am to anyone, so I recruited other people from small group to come too. You can blanket introduce us as your church friends

I try but fail to fight off a smile. His thoughtfulness has the temperature of my heart increasing by several degrees. Not only does he want to come see my world, but he also considered how his presence there might affect me. He's taking that extra step to make sure I feel comfortable, and that's just plain hot.

After spending an extra twenty minutes choosing an outfit and curling my hair, I head to the student union early. The welcome team girls haven't arrived yet, so I pace the lobby.

This is great, Teegan! It's so kind of your friends to want to see such a big part of your life. Things won't be awkward at all. It's all fun and games, end of story.

Thankfully, girls start to arrive and distract me from my solitary, frenetic thoughts. We discuss the campus-wide disappointment about the men's soccer team not making the playoffs this year (a fact that devastated Mateo, I'm sure). I'm fully engrossed in conversation with a large circle of girls when I feel a tap on my shoulder.

I spin on my heel to see Joy smiling widely, surrounded by Caleb, Natalie, Catherine, and Will.

And Brooks. An entirely too handsome, too familiar, too comforting Brooks.

"Hi, guys! Welcome to Arrow!" I say, stuffing down any conflicted feelings about the increasing pull I feel toward that man. "It's so amazing of you all to come!"

"I've been curious to see what this is all about," Catherine says. "I'm still trying to get a handle on what exactly it is that you *do* for your job."

I laugh heartily along with everyone else. "I confess it's a tough job description to sum up." I guide them into the meeting room and choose a row of seats close to the back. The band leads the group through the worship songs, and Kent shares a message about living a life filled with purpose. Nothing about this format is all that different from our regular Sunday church service, but I still find myself unduly anxious about their impression of the meeting.

"So, what did you think?" I ask after the band finishes the final song of the night.

"This was awesome! I'm so glad we came!" Natalie says.

Will chimes in next. "Yeah, I totally wish I had been involved with a group like this when I was in college. What a great community."

I'm listening and smiling, but my eyes keep darting to Brooks, trying to gauge his reaction. Despite my attempts to be subtle with my glances, his growing smirk assures me that he's fully aware of my attention.

"Hundreds of college students sitting in a room to grow in their faith together? What's not to love about that?" he finally says. "This is like my college FCA experience on steroids. Lots of steroids."

Everyone laughs and throws in additional comments of agreement.

"So, you have to go hang out even later than this?" Catherine asks after stifling a yawn. "The After Party deal?"

"Yep!" I nod. "Every week we do something fun after the meeting to give students the chance to continue hanging out and build more connections. Tonight, we're going to the specialty donut shop in Center Square."

"I'm afraid we're going to have to bow out of further festivities," Joy says, also yawning. "Us old folks need to hit the hay."

One by one, other members agree with Joy's logic. I can see the turmoil in Brooks' eyes, wanting to come and continue hanging out but not wanting to put me in an awkward position.

"Yep, the alarm bell rings early for teachers," he finally says jovially. "Thanks for letting us come crash your party."

"You're all welcome any time." I motion my hand toward the whole group as I say it, but my eyes are locked on Brooks.

Chapter Eighteen

By the time Thanksgiving week rolls around, Brooks has slowly chipped away at my hesitations one swing of the ax at a time.

Leaves a note on my door with his reflections on the thoughts I shared in small group that week? *Whack.*

Emails me a digital gift card to Raelynn's for coffee? *Whack.*

Scrapes the ice off the windshield of my car *before* my early Friday morning Bible study? *Whack.*

Continues sending goofy dance trend videos? *Whack, whack, whack.*

He's turned his full-court press hashtag into a way of life.

I spend the drive to KC for Thanksgiving with the music turned off, something I never, ever do. But I need some time to vocalize my many thoughts to God, hoping to untangle the thread to the right path forward.

"Okay, God. I really need you to shoot me straight here. I don't know how much longer I can stumble through the confusion. My heart is getting too tangled, too wound up with anxious energy. Brooks did everything wrong in high school, but now he's doing everything right. I can see the evidence of how you've changed him. I see the way he loves you, the way your love is guiding how he lives. He's apologized for the past. And I believe his sincerity."

I smile as I think about the Bible verse he texted me this morning, saying it reminded him of something I said during small group. Little did he know that Psalm 16 is one of my favorites.

"He's doing everything right to show me that he cares about me now. That he wants a relationship again. But I'm still so scared. I guess that's what it really comes down to . . . I'm afraid of losing him again. If I let him back into my life in that way, and it doesn't work out for one reason or another—how will I survive that?"

I exhale. "I mean, I know I'd survive, I suppose. But I don't *want* to experience that kind of agony ever again. It feels like Brooks is uniquely designed to make or break my heart.

"He said he's been trying to earn his way back to me, and I know that's not how forgiveness works. That's not how your grace works. But I also know that forgiving him for the past doesn't necessarily mean we have to have that kind of relationship again."

I sigh. "But I think I might *want* that kind of relationship with him again. Am I playing with fire by chasing after something I want even if it might burn me a second time?"

There's nothing but silence surrounding me in the car, but my heart also feels surrounded by a peace I haven't felt since seeing Brooks again. I don't exactly know what it means yet, but I sense God's command. "Don't be afraid. I am with you."

"Help me not walk in fear," I whisper.

On Thanksgiving morning, I shower and put on a navy floral dress that's the perfect combination of comfy and cute. By the time I head downstairs, my mom is already there, dressed in a blouse and dress pants with an apron secured over the top. She greets me as I pour a cup of coffee.

We chat while I eat an English muffin and drink my coffee, then Mom tosses me a second apron. "We'd better get to work if we're going to have everything ready by noon," she tells me. The counters are already covered with an array of Thanksgiving feast ingredients. None of my grandparents live in town, so it will just be my parents and me this year.

"Why are we eating at lunch this year instead of dinner like normal?" I ask, tying the strings of my apron.

Mom's brow furrows, but I can't tell if it's because of my question or the can opener protesting in her hands. She reattaches it to the top of the can of green beans, and this time, it turns without a problem.

"Your dad asked if we could eat earlier this year, and I didn't mind. This way, we could go down to the Plaza for their Christmas lighting ceremony, if you want," she says.

My eyes brighten. "Yes! I'd love to do that!" I start humming as I wrap sweet potatoes in foil. The *ping* of my phone pulls my attention away, and I open my text messages, only to find a novel from Brooks.

BROOKS

> Happy Thanksgiving, Sneaks. Things I was thankful for about high-school-Teegan: 1) The way you relish life with enthusiasm. 2) Your smile that could turn any bad day around. 3) Your willingness to go along with any of my crazy ideas spur of the moment. 4) Your killer dance moves. 5) The way I could be goofy but also be serious around you, and you liked both versions of me. Not just the fun-loving one.

Before I've even finished reading the first text, more come through.

BROOKS

> Things I'm thankful for about now-Teegan: 1) All of the above. 2) The way your love for Jesus influences every relationship in your life. 3) Your loyalty to your friends. The depth of your friendships speaks to your character. 4) The way your thoughtfulness about the Bible passages we discuss each week challenges me to think more deeply. 5) Your forgiveness. Even if we're never more than friends, I'm so grateful that you forgave my idiocy. But also, I absolutely want to be more than friends, in case that's been unclear till now.

> Also, your enthralling eyes and dazzling smile that I fall asleep thinking about every night

> Have I mentioned your laugh yet? Because it's a song with so many remixes, I'll never get tired of hearing it

BROOKS

I know I'm blushing as I grin at my phone.

"What's all this smiling over?" my mom asks.

Flustered, I hide my phone behind my back like a teenager. *Real smooth. Not suspicious at all.*

Mom's eyes narrow at me.

"Um, just a 'Happy Thanksgiving' text from a friend," I evade, turning back to the sweet potatoes.

"Uh-huh," Mom responds. Out of the corner of my eye, I see her lean a hand on the counter next to me. Her fingers start drumming against the counter, and it only takes two seconds for my willpower to lose patience.

"It's possible the friend might have been Brooks," I say, then bite my lip.

Her fingers still.

"That smile looked like more than friends, hon," Mom observes quietly. I put the foil down and turn to face her.

"Maybe? But maybe not?" I reply, then sigh. "It's up to me to decide."

"*Hmmm*," Mom hums. "And when are you supposed to decide this by?"

"I have as much time as I need," I answer. I quickly add, "I guess I don't know how to know, you know?"

Mom nods thoughtfully and turns back to mixing up the green bean casserole. "You know I loved Brooks right up until . . ." She trails off. I never told her the precise reason that Brooks ended things. I didn't really tell anyone.

Mom clears her throat and places a hand on mine. "But I love *you* most. The full you. I don't want to see the flattened photocopy version of my daughter who roamed around here for so long after things ended with him."

I'm stunned. "I didn't think you . . . I thought I . . ."

She raises an eyebrow. "You thought you hid how devastated you were? You probably did fool most people, but I'm your mother, honey. I know my daughter. And that shadow wasn't my daughter. Not for a long time."

I'm quiet, unsure what to say. *Do I come to Brooks' defense, explain all the ways he's different now, even though I'm scared of the exact thing that she voiced?*

"I trust your judgment, sweetheart. You're fun-loving and light-hearted at first glance, but there's so much depth and maturity to you. I know you'll do the right thing for your heart," Mom says, squeezing my hand. "I'm on Team Teegan no matter what."

I lean forward to give her a short hug, mumbling, "Thanks, Mom." Then, I quickly change the subject to ask how Logan is doing. We continue chatting and working side by side until everything is in the oven.

A little before noon, the doorbell rings, pricking my heart. Even though it's been years, I've never quite gotten used to my dad ringing the doorbell at the house he used to live in. The house that sheltered us as a family unit for most of my life.

"Hi, Dad!" I exclaim when I open the door.

"There's my girl!" he responds, wrapping me up in a hug. His tan sweater and navy pants give him a very dignified look, especially coupled with the addition of facial hair.

"A beard, huh? That's new!" I observe, and his hand rubs against the hair on his jaw. Nervously.

Weird.

"Yeah, trying something different," he responds before his dark eyes crinkle at the edges. "You look beautiful today. Not surprising when you've looked beautiful every day of your life."

I roll my eyes. "You have to say that—I share your genes."

"Nah, you got your good looks from your mom," he replies, hanging up his coat on the rack by the door. "Speaking of!" he says, looking behind me.

Mom sidles up to us at that moment. "Happy Thanksgiving! Good to see you, Morgan."

They give each other a hug before we head back to the kitchen. I help my mom pull dishes out of the oven, whispering under my breath, "Can we not mention anything about Brooks to Dad?"

She gives me a wink and purses her lips. I have a feeling she would have mimed zipping them shut if her hands weren't laden with hot pads and a casserole dish.

While we eat, I catch my parents up on the semester. I also share how uplifting my church small group has been (conveniently leaving out Brooks). Mom shares a story from work this week about how she solved the problem when her boss double-booked two important appointments. I smile as she shares because it's so evident that she's thriving in this position.

"Any more raises since September?" I ask coyly, knowing Mom will be too humble to brag about herself.

Her cheeks pinken. "Not since September. Although, my boss did say I'd be getting a significant end-of-year bonus, so we'll see what that translates to."

"That's fantastic, Reagan," my dad says after swallowing a bite of ham. "Good for you."

Mom blushes again, and my eyes dart back and forth at the lingering look between them.

"So, Dad, we were talking about going down to the Plaza to watch the Christmas lighting tonight. Would you want to come with us?" I ask, hoping he'll join.

"Oh, um, I don't think I'll be able to, Teegan. Thanks for including me though." He coughs, then takes a sip of water.

Logan interrupts the moment by calling my mom on her Echo Show, so we virtually seat him at the table to catch up. He's all smiles as he talks about the fish he and his buddies have been catching, and I can imagine the fish smell from here. *Yuck.*

The rest of the day passes by smoothly. I manage to avoid mentioning Brooks around my dad, and Mom doesn't bring it up for discussion again. Even though she would have had the perfect opportunity in the car on the way to the Plaza, or during the *long* walk from our parking place to the retail buildings. We arrive with enough time to grab hot chocolate to warm our hands before joining the countdown.

"We should do this every year!" I announce on our walk back to the car. "That was magical to see the lights and be around so many happy people! Too bad Dad couldn't have come—he would have loved it too."

"What's not to love?" Mom responds quietly. "Perhaps we've stumbled upon a new Thanksgiving Day tradition."

Later that night, I'm bundled up in bed with my coziest pajamas and blankets. I unlock my phone, staring at the text threads. I've already messaged several times with Lana and Amaya today—Amaya is in Wichita with her mom, while Lana and Mateo stayed in D.C. this year. They'll be in Michigan with his family for Christmas, which means I don't know the next time I'll see Lana in person. It makes me sad, but also grateful that she came to my birthday party. Which leads me back to Brooks.

I click open his text thread, contemplating what to say. How much to say. If I should even say *anything*.

> Was busy all day, but thank you for all your kind words this morning. I'm grateful that you wound up in Brooklyn and walked through the door of Joy and Caleb's house

Seconds later, the three dots start bouncing.

BROOKS

> I'll never stop thanking God that I got to walk through that door

Chapter Nineteen

I head back to Brooklyn the Saturday after Thanksgiving so that I can attend church on Sunday. Brooks isn't here, not that I'm watching for him. Simply a casual observation.

When the service ends, Joy finds me. "Teegan! Did you have a good Thanksgiving? Who did you celebrate with?" she asks.

"I did! Just my parents in KC, but we had a good day. How about you?" I return the question.

"We did have a great time. We traveled to see Caleb's family a few hours away, and it was good to see everyone," Joy answers. "Hey, would you be free for lunch today? I know I see you every week at small group, but we haven't been able to talk one-on-one in a while."

"I'd love to! I don't have anything going on. Caleb won't mind?"

"Oh no, he'll be fine," she says. "He'll be content to sit and watch football in the silence all day. He enjoys people time, but he's an introvert at his core. So some alone time after seeing extended family will be good for him."

Joy rides with me to Sandy's, a sandwich shop in Center Square that's a local favorite. We order food and find a table in the corner. She asks me lots of questions about campus, which I'm well-prepared to answer after sharing so many of the same stories with my parents. But then she asks a question that I'm not prepared to hear.

"So, have any of the guys from our small group caught your eye in a more-than-friends way?" There's a twinkle in her eyes as she asks.

I swallow my bite of sandwich before chewing fully, and it goes down with a fight. Gulping water, I cough and clap my chest.

"Sorry, didn't mean to choke you," she apologizes. But the twinkle in her eye has only grown at my flustered response. "I mean, you don't have to answer. I think that all of you are so amazing, and I *love* love, so I can't help but hope that some matches might be made. I apologize if I overstepped our friendship in asking."

"Ummm, ahhh, no, you're totally fine, Joy." I stumble over the words. "I mean, you *are* a friend I trust and would want to talk about these kinds of things with."

My eyes shift around the restaurant as my knee starts bouncing under the table.

"I just wasn't expecting that question. You caught me off guard, that's all," I say, trying to buy more time to decide how to answer.

Joy takes a big bite of her buffalo chicken wrap, giving me ample opportunity to continue talking.

I take another drink of water, desperate to cool down the flush heating my face. "So, yeah, I guess there's a connection," I say with false levity in my voice. "Or there *might* be one. Still to be determined."

She silently regards me with encouraging eyes. I blow out a long exhale. "Brooks and I are . . . well, we've talked, and there's the possibility of something, maybe."

"I knew it!" Joy exclaims, raising her fists and shimmying her shoulders with delight. "You two seem so perfect for each other, and I thought I sensed something in how he looks at you."

The heat returns to my cheeks at her comment. *How much do I explain? Leave it at that, or fill her in on the bigger picture?*

I bite my lip before deciding to dive in. "It's a little more complicated than that," I begin hesitantly. "Um, Brooks and I, well, we have more history between us than just small group this semester."

"Right, you knew each other in high school," Joy states. I give her a meaningful look. Her eyes widen as the light bulb flips on. "Ohhh, you *dated* in high school."

Nodding, I blow out a breath. "As Brooks shared already, he wasn't a Christian in high school. And he ended our relationship very . . . poorly."

Joy's face softens with empathy. "I'm sorry to hear that, Teegan."

"It's okay. It was a long time ago. And he's obviously changed a lot since then. We both have," I reason. "But it did mess me up for a long time when our relationship ended. It was . . . well, the most painful thing I've ever experienced. So I'm trying to figure out if I'm willing to risk a repeat."

"I take it Brooks has already indicated his interest in pursuing a relationship again? At least, the amount of planning and coordinating he did for your birthday certainly leads me to that assumption," Joy says.

I nod. "He's giving me the time to decide what I want. But he's leaving no stone unturned in the meantime."

Joy smiles. "As he should be. You're an incredible woman, Teegan. He'd better be pulling out all the stops to win you over." Her smile softens. "But also—it's okay if you decide to say no. Don't mistake me saying you'd be a great match with me pressuring you into it."

I look down at the table. "I've really enjoyed our small group, though. It's filled this hole in my life that I didn't realize was there. I'd hate to mess up the vibe of our group by turning him down. Or by saying yes and then having things end badly." I cover my face with my hands. "I think we've passed the point of no return, though. No matter what happens, there's a risk of things exploding."

"Teegan, there's always a risk of things exploding," Joy says, and I peek out from behind my fingers. "Each day holds the threat of something terrible changing life as we know it forever. But every day also holds the potential for beauty you didn't see coming. You never know what kind of day it's going to be. Sure, you can calculate risk, but you can never fully avoid pain."

I mull over her words. "I'm not quite sure how to calculate this risk. Math was never my strongest subject. My mental calculator is the kind that looks like a bar of chocolate you buy from the school book fair, not the graphing type," I joke.

Joy laughs. "I think you'll do just fine figuring things out. Let me reiterate: I'm not telling you that Brooks is a risk you *should* take. That's up to you to decide. I'm only reminding you that there's risk everywhere. Live bravely, even when you feel afraid."

————

Joy's advice echoes in my thoughts throughout the week. It's always in the back of my mind—during my Bible studies, while I'm visiting the sororities, even while I'm dancing my stress away at gym class. I decide I should text Joy and thank her again for all of her thoughts and encouragement.

Before I click my phone off, I open my latest text from Brooks. It's a photo of the sunset over the Flint Hills at the prairie reserve on the outskirts of Brooklyn. The vibrant pinks of the sky swirl with lavender clouds over the rolling plains.

BROOKS

Made me think of you. It's almost as beautiful

At small group on Wednesday, we're discussing the fourteenth chapter of John. We spend a lot of time talking about what troubles our hearts and what it looks like to rely on the peace that Jesus gives. A peace that's unlike what the rest of the world has to offer.

I'm quieter than usual throughout the discussion. But I can't exactly delve deep into what's troubling my thoughts and disrupting my peace right now. Not when he's across the circle from me.

Sleep comes in short bursts throughout the night as my mind tosses and turns over Brooks. At this point, it's useless to deny that my heart *wants* to be with him again. My Brooks. And yet, not the same Brooks. The updated version of Brooks that feels like it belongs with the updated version of me. As though every updated version will forever fit together, regardless of how we grow and develop with age.

Can I risk the possibility of a virus corrupting everything between us? Irreparably damaging my core processor? Since when do I think in computer software metaphors? I've been hanging around Will too much.

Because sleep was fitful, it doesn't take much to wake me early Thursday morning. The sound of an ice scraper outside my window pulls me to full consciousness in record time.

Somehow, that sound scrapes away any lingering hesitations. I race to throw a sweatshirt over my pajama top and slide my feet into slippers. Opening the front door, I see that it's actively sleeting.

And still, Brooks is scraping what ice he can off my windshield. Gina's car is already cleaned off, aside from the fresh pellets still falling. He's bundled up in a winter coat and gloves, but he still must be freezing.

Not even bothering to change into real shoes, I carefully make my way to Brooks, noticing that he sprinkled ice melt on the sidewalk.

"Teegan, what are you doing? It's freezing out here! Get back inside!" Brooks tells me when he sees me approach.

"I want this."

Brooks stares at me, hints of disbelief and hope wrestling in his eyes. "I really need you to clarify that statement," he says, a desperate huskiness lacing his tone.

My body trembles from a combination of fear, adrenaline, and frozen rain, but I plunge ahead through the discomfort. "You. Us. Everything. I want this," I state. "At least, I want to try. To see if there's a second chance for us."

The ice scraper clatters to the ground as Brooks exhales a shaky breath. He steps forward, closing the space between us. Pulling off his gloves, he cups my face in his hands. Pellets of ice continue falling around us, but the heat in his gaze sparks a fire in my core.

"This isn't just a second chance to me, Sneaks." His voice is tender, little more than a murmur. "This is the only chance I ever want. Before you say yes to this, you should know that I'm not just trying. It's not going to be a half-hearted 'it works or it doesn't' shot to me. We're talking next-level full-court press, Teeg. Is that still what you want?"

I can't look away from his eyes, from the intensity and pleading and fervor housed in those pale blue pools. Willing myself not to blink, I slowly reach my hands up to cover his.

"Yes." It's a whisper and a scream.

A smile twitches at the center of Brooks' lips, slowly spreading to take over his entire face. His eyes briefly drop to my lips before returning to hold my gaze.

"I'm going to work really hard to not get ahead of myself with you, Sneaks. But know that in my mind, I kissed you senseless just now," he says with a smirk.

I drop my head back, breaking eye contact, if only to stop myself from kissing *him* senseless. He's right—it would be far too easy to get ahead of ourselves. Far. Too. Easy.

"Can I take you on an official date this Saturday?" Brooks asks, and I nod a yes. "I'll think of nothing else till then."

"Your poor students," I tease.

"They'll be fine. They can read the textbook. It's riveting," he teases back. "Now go inside before you freeze and get sick again."

"That wasn't the end of the world, you know. I had a pretty good caretaker," I tell him with a smirk of my own, reaching up to tap my finger against the cleft in his chin.

He groans. "You are *not* helping the self-restraint, Sneaks. Get outta here!" He shoos me toward the house, picking up the ice scraper to finish the job.

Once inside, I close the front door and lean against it. The ice clinging to my hair starts melting instantly. I need a hot shower and dry clothes stat, but I take a moment to close my eyes and smile in the silence.

All traces of fear are replaced by the joy that wells up in my heart and spills out from my eyes.

This is the only chance I ever want.

Chapter Twenty

I stare at the messages, grinning ear to ear. Normally, I'd sleep late on a Saturday morning with nothing planned. But the anticipation of our date tonight has me awake far earlier than usual.

I can count on one hand the number of people who know that I'm going on a date with Brooks tonight: Mom, Amaya, Lana, Gina, and Joy. Usually I'm much more of an "announce everything to the world" type of person. In fact, I gave Lana so much grief about her reluctance to tell anyone about Mateo for their first few dates.

But I'm trying to wrangle my heart into submission when all it wants to do is get way, way ahead of itself. So I'm keeping things on the quiet side until I know with a little more certainty that this could really pan out.

Would it *actually* hurt less if things end poorly and I've told fewer people?

No.

But I wouldn't have to fake it around as many people.

So my lips are mostly sealed. Even if that means the buzzing energy is exploding my insides.

I spend the day doing grown-up tasks like grocery shopping and cleaning so that my mind has something else to focus on. At 4:30, I take a long shower and begin the process of getting ready. Standing in my robe in my closet, I consider my wardrobe choices. *Casual attire.* So, not a dress, I suppose. I eventually settle on a pair of light wide-leg jeans and a pink long sleeve top.

In the middle of applying makeup, a video call from Amaya rings on my phone. I answer the call and prop the phone against the mirror right as Lana joins.

"Hey, Beefs!" I say.

"How are you feeling about tonight?" Lana immediately asks.

"I'm feeling good!" I answer.

Amaya questions me next. "You feel good for real, or you're just saying that to hide that you're nervous?"

"Ummm, can it be both?" I reply after a pause.

"I guess so," Amaya responds. "I suppose Lana was that way at first with Mateo."

Lana nods. "True. But this is a slightly different situation. We want to make sure that your heart feels safe going into a date with Brooks."

I pause, staring at my mascara wand. *Does my heart feel safe? Is it possible to feel entirely safe when Brooks broke my heart once before? That doesn't feel safe at all. But Current Brooks does feel safer. Should I back out of this before it's too late if I'm not completely safe?*

"I can see the wheels turning, Teeg," Amaya says. "Care to share what's buzzing around the thought mill?"

"*Mmm*, it's complicated. And confusing." I pause. "Part of me feels terrified of repeating the past. That doesn't feel safe at all. But part of me feels overjoyed to have this chance with *this* Brooks. That feels safe-ish. So, what does that mean?"

"That was probably a bad way to phrase the question," Lana jumps in. "Relationships are never risk-free. Even without past hurt to consider. As you get ready to walk out the door to go on a real date with Brooks—possibly the start of a real relationship—are you feeling peace about it?"

Our small group discussion from Wednesday about peace fills my mind. And I have my answer.

"Yes. I feel peace about it."

"Then we're pumped for you!" Lana squeals.

Amaya nods. "Know that we're praying for you tonight, Beef."

"And we expect a full report," Lana adds.

"Scout's honor," I reply. "Now I need to finish getting ready. Love you both!"

At 6:25 p.m. I give my reflection one final perusal. Satisfied with my appearance, I head to the living room to pace until Brooks shows up. I'm thankful that Gina had plans tonight, giving me space to be alone with my frenzied energy. Even though my heart feels at peace with my decision to date Brooks, it's still working overtime, beating twice as fast as usual.

At 6:31 p.m., the doorbell rings.

I blow out a breath and open the door.

Brooks stands on the porch, dressed in dark jeans and a blue Henley shirt under a half-zipped fleece jacket. His hair looks extra-perfectly styled tonight, and his eyes regard me with a mixture of intensity and playfulness. His smile grows as he holds out a coffee tumbler with an intricate floral design.

"I thought about bringing flowers, but decided a hot cup of sugary caffeine might be the better offering for tonight," he says. I reach out to take the tumbler from him, and he allows his fingers to linger against mine for a split second before letting go.

"Ready?" he asks, and I realize I've been smiling at him without saying a word.

"Yes! Ready! Let me put on my jacket," I reply.

Brooks takes the coffee while I slip my arms through my jacket sleeves, then hands it back to me. It may have been a gentlemanly move, or it may have been an excuse for extra physical contact. Either way, I'm taking it.

We walk to the sidewalk, and Brooks opens the passenger door for me.

"Do I get to know where we're going now?" I ask once he sits in the driver's seat.

"What? And ruin the fun of the surprise? No way," he replies cheekily. I smile in the darkness as he pulls into the street.

"You can even close your eyes if you want the full shock factor," he adds. I happily comply. "And I'm not even suggesting that just so I can stare at your beautiful face while you're not looking."

"You'd better keep your eyes on the road," I scold, swatting his arm. Except, since I can't see, I miss, and hit his firm chest instead. I feel my cheeks warm.

"I'm an excellent multi-tasker," is the only reply he gives.

As we drive, Brooks tells me funny stories about his students from the week, filling the short car ride with laughter. He tells me to stay put after parking the car then opens my door and guides me out.

"One step up onto the curb here." He leads, holding me steady.

"This was an excuse to hold my hand, wasn't it?" I tease, eyes still closed.

There's a small pause, and I can feel Brooks' gaze without seeing it. "I'll make up every excuse I can, Sneaks." He clears his throat. "Now open!"

My eyes fly open to take in the sight of Brooklyn's only bowling alley. I burst out laughing.

"Cosmic bowling?"

"Not *just* cosmic bowling. Get ready for the most intense game of trick shot HORSE bowling you've ever played," Brooks says with a mischievous grin. "Let's go!"

After donning the rental shoes and picking out bowling balls, Brooks leads me to the lane he reserved for the night. The bumpers are up, and Brooks explains the "rules" of his made-up game to me.

"Like the game of HORSE in basketball, we take turns taking shots, and the other person has to replicate. If the second person knocks down fewer pins, they get a letter. If they knock down more pins, the first person gets a letter," he says.

"I agree to the terms," I say, holding out my hand to shake his.

"Now who's making up excuses to hold hands?" Brooks says with a wink. "Ladies first," he adds, handing me my bowling ball.

I walk up to the start of the lane, do a backward granny shot through my legs, and watch as six pins fall down. Brooks hits the reset button to set them all back up.

"Piece of cake," he scoffs, getting in position to replicate my shot. He holds his hands up in victory when eight pins are knocked over. "That's an 'H' for you."

I huff and roll my eyes. "I'm just getting warmed up. Let's see what you got."

Brooks takes his ball again after the pins are reset. He saunters toward the line but swivels at the last minute and flicks his wrist backward to send the ball rolling down the lane. After a couple of bounces off the bumpers, all ten pins miraculously fall.

I narrow my eyes at him. Competitive Teegan is rearing her head.

He throws me a lazy grin as I pick up my bowling ball and mimic his moves. Unfortunately, I miss the timing of the backward wrist release (it's harder than it looked!), and *several* bounces off the bumpers later, only two pins are down.

Stomping a foot, I whirl around to find Brooks standing right behind me. "Don't take it too hard, Sneaks," he says, voice low. "I could let you win, if you want."

The teasing in his gaze sparks something inside me. I poke a finger into his chest. "You're going down, Brooks Murphy."

Our antics escalate, feeding off of each other's outlandish energy. There are dance moves converted into bowling shots, no-look throws, and one shot by Brooks that requires lying down on the greasy bowling alley floor. I only go along with it because Competitive Teegan has taken over my body.

An hour later, I've epically lost two rounds of trick shot HORSE bowling and managed to eke out one narrow victory. We've trash-talked, cheered, and laughed so much, my cheeks might permanently freeze in a smile.

"Okay, refueling time. Let's head up to the snack bar," Brooks announces after my third-round win.

"You're just sore because you finally lost," I tease, poking him in the side.

"I'm absolutely a sore loser. I'm going to distract you with fine dining so I can reclaim my bowling conquest," he teases back.

Standing at the snack counter, we peruse the menu. "Order anything you want, Sneaks. The sky is the limit," Brooks says. "No amount is too much."

Laughing, I narrow down the edible-sounding options. "How about we share loaded nachos, a soft pretzel, and mozzarella sticks."

Brooks nods. "Acceptable variety," he says then turns to place our order. After paying, he looks back over to me. "We should go wash our hands while they get the food ready."

"I thought you had an immune system of steel?" I say, raising an eyebrow.

"Even Superman has kryptonite," Brooks states, shrugging his shoulders. "And bowling alley germs might be mine."

After a thorough hand-cleansing, we take our food to the small table by our lane. Between bites, we share more about our college experiences and careers, slowly filling in more gaps of the lives we lived apart from each other.

Each snapshot that Brooks shares simultaneously adds water to two emotional buckets: bitterness over missing out and gratefulness to not be missing any more.

"What was your major in college?" Brooks asks. "You've talked about deciding to go on staff with Arrow but never mentioned what your original plan was."

I huff a small laugh. "Education, actually."

The nacho in Brooks' hand stops midway to his mouth. "Are you serious?"

I shrug. "Dead serious. I was a special education major, and I hoped to teach in a resource room for elementary students who had learning disabilities or were on individualized education plans."

Brooks slowly chews the nacho, eyes slightly narrowed and head cocked to the side. "I can absolutely see that. What originally got you interested in that path?"

"Do you remember Megan Sanders from high school?" I ask, and Brooks nods. "She was one of my friends in elementary school, and she used to struggle a ton with school. She was always so discouraged and would get in trouble in class for not paying attention, but I think it's because she didn't want to admit that she wasn't getting it. They eventually tested her and discovered she had dyscalculia. Her brain didn't process math concepts the way a typical student's brain does. Megan started going to the resource room and learned strategies that were tailored to the way her mind worked, and it made a huge difference."

Brooks is nodding along, understanding on that educator level. I continue explaining. "I loved the idea that I could make that kind of difference for kids, to open the world of learning to them in a way that fit their individual needs. To help them *enjoy* school, *love* learning. And I loved all of my in-classroom experiences during college."

"You would have been great at that, Teeg," Brooks affirms. "I mean, you're clearly amazing at what you're doing with Arrow, but I could totally envision you in that kind of education setting."

I look down, nudging chips around the nacho plate. "I've . . . well, I've been sort of considering trying teaching instead of continuing on staff with Arrow." I murmur it quietly, not making eye contact.

"Then try it," Brooks states matter-of-factly. I look up at him. "Give it a shot if that's what you want."

"I don't know. I may have missed my chance." I sigh. "Even though I completed student teaching and got my degree, I never got my teaching license."

Brooks bursts into laughter. "Teegan, you have not missed your chance. Getting your license wouldn't be hard. Schools are dying to have more quality educators. Plus, you're amazing. You'd have a position offered to you the second your license came through."

I eye him, trying not to let my thoughts run away with themselves. "It really wouldn't be that hard?"

"No. I promise it would be easy. And I'd help you through all the steps," he assures me.

I pop a chip in my mouth to buy time. After chewing slowly, I shrug again. "It's just something I've been thinking about. I'm not sure yet what I'm going to do."

"It's not like you're making a lifelong vocation decision," Brooks muses. "It could be the *next* right thing that God's moving your heart to, like staff with Arrow was the first right thing out of college. He places passions on our hearts, gives us talents and gifts for a reason. If you have this burden to help kids learn, it might be there for a purpose. So keep thinking about it. I'm always here to give you a clear picture of the education world—the fulfilling and the frustrating," he finishes with a grin.

I grin back at him. "I mean, you do have all that 'Mr. Murphy rizz' the middle schoolers were raving about."

Brooks groans and bangs his head against the table. "I'll never hear the end of that from you, will I? Just like I'll never hear the end of it from them until you and I are dating." He pops his head up with a smirk. "Oh wait—I can hear the end of it from them now."

Playfully smacking his shoulder across the table, I give him an exaggerated glare. "Let's not publicize this to the whole middle school quite yet."

"I won't do anything until you tell me to, Sneaks," Brooks says. His gaze turns sober, heated. "Not a single thing. I won't risk screwing this up."

———

After two more rounds of insane trick shot HORSE bowling (winners redacted), Brooks drops me off at home. He walks me to the front porch, and so many memories of this exact scene play out in my mind. It's a familiar groove, yet distinct at the same time. Like déjà vu, where you have the same vibes but different precise details.

We pause on the porch, both reluctant for our time together to end. Brooks rests his hands in his pockets, and I know it's a move designed so he'll keep his hands to himself. It's the *right* move for our first date, but it also feels unnatural since it feels more like a hundredth date.

These second-chance waters are so murky right from the start.

I draw in a breath to thank Brooks for the date, but he beats me to the punch. "Teegan, thank you for going out with me tonight. Thank you for . . . for everything."

There's so much heat, so much intensity radiating from his steel blue eyes that I'm milliseconds away from plunging head first into the murky waters. *Would it be so bad to kiss him on a first date that's only kind of a first date?*

Yes, Teegan, it would be bad. A week ago, you weren't sure if you were going to date him at all. Control yourself.

"I had a really, *really* good time tonight," I answer. "Although, you set the fun date bar pretty high—not sure where you'll go from here."

Brooks smirks. "Oh ye of little faith. But speaking of next dates, I did want to let you know that the next two weeks are a little crazy for me. I have my finals for my master's courses this coming week, and then I give midterms to my students the following week. So if I'm less available or attentive, I swear it's not because I'm not thinking about you. That's literally all I do these days, which is both elating and exasperating."

"Look at you with the fancy adjectives and alliteration," I tease, but then my expression softens. "I promise not to take it personally."

Brooks steps down off the porch, turning one final time to call "Goodnight" over his shoulder.

Once inside, I grin like a fool in the emptiness. Despite the semi-late hour, I text the Beefs.

> Awake? Video call?

AMAYA

> I'm still up, but Lana might be asleep an hour ahead

A minute later a video call rings through from Lana, and Amaya immediately pops on after I answer.

"Yeah, right—you forget I have finals to study for," Lana says before yawning.

"But it's Saturday night! You shouldn't be studying!" I exclaim.

"This final year of law school is kicking my proverbial booty," Lana says. Her messy bun is disheveled, and her eyes are droopy. "But Mateo is staying awake with me playing FIFA while I study, so I have his running commentary to keep me from falling asleep." She adds this last part with a wry smile.

"I do what I must in order to help," Mateo's voice yells in the background.

"But even studying for finals takes a back seat to a date recap. Start talking, Teegs," Lana says.

Filling them in on the entire night only causes my grin to grow wider and wider. Reliving every playful moment, every serious conversation makes my heart flutter with giddy butterflies.

"I even mentioned that I'm considering moving on from staff to try teaching, and Brooks told me it would be easy to get my teaching license and find a job," I say.

"Are you leaning that way?" Amaya asks. Lana looks at me expectantly.

"Maybe? Unsure. It's still more the inkling of a thought, but it certainly isn't going away," I answer with a shrug. "But I can't lie and say that hearing Brooks talk about his job and seeing him interact with students doesn't sway me more in that direction."

"Wait, when have you seen him interact with students?" Lana questions.

I tell them about my visit to The Hangout, complete with all of the exaggerated praise for "Mr. Murphy" laid on thick by the students.

"I am zero percent surprised that Sofia egged on the attraction between you two. That girl. Ahhh, I miss her! I love that you got to visit and see Sofia in action there!" Lana says, a hand over her heart. "Oh my goodness, I miss The Hangout so much. I'm totally jealous right now."

We continue chatting for a few more minutes before I wrap things up. "You need to finish studying, LaLa, and you need to go to sleep, Amaya," I say. "And I need to lie in bed and replay my date with Brooks over and over."

They laugh at me, and we say our goodbyes.

I change into pajamas, remove my makeup, and then lie in bed, replaying my date with Brooks over and over—smiling the entire time.

Chapter Twenty-One

B rooks wasn't kidding about having a chaotic schedule following our date.

I know he's studying hard for the two finals he has to take, while also teaching all day. He still made time to text me throughout the week, but he skipped small group last night.

We've only been officially dating for one week, and I'm already feeling pouty about not seeing him. I assume he'll check his phone during his lunch hour, so I send a quick text message.

> Could I bring over dinner and help you study tonight for your final tomorrow?

We don't have an Arrow meeting tonight due to finals week, so I have a rare Thursday night off. I decide to pick up some cookies to deliver to AOPi as study fuel rather than pace my house waiting for his reply. Bakery box in hand, I'm walking up the steps to my old sorority house when my phone dings. I quickly pull it out to check the message before I go inside.

BROOKS

> If you come over, the only thing I'll wind up studying is the facets of blue in your eyes

> <GIF of Robert Downy Jr. rolling his eyes>

BROOKS

> You're deluding yourself if you think I'm joking

I will hold your feet to the fire and force you to study. I used to quiz Lana with note cards all the time in college. I'm a pro

I'm not underestimating your quizzing skills. You're underestimating how bewitching you are

I'm grateful that these are text messages and not a video call when my cheeks start flaming. *Did the sun just get hotter? Wasn't it forty degrees a second ago?*

Of course you can come. See? You've bewitched me via text, persuaded me to agree to your wishes

<magic wand emoji>

What time?

5:30 work?

I'll be there

Just 313 minutes away

I pick up Chinese takeout on my way to Brooks' apartment. After touching up my hair and makeup, of course. And changing my outfit twice, settling on leggings and an old AOPi hoodie. Keeping things casual and minimally bewitching.

When Brooks answers the door, his expression tells me that I've failed at my bewitchment-minimalization effort. His hair looks like he's absentmindedly tangled his fingers through it, adding to the leisurely look of his black joggers and plain gray t-shirt.

Apparently, Casual Brooks is also exceptionally bewitching. Because I stand there staring, not moving. I'm pretty sure my lips have parted wordlessly, a movement which draws Brooks' attention to my mouth. When he draws his eyes back up to mine, the unbridled longing in his gaze threatens to pull my lips straight to his.

Maybe this was a bad idea.

I abruptly hold up the bag of food, needing to break the spell in the air between us.

"Sustenance!" I chirp, my voice awkwardly high-pitched.

Brooks clears his throat and gestures me inside. "I'll get some glasses of cold water," he says.

Yes. Gallons of cold water, please.

I move to set the food out on the small dining table. There's a laptop on the table but no note cards or papers or highlighters. Zero useful study accessories. "Brooks? How am I supposed to quiz you if there are no note cards?"

Brooks comes out from the kitchen holding two glasses of ice water, a slight grimace on his face. "I need to confess something. I don't really use note cards to study."

Crossing my arms, I narrow my eyes. "What am I doing here then if I can't test your answers?"

With two long strides, Brooks closes the space between us, leaning around me to set the glasses on the table. His voice is a velvet murmur when he speaks. "I told you, Sneaks—if you came here, I'd spend my time studying you."

Our nearness, the low tone of his voice, the intimacy of his breath so close to mine—the combination freezes my lungs. With great effort, I pull in oxygen through my nose, slowly blowing it back out. "And I promised to hold your feet to the fire, so you'd better find me some paper to cut into rectangles."

One corner of Brooks' lips twitches then oh-so-slowly turns up into a half-smile. "Let's eat, then I'll show you my online study guide." He moves to sit down, giving me space to turn back into a fully-functioning human.

We pass cartons between us, eating directly from them with chopsticks. I tell Brooks about my change of pace during Townsend finals week. He reluctantly admits he aced his first final this week when I prod him. Brooks wasn't a *bad* student in high school, but he wasn't exactly the poster child of academia. This updated version of Brooks is clearly committed to both teaching *and* learning.

Which means he doesn't really need help studying.

I needed an excuse to see him.

When we're both stuffed, Brooks brings the laptop over to me. "Here's the study guide I've filled out for my School-Community Relations class. The biggest chunk of our grade came from a case study mock plan that we turned in yesterday. But we do have a test over some of the material. Ask me anything."

He takes his seat across from me, and I skim over the document all about philosophies and strategies for engaging the broader community with the school district. Brooks has filled this in with plentiful, meticulous notes.

"You love this class, don't you?" I ask, raising an eyebrow.

Brooks gives a soft smile. "I have enjoyed this one. It's filled me with more ideas than I could ever successfully implement."

I draw my knees up to my chest, resting them against the table. I proceed to "quiz" him on the material, which is really me asking minimal questions and Brooks giving mini-dissertations on each topic. A simple question about community partnership strategy has him talking for a solid four minutes straight.

"Everyone assumes that community partnerships are only about getting goods and services donated to the schools. And, of course, those are crucial to supporting the staff and students, to fill in gaps that official funding doesn't cover," Brooks explains, voice increasing in speed and strength. "But that's the tip of the iceberg of what community partnerships could be, *should* be. It's about getting real people from the community around students to provide models for them of what it means to be contributing members of society. To see how our community is shaped by a variety of people with different vocations, skill sets, hobbies, passions, and experiences—that together we contribute to a whole that's greater than our individual selves. Students need to see positive role models of varying shapes and sizes, metaphorically speaking. Help them picture themselves as one of those contributors."

Brooks is on the edge of his seat now. His passion for not only his specific students, but education in general, oozes out of every word he speaks, every inflection of his voice, every raise of his eyebrows and gesture of his hands.

The passion is contagious. I feel it swelling in my chest, whispering in my mind.

You could do this. You might be made to do this.

My thoughts have tangled themselves and distracted me from what Brooks was saying. I snap my attention back to him when my ears register silence. He's smiling softly at me.

"Sorry, what were you saying?"

"Doesn't matter what I was saying. I'd rather watch the expressions that dance across your face while you're lost in thought," he says.

I drop my head against my arms resting on my knees. "Brooooks," I groan. "Now I can't look at you with a straight face."

Seconds later, his smiling face peers up from the floor next to me. I smile back, and he playfully pinches my side before taking the chair next to me. "So, will you be in KC for Christmas?" he asks.

"Yep. I'll be staying with my mom, but I'll see my dad too. You?"

Brooks nods his response. "Could I see you for Christmas some-time?" he asks. There's a note of anxiety in his voice. Like he actually thinks I could say no.

I smile softly at him. "Yes. Let me check with my mom on the plans."

His typical playful spark crowds out the anxiety in his eyes. "Good. 'Cause baby, all I want for Christmas is you."

I roll my eyes to hide my mutual feelings.

Christmas Eve holds an extra thrill of anticipation this year because Brooks will be joining us for dinner.

Mom said he was welcome to come any time, but it made the most sense to have him come tonight. Logan and I will be spending most of the day with Dad tomorrow, and Brooks needs to spend Christmas Day with his dad, brother, and sister-in-law.

I've been staying with my mom for a couple of days now, and we've had multiple conversations about my new relationship with Brooks.

Despite her caution at Thanksgiving, my words and actions have provided her enough assurance to feel happy about it now. She agreed not to mention anything about it to Logan or my dad yet. Those seem like they should be in-person conversations.

Unfortunately, Logan got delayed and is still on his way to KC from St. Louis. He'll probably arrive shortly before dinner, so hopefully I have enough time to prepare him prior to Brooks' arrival.

I'm extra meticulous applying makeup, going for a light smoky look complete with a subtle cat eye. It should pair well with the jade green dress I'm wearing. The sound of the front door opening reaches my ears right before Logan calls out greetings. "Hey, big bro!" I call from my room as I hear Mom welcoming him in the foyer.

I need to run down and quickly fill him in on all that has transpired with Brooks, but I decide to add one finishing touch to my outfit first. Pulling half of my hair back, I secure it with a deep maroon hair bow, adding a softer feminine touch to my darker eye makeup.

Zipping up my ankle boots, I give myself a mental pep talk before going to tell Logan about Brooks. Logan overlapped with Brooks on the varsity basketball team for a year, but he was a grade older and Logan was already away at college by the time our relationship ended. But he's still the stereotypical protective older brother, so he might need more convincing than Mom did to let the past go.

I reach the top of the staircase at the same moment the doorbell rings.

Oh no.

My brain tells my feet to go down the steps as fast as humanly possible, but Logan is already almost to the door.

"I'll get the door, don't worry about it," I'm practically shrieking as my feet nearly trip over themselves on the stairs.

I reach the door a second *after* Logan opens it, just in time to hear Logan's icy voice. "You."

Just in time to watch in slow motion as Logan punches Brooks across the jaw.

Chapter Twenty-Two

"LOGAN! Stop it! What are you doing?!" I yell, grabbing fistfuls of Logan's shirt to try to pull him away from Brooks.

"No, I deserved that," Brooks states, rubbing his jaw.

"You deserve a lot more than that, you little punk," Logan spits, eyes still blazing. "Just because I was at college, you think I didn't still have friends from the team who told me all the crap you talked about my sister? How dare you show up here?"

I'm desperately pulling on the crook of Logan's arm, attempting to drag him away from Brooks. "I invited him! We're dating!" I exclaim.

Logan's biceps tense even further under my grasp, and he slowly swivels his head to look me in the eye. "What did you say?"

I blow out a breath. "Brooks is here because I invited him. Because we recently got reconnected and started dating again."

Logan's eyes narrow on mine. "Teegs . . . what are you thinking? Are you forgetting what he put you through? The things he said—the things he *did*?"

Apparently, Logan is aware of why Brooks broke up with me. Fantastic.

"Are you failing to remember the nights crying alone in your room over winter break?" Logan adds, voice still simmering with rage.

Apparently, I was less adept at hiding than I thought I was. Awesome.

"You're right. You're absolutely right," Brooks speaks up again. He stands up straighter and fully faces Logan. "I was a jerk. And so stupid. I'm worse than scum for the way I treated Teegan. I don't deserve her forgiveness, and I certainly don't deserve another chance to be in her life."

"But I forgave him," I jump in. Tugging on Logan's arm to get him to look at me, I continue. "Brooks and I joined the same small group at our church without knowing it. We slowly reconnected as friends, and Brooks apologized profusely for the past. And I chose to forgive him. And I'm choosing a relationship with him now. I'm not letting the past dictate the present."

"But Teegan, sometimes we learn from the past to know what *not* to do in the future," Logan counters.

"I know. The past informed my choices, which is why I took things slowly. We started off as fellow small group members, then as friends. But Brooks has changed. He's not the same guy he was in high school." I look over at Brooks with soft eyes and see a similar soft expression in his. "We've both grown and changed. And I like who he is now." I end with a smile at Brooks before looking back to Logan.

"Teegan, I don't want a repeat—" Logan begins.

"I swear I'd never hurt her like that again," Brooks asserts.

"Yeah, you probably thought that when you started dating the first time, though," Logan says. His eyes narrow again. "And look how that ended."

"I trust him," I declare, pulling Logan's attention back. "I've matured a lot since high school too, Logan. I've learned not to completely tie up my sense of self in another person, to keep myself grounded in my relationship with God. I've learned how to maintain my individual identity. I trust Brooks, and I trust myself to take care of my heart."

There's stillness in the air as we stand there, each processing our own slew of thoughts. The evening is cold, and I shiver for the first time as my adrenaline wears off.

"Why don't we come inside and talk about this over dinner?" Mom's voice cuts in from behind us.

Logan glances back at her. "You knew about this?" Mom nods in response. "And you're okay with it?" Another nod. He meets my eyes one more time, and I squeeze his arm, trying to channel reassurance through my eyes.

He sighs. "Fine." Logan follows Mom to the dining room, and I rush to usher Brooks inside.

"I'm so sorry. He was late getting here, and I didn't have time to tell him," I whisper. "I'm so, so sorry."

Brooks wraps me up in a hug, breathing against my ear. "It's okay, Sneaks. Like I said—I deserved it." He pulls away, though there's reluctance in the removal of his arms from around me. "I wouldn't say no to an ice pack, though," he says with a smirk.

It's the most natural thing in the world to reach down and take Brooks' hand, to lace my fingers through his. A movement so second nature, so familiar, you'd think any surge of delight at the touch would have long since vanished.

And you'd be wrong.

A shiver of warmth races through my body in response to Brooks' hand possessively curling around mine. My pulse skitters when I meet his eyes and see a mirrored reaction in them. "Let's go get you some ice," I murmur.

Brooks holds a bag of frozen corn against his jaw as we carry food from the kitchen to the table. I volunteer to pray for our meal, and then we begin passing dishes and spooning food onto plates.

"How's work been going, Logan?" I ask, hoping to give Brooks a little recovery time before the grilling session I'm confident is coming.

Logan shares a minimal response, but my mom asks several follow-up questions. She must be picking up on my strategy. I also volunteer ample information about how my semester went, elaborating on each Bible study I led, as well as describing the dynamics of our church small group.

We're mostly finished eating by the time Brooks' inevitable turn in the hot seat comes. Logan's eyes narrow, and I have the urge to throw my body in front of Brooks as though to protect him from the bullet that's coming.

"So, Murph, how exactly did you go from being high school jackass Murphy to—" Logan gestures across the table at Brooks, "—this Brooks?"

"Language, Logan," my mom chimes in. "Not at the dinner table. And let's not forget that high school Logan did some rather immature things as well."

"I never pressured a girlfriend physically, broke up with her when I wasn't satisfied, then said degrading things behind her back. So, I wouldn't say my brand of immature was quite the same," Logan jabs.

Our overlapping voices create one simultaneous mess.

Mom—"Logan!"

Me—"Stop it!"

Brooks—"He's right."

We're all quiet as Logan continues glaring Brooks down. Brooks tugs on my hand, which is when I realize that I'm standing. Brooks slides my chair back to me as he continues speaking, "Logan's right, and it's a fair question. The simplest answer is that Jesus is why I'm a different man. In high school, I had no faith, nothing beyond myself that I was living for. In college, a couple of my teammates, Brody and Rylen, were involved in FCA, and their lives sparked my interest.

"They were the hardest workers on the team, even if not the most talented. They treated women with respect—everyone with respect. They were the first to show up to drive guys home from parties during the off-season, were always there to listen without being judgmental. And they had a genuine contentedness that I knew I lacked. I started attending the FCA meetings with them and reading the Bible, and God slowly transformed my life. He's still transforming me day by day," Brooks concludes.

Logan's face has softened slightly, but he still looks skeptical. "And teaching? How exactly did you wind up in education? Doesn't seem like the thrilling type of career I would have guessed for you."

Brooks gives the same explanation I've heard him share, and Logan continues drilling him with question after question about his life (and dating) experiences since high school. I assume Logan's still searching for loose threads to pull on, but so far, he's coming up empty-handed. Brooks answers with candor and confidence, not flinching back from explaining any of Logan's interrogations. The only sign he's nervous is his grip on my hand, which is propped on his knee under the table. He's clutching my hand like I'm a helium balloon that might float away if he's not careful. I try to rub a reassuring message along the side of his hand with my thumb.

I'm with you. I'm not leaving. We're okay.

As Brooks shares about his life, about all the ways that God has changed him, Logan visibly relaxes. Logan shares my dad's darker hair and eyes, which can project an intimidating demeanor when he's irritated. Thankfully, his hackles are fully disarmed by the time Brooks mentions his mom's passing.

Shock and sadness mingle in Logan's brown eyes. "I'm really sorry to hear that, man. Your mom was always so nice to the team when we'd hang at your house."

My mom adds her condolences, and I feel Brooks' escapist energy building up, eager to move on from the sadness.

"We're supposed to get to Dad's house in time for a late brunch tomorrow," I tell Logan, abruptly changing the subject. "We'll have time to open presents here with Mom before we go over."

"Yep. Got it," Logan replies.

Brooks squeezes my hand under the table.

We round out the meal with my mom's homemade apple pie and vanilla ice cream. Everyone pitches in to put away leftovers and load the dishwasher.

When it's time for Brooks to leave, Logan walks with us to the foyer. "Sorry about earlier, man." Logan looks sheepish as he apologizes. He holds a hand out to Brooks, who shakes it firmly.

"You were just being a good brother. I don't fault you at all," Brooks replies.

Logan stays inside as I walk Brooks out to the front porch, crossing my arms to fend off the chill.

"Thanks for coming tonight. I'm glad I could see you for the holidays," I say. Untangling my arms, I brush a thumb across Brooks' jaw, where a faint bruise is forming. "I really hope this doesn't hurt too much."

Brooks leans into my touch then reaches a hand to grip my waist, gently pulling me closer to him. His other hand clasps around my fingers on his jaw, and he turns to press a kiss to my palm.

"Trust me—I'm not feeling any pain right now," he says, voice thick. "Thanks for letting me back into your life. I don't deserve to be here."

My brow furrows. "Brooks, you have to stop saying things like that."

"What do you mean?" he asks, brow now similarly furrowed.

"You constantly talk about how you don't deserve to be with me now, or how you were trying to earn your way back to me. That's not how forgiveness works. You know that," I say, but his expression remains troubled.

"I know that in theory." Brooks sighs. "But in reality, I can't erase the memory of what I did to you. That ugly side of who I was then. The effect it had on you. Like William Faulkner said, 'The past is never dead. It's not even past.'"

My eyebrows raise. "You're just pulling William Faulkner quotes out of your back pocket now? How do you even know that?"

"History teacher," he says with an attempt at a light-hearted shrug. But his fingers are tight against mine as he swallows hard. "It may have been a past version of me, but it was still me. *I* hurt you. And I can't escape the feeling that I need to somehow justify the grace you've shown me."

"But it's not grace if you earned it." I pause to raise my other hand to the side of his face. "You are sincerely sorry, Brooks. You've changed. You've apologized numerous times. And I've chosen to forgive you. That's it. You can be sweet to me because you care about me, but not if you're viewing it as a form of penance, okay?" My voice is unwavering, and I hope the words sink in.

He sighs again but nods. Then he quirks one eyebrow before asking, "Just so we're on the same page, I *can* be sweet to you in over-the-top, obnoxiously sugary ways, right?"

I roll my eyes and let my hands drop from his face, but he catches them in his. "Baby, let the games begin," he teases, gently squeezing my hands.

I roll my eyes harder, but I can't help but grin. "You and your song lyrics. The gift that keeps on giving."

"Speaking of, I did not bring you a Christmas gift tonight, per your strict orders," he says, giving me a disapproving look. "But that doesn't mean you won't be receiving something soon that is completely unrelated to Christmas gift-giving traditions."

I bite my lip to contain my smile. "You are impossible. Merry Christmas, Brooks."

"Merry Christmas, Sneaks."

———

Logan and I have an enjoyable Christmas morning with Dad, although he seems a little distracted the whole time. We eat brunch and open gifts before watching *Home Alone* together, just like we did growing up. It's been several years of this new normal of split traditions, so I should be used to it. But I'm more despondent about it this year than usual. Maybe it's my reconnection with Brooks? But something has made me wish for the old days together as an intact family unit more than I have in recent years.

I stay at Mom's house for an extra couple of days after Christmas because we have our annual Arrow staff planning retreat at an AirBnb at the Lake of the Ozarks. While students are on the extended winter break, we take a few days away as a staff team to plan for the upcoming semester. It doesn't make sense to drive back to Brooklyn only to turn around and drive to Missouri again a few days later.

I'm in my room packing to leave when Mom comes in holding a package. "You got a delivery!" she says, handing it over to me with a wink. "You'll never guess who sent it."

A smile jumps to my lips, and I accept the bubble mailer from her.

"I'm glad that Brooks could come over on Christmas Eve," Mom muses. "Well, minus the punching incident. Although, maybe it was good for Logan to get that out of his system. He might have a more open mind now."

I huff. "It better be out of his system, and he'd better have an open mind now. Because this is happening whether he likes it or not."

Mom unexpectedly wraps me up in a hug. "It was good for my heart to see you two together. To hear you explain how you arrived at the decision to give him another chance. To hear Brooks explain how his life has changed over the past several years. To see the growth in him—in both of you. It put my mind at ease."

I hug her tightly before pulling back to look her in the eyes. "You know, I think it was good for me too. To articulate everything to a skeptical crowd. And I meant what I said—I trust Brooks, and I trust myself. But more than that, I trust God to help both of us have a healthier relationship than the first time. I'm grateful that we have the chance."

Mom smiles, and then she shoos herself away so I can open my package from Brooks. He did promise a "non-Christmas" gift was on the way.

Opening the bubble mailer, I find what looks to be a book wrapped in brown craft paper. It's an intricate wrapping job, made to look like an overlapping "v" pattern on the front. There are multi-color Flair pens tucked into the flaps along with pastel page tabs. It's tied with a festive ribbon, and he's written my name on the front. When I flip the package over, I snort a small laugh at the excessive amount of tape holding it together. I can picture Brooks muttering under his breath while attempting to copy some book-wrapping tutorial video. The thought makes my heart do a series of back flips.

I take a photo of the finished product before untying the ribbon and tearing open the paper. Inside, I find a guided decision-making journal. Flipping open the first page, his inscription reads:

To Teegan -

I don't think you can make a "wrong" decision in this case, but I hope this helps you sort out your thoughts about your future. I believe in you no matter what you choose.

- Brooks

Skimming the pages of the journal, I see prompts to evaluate past experiences, inventories of emotions and passions, twists on pro/con lists, and lots of guided reflection questions.

This is exactly what I need to help me pull the chaos out of my thoughts.

> Your not-Christmas gift arrived. Thank you so much! This is absolutely perfect!

My text doesn't show as read right away, so I continue packing until Brooks responds several minutes later.

BROOKS

> I hope it's helpful and not overwhelming. Feel free to use it as fire kindling if it tips to the "too much" side

> No! It looks like exactly what I need. I think my typical "walk around talking aloud to myself" method may not work in this case. I might even go to a coffee shop today and start filling some of it in before I drive to staff retreat. Orrrrr I might spend the couple of hours shopping to get you the perfect "not-a-holiday" gift

BROOKS

> Absolutely not. Don't waste your time on that. I order you to go to the coffee shop. That is my gift from you

> Well, it's definitely NOT your gift. But I will do it. You'll just be surprised and unsuspecting when your unexpected present comes

BROOKS

> It can't be unexpected because I know you're arriving back to town on January 1st. My present already has a countdown

He sends a screenshot of his phone lock screen with a countdown widget labeled "Sneaks is back!" My heart is no longer doing back flips. It has officially liquefied into a puddle of gooey warmth.

BROOKS

> I really miss you, just so you know

> I miss you too. A lot

Chapter Twenty-Three

Our staff retreat is a little more chaotic than usual this year with two crawling babies constantly interrupting. Rachel is apologetic, but we all love having her and the twins present. It's more important for her to feel included than for us to be efficient.

On day two of the retreat, we take a walk along a nearby park trail to break up the "sitting and planning" portion of the meetings. Kent stayed home with the napping twins, and Gina is deep in conversation with Lucas and Connor, the two single staff guys.

"So, how was the twins' first Christmas?" I ask Rachel.

"They won't remember any of it, but Kent and I had a great time celebrating. And our families had a *great* time spoiling them," she says with an eye roll. "The amount of presents was a little ridiculous, especially when they're too young to appreciate them. How was your Christmas?"

"It was great! A little more eventful than expected, with my older brother punching my old ex-boyfriend who I'm currently dating again. But other than that, just your typical Christmas!" I joke. Then, I mentally punch myself in the face. Because I haven't mentioned a single thing about Brooks to Rachel or Kent.

Rachel stops walking, looking rightfully shocked and confused. "Your . . . ex-boyfriend who you're currently dating? I didn't know you were dating anyone." Her posture sinks slightly, and her expression borders on hurt.

Gah. Teegan. Why don't you think before throwing jokes out?!

"Yeah, it's pretty new-ish," I say. "I'm sorry I didn't mention it sooner. It's been a slow development." I give her a very basic version of our relationship. I'm trying to act nonchalant, like this isn't a revolutionary turn of events, but I can't keep the Brooks-induced grin off my face.

"You really like him, don't you?" Rachel asks, face softening.

"I do." My heart does a little skip-hop heel-click move.

"You mentioned he's in Brooklyn teaching. Is that a permanent position? Would he be in town long term as you're working on campus?" Rachel asks.

It's a perfectly valid question. Entirely fair. But I'm epically unprepared for the uncomfortable conversation with Rachel (or Kent) about my future. A conversation that would certainly be prompted by the honest answer to her question.

"I'm not exactly sure," I evade. "It's still such a new thing, us dating. We're enjoying taking it one day at a time!" I quickly change the subject, "Hey, I wanted to ask if you want me to continue leading the Friday morning senior group, or if you'll be taking that back over this semester?"

Rachel's face still looks slightly disconcerted, but I successfully steer conversation away from Brooks. Or any mention of my undecided future. I'll be avoiding that for as long as possible.

Forever sounds like a reasonable avoidance goal.

———

After the retreat, I return to KC on the thirtieth, but I'm staying with Amaya instead of my parents for a couple of days. She's taking off work on New Year's Eve so we can hang out and then go to a party together. Amaya lives in Westport but works in the Crossroads district downtown, so I decide to find a coffee shop downtown to hang out and do a little more reflection in my journal from Brooks.

Searching the map for "coffee shops" returns an overwhelming plethora of options.

I parked in a random lot in the Crossroads to find a coffee shop. Looks like I need to plan a coffee shop crawl with all of these cute places! But for today I need a quick decision, so where should I go??

AMAYA

If you want a cool architectural ambiance with lots of open space, go to Messenger. If you want a smaller, unique vibe, Café Corazón is a local Latin American/Indigenous inspired coffee shop with an awesome menu

I quickly compare the two listings on the map. They both look appealing, which makes this coffee crawl idea seem all the more necessary.

!! Café Corazón has a latte flight!!! Winner!

AMAYA

I'll come meet you there when I get off work

My parallel parking skills come in handy once again when I'm able to pull into a small spot directly in front of the café. Walking inside, the vibrant mural painted on the wall above the counter immediately makes me happy I chose to come here. The display case of unique pastries further affirms my decision.

I order a latte flight and tell the barista to surprise me with a pastry of her choice. Choosing a table near the large windows, I get out my journal and pen. The barista brings over the latte flight, pointing out three different flavors. My mouth is watering already, but then I eye the giant pastry on the plate. "Okay, tell me what you picked."

"It's one of our *alfajors*, the *maicena* flavor. Think a shortbread cookie sandwich filled with creamy *dulce de leche*. It's one of my favorites," she tells me. Now, I'm full-on salivating.

"Thank you!" I call as she walks away. Pulling out my phone, I quickly snap photos of the pastry and the lattes. I prop the journal open on the table, then take another picture of the full setup to send to Lana.

I take a sip of each latte, relishing the different flavors. A single bite of the pastry has me moaning with delight and calling out a loud "Thank you!" to the barista.

Every crumb of the *alfajor* is gone and the latte glasses are empty by the time Amaya comes in two hours later. I jump up to give her a hug, fueled entirely by my excitement to see her and not at all by the caffeine and sugar.

Amaya orders a coffee to go, and then we decide to walk to a nearby Thai restaurant for dinner. We share Pad Thai and yellow curry as I catch her up on staff retreat.

"You're going to have to talk to Kent and Rachel eventually, Teeg," Amaya says in response to my story about the narrow miss with Rachel.

"But will I? Casually disappearing seems like a valid option if I do decide not to return to staff," I joke.

"I know you think the conversation could be slightly uncomfortable—"

"Or straight up excruciating," I cut in.

"*Mildly* uncomfortable," Amaya emphasizes with an eye roll. "But you can't avoid it forever. You could give them a heads-up that you're considering other options before you officially decide anything and stop it from looming over your head."

"I will take that option under advisement," I comment before taking a huge bite of curry and rice. "How's that big pitch coming?" I ask around the food in my mouth.

Amaya graciously takes the reins of the conversation to talk business. It's not a language I'm fluent in, but hearing Amaya talk about her job makes me feel passionate about it nonetheless.

"Wow—it sounds like you've got a lot going on," I reflect after she outlines the multiple clients she's juggling. There's a weariness to her eyes and her voice as she drops the mask in response to my observation.

"It is a lot—which I'm fine with. I like having a lot on my plate, but I do miss having you and Lana around every day to have a safe place to breathe for a minute," Amaya says before giving a slight shrug. "Even though I have friends I enjoy hanging out with, and I get along fine with my roommate, I still feel like I need to be 'on' all the time."

I nod in understanding. Lana and I are maybe the only two people who ever see behind the image of Amaya that most people know. The confident, charismatic, high-achieving leader with drive and ambition for days. It's who we saw for the first several months of our friendship, until Amaya slowly trusted us enough to voice the moments of self-doubt and insecurity.

"How are you feeling about the corporate ladder grind?" I ask quietly, leaning forward over the table.

"Feeling about it? I don't know that I have feelings about it. At least, not that I've actively thought about," Amaya replies. "Maybe I'll think about it. I love what I'm doing—love what I'm achieving. I'm just feeling a little nostalgic about our late-night slushie runs or movie nights that turned into talking for hours."

I nod in understanding again. "Same, girl, same."

"But life moves forward. We keep moving with it," Amaya says with another shrug.

"Any special man in your life that I'll be introduced to at the New Year's Eve Party?" I ask, eyes sparkling. I'm overdoing the teasing tone so that Amaya will answer me because I really do want to know.

"Yeah, right," Amaya scoffs. "Like I have time to even think about dating. You'll meet several of my friends but no romantic connections. That's the furthest thing from my mind."

Amaya outlines our plans for New Year's Eve at the Power and Light District tomorrow, listing off the friends who will be there and emphasizing the *only friends* designation. I'm excited to meet more of Amaya's KC circle so I can better picture her life when she gives updates on our weekly calls.

The next day, Amaya and I video call Lana to catch up, but otherwise spend a leisurely day hanging out until it's time to get dressed for the party. We meet up with Amaya's friends and get the wristbands designating our ticket level. It's a fun evening hopping from one venue to another and getting to know some of Amaya's friends. Some are from work, some from church, and others from her women in business group.

I entertain them with stories about College Amaya and laugh at their tales of Grown-Up Amaya. We dance, share good food, and generally have a blast. The only cloud hanging over my head is that I don't get to share this night with Brooks. Or kiss him at midnight.

At 11:40 p.m., we're squished in a crowd at the same venue where Brooks and I danced at the silent disco. I pull out my phone and take a selfie to text to him.

> Wish you were here

He hearts my photo and then sends his own selfie. Will, Jason, Sarah, Catherine, and Bailey are all smiling in the photo, standing in a crowd in Center Square.

BROOKS

> Wish you were HERE. No, I'm glad you're having fun with Amaya. Wish we could both be in both places. Or teleport back and forth. Why doesn't that technology exist yet?

> Valid question. Also, I love that Bailey is hanging out with you guys! Tell everyone hi from me!

BROOKS

Can't wait to see you tomorrow <kiss face emoji>

<pink heart emoji>

Chapter Twenty-Four

After having the greatest time with Amaya, I drive home to Brooklyn on New Year's Day. As sad as I was to say goodbye to her, it wasn't a secret how eager I was to get back to a certain someone.

Brooks and I have dinner at an Italian restaurant in Center Square, catching each other up on the remainders of our winter breaks. He has to go back to work tomorrow for two professional days prior to students returning for second semester. Thankfully, the bruise on his jaw has faded completely. I would have felt *really* bad if he had to explain that to his colleagues, much less his students.

"Tell me about the master's classes you're taking this spring," I say before taking a bite of a breadstick.

"I have two classes again this semester. One focused on ethics and one about leadership in curriculum. Not quite as interesting as the community relations class, but still important topics I need to know about," Brooks answers. "The ethics class is virtual, but the curriculum class meets in person on Monday nights. Will your schedule stay the same for the Bible studies you lead?"

"Mostly. Except Rachel is taking over the Friday morning group this semester," I reply.

"Which means you can get a little more beauty sleep, Aurora." Brooks winks.

"It's not my fault I was born to sleep in. Some genetics can't be altered," I tease back. "I'll miss being with those girls, but I'm glad that Rachel feels like she has the capacity to meet with them again." I push pasta around my plate, dropping my eyes. "I did a lot of writing in the guided journal you gave me. It's helped me dream more concretely about teaching."

My eyes flit back up in time to see Brooks pause mid-chew. "Yeah? You're thinking more seriously about teaching?" He can't hide the spark of hope in his eyes, and I can't stop the increased temperature of my heart in response to that spark.

I bite my lip and twirl a finger through my hair. "I wouldn't say I've made an official decision, but the journal has been really helpful to get my thoughts organized. And I can't stop thinking about it. Imagining myself in a classroom with small groups of kids, teaching them multiplication strategies or reading comprehension foundations. And it makes me feel . . . calm when I'm picturing it. Calm but eager at the same time. That has to mean something, right?"

Brooks' intent gaze breaks into a droll smile. "I'll throw a dose of reality at you—there's practically nothing about education that could be described as 'calm.' It might be the dictionary antonym of 'calm.'"

I laugh in response, and Brooks props his chin in one hand on the table. He slides his other hand across the tabletop, reaching for mine. I happily meet his request, lacing my fingers with his.

"All jokes aside, I do think that any student needing a little extra help and attention would hit the jackpot to wind up in your class. And the fact that you feel drawn to it could certainly mean something. But that's ultimately up to you to discern," Brooks says. "I'm not an unbiased advisor."

His thumb gently traces mine, lulling me into a hypnotic state.

"Need any to-go boxes over here?" Our waiter's voice jolts me to full consciousness again.

"Yes, please," Brooks and I respond at the same time. He hands his credit card over to the waiter in exchange for the boxes. We're silent as we scrape leftovers off of our plates, and the waiter brings back the receipt for Brooks to sign.

"Now that the table is clear, I have a not-Christmas gift for you," I proclaim with smug excitement. Brooks tries to tell me I didn't need to get him a gift, but I can see the eager anticipation in his eyes.

I slide the thin box across the table, and he quickly unwraps it. Pulling out the desk plaque inside, he reads out loud, "Principal Murphy." His eyes are both soft and dancing when he looks up at me.

"Teegan, this is perfect. I don't know when I'll get to use it for real, but you better believe I'm going to display it on my dresser for now," Brooks says, voice warm.

"I believe in you. You're going to make an amazing administrator someday," I respond. "But that's not all. I got this specially made on Etsy." I slide the Principal Murphy plaque out of the holder and pull the additional options out of my purse, which I hand over to him.

His smile grows as he reads them. "Dean of Student Fun, Chancellor of Chaos, and Headmaster of Hijinks. Teeg, this is too good. Now it's *really* perfect," he says with a laugh.

"I figure you can decide which vibe fits the day," I tell him with a grin of my own.

As we exit the restaurant, Brooks is quick to pull my hand into his. We stroll slowly toward the parking lot, neither of us eager to part ways.

Brooks clears his throat. "Hey, I've been thinking about something. We're going to see each other at small group next week—well, every week actually. And I've been wondering when we might want to tell the group that we're dating?"

I look over at Brooks, his hair golden under the street lamp, profile striking in the half darkness. It's too dark to see his eyes clearly, but I have his particular shade of blue memorized.

"Right now!" I say, pulling out my phone.

"Right now?" Brooks repeats.

"Yes! Act like you like me for a selfie," I tease, pulling him to me.

"Zero acting required," he says. I catch a photo of him softly smiling at me before he turns to face the camera. *That will be my little treasure.*

Brooks squishes his face against mine, and we both give cheesy grins to the screen. He hovers over my shoulder as I pull up our small group chat to send the photo. The cheesy smiles don't even look cheesy—we just look elated.

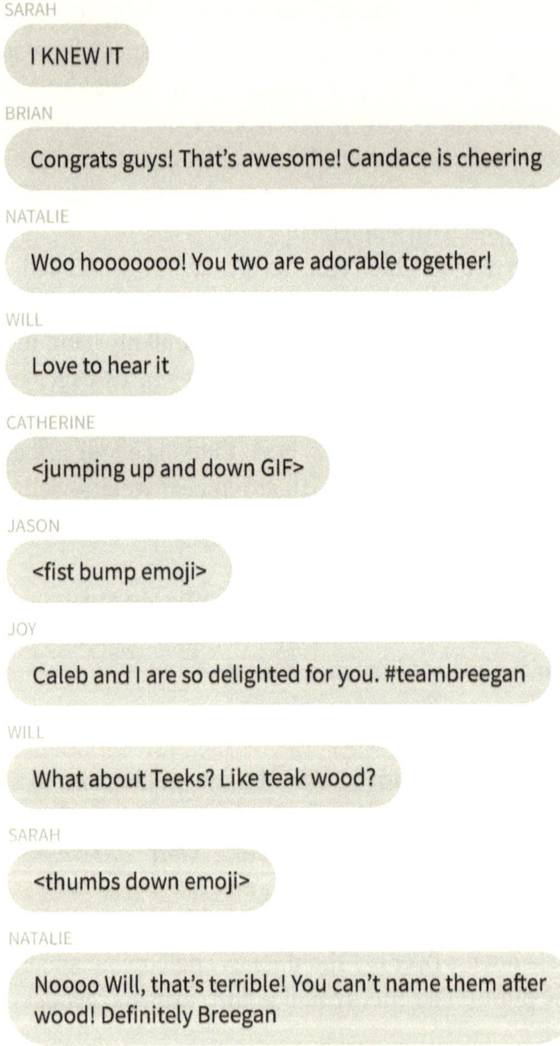

It's mere seconds before a message flurry starts dinging through, but that's long enough for Brooks to press a firm kiss to my temple. And my knees to go weak. I guess clichés become cliché for a reason.

My phone continues dinging, but I pocket it and smile up at Brooks. He gives a mock sigh. "Look what you've started."

"Look what *we* started," I emphasize. Whatever sarcastic reply Brooks had dies on his lips when I lean up to kiss his cheek. The feel of his skin beneath my lips sucks me into a black hole of wanting more. I'm suddenly dying to kiss him for real, for him to kiss me *for real.*

I tug on his hand to start walking instead. "Time to get you home before your big day back to work tomorrow. Let's go, Breegan."

When Brooks pulls up to my duplex, he lingers in the car. "Teegan, there's something I think that I should probably tell you really plainly."

Swiveling my body toward him, my mind races with potential scenarios that could make his voice so serious. I start to panic until he takes my hand and traces soothing circles on my palm.

"Given our history," Brooks begins, voice tight. "I want you to know that I've personally committed to waiting until marriage to do anything more than kiss a girl I'm dating. Including you."

I slowly exhale the breath I didn't realize had ballooned in my chest. "Thanks for telling me that, Brooks," I say, squeezing his hand.

He gives me a tentative smile as he fidgets with my fingers. "I know you've told me to stop apologizing for the past, and I promise I'll stop after this one final time. I'm sorry for how disrespectful I was to you and your boundaries in high school. I regret everything about every decision I made during that time in my life, but I promise I'm committed to doing better this time, treating you the right way. We're on the same page now, and I felt like you deserved to hear that from me."

"I do appreciate it," I affirm. I tilt my head to one side as I reach up to trace my finger along his jaw. "But now you really do have to stop apologizing," I add with a smile, gently pressing the cleft in his chin.

Brooks catches my hand and presses a kiss to my fingertip. "Promise."

CHAPTER TWENTY-FIVE

The following week, our small group practically throws a party in our honor. Even though we drive separately, Brooks waits for me outside of Joy and Caleb's house so we can walk inside together. Our entrance is met with cheers and enthusiastic hugs. Sarah even has a cookie cake with "Breegan" written in frosting.

"Hey, I thought we were taking an official vote tonight!" Will whines.

"You're the only one voting for Teeks," Catherine says, rolling her eyes.

"If we made it an anonymous vote, you might find out there are others who are secretly with me," Will counters.

Brooks unabashedly claims the loveseat, pulling me along to sit next to him. The group eventually settles in, and we begin our discussion of the first chapter of Hebrews, the book of the Bible we'll be studying this semester. For the hundredth time, I find myself thinking about how grateful I am that Lana and Amaya pushed me to join this group. For so many reasons.

That night, I fall asleep smiling. The smile is still plastered to my face the next morning when my alarm goes off at 7:30. I'm reluctant to get out of my cocoon of blankets. The air feels too frosty.

Grabbing my phone off the nightstand, I feel it vibrate with a notification.

He sent the text an hour ago. I wrap myself in a blanket before padding over to the window to peek outside. Fluffy layers of white cover everything in the morning light. The sliver of the yard bathed in full sunlight, just beyond the roof's shadow, glimmers with snow diamonds.

I check Townsend's social media and see that they've canceled classes for the day as well, which means I won't have any of my meetings on campus.

> Give me an hour to eat and get dressed, and then I'm in! But I don't have a sled

Brooks sends a photo of himself with two sleds in the checkout line of the store.

BROOKS

> Got it covered.

> What are you doing out driving already?! Be careful!!

BROOKS

> The apartment parking lot was dicey, but the main roads were fairly cleared. Ish. I promise I drove slowly

> See you soon!

I head out to the kitchen to make some breakfast, grateful for the scent of fresh coffee in the air. Gina is sitting at the table eating eggs and toast.

"Classes are canceled today," she says around a bite of toast.

"I know—Brooks texted me this morning that it was a snow day. It's so pretty outside!" I respond, my voice surprisingly chipper for Morning Teegan.

"Only Brooks could make you sound so human prior to your first cup of coffee," Gina teases.

I shrug and smile. "Can't even deny that. He's going to pick me up in an hour to go sledding."

"Aw, that's fun!" Gina says. "You should go to that church on the hill. Well, if his car can manage to get up the street. Not as many people sled there. For sure only college students, not the little kids."

"Ooo, good thought." I hum as I pour peppermint mocha cream-er into my coffee.

Gina laughs. "You are one smitten kitten." I shrug, offering no denial, which only makes Gina laugh more. "I'm going to go over to one of the dorms for a movie marathon with a group of girls, so I'll probably be out until this evening."

Since Gina is awake, I blast music from my phone while I get ready for the day. After food and caffeine, I get dressed in the warmest clothes I have. I don't own snow pants, so jeans layered over leggings will have to do. I'm grateful that I bought a good pair of snow boots last year for walking around campus in the winter.

Even though we'll be outside sledding, I still apply light makeup. I dig a winter hat out of my closet but can't find any gloves for the life of me. I'll have to clean up the tornado of a mess I've created in my room tonight because Brooks should be here any minute now.

Right on cue, the doorbell rings. I rush to open the door, swallowing a gulp at the sight of Brooks. The longer strands of his hair are poking out from his beanie, and his cheeks are flushed from the cold air. His grin resembles a five-year-old on Christmas morning. "Ready?" he asks eagerly.

"Almost! Come inside while I put on my boots and coat," I say, closing the door behind him. He comes in and holds up a grocery bag. "I picked up some waterproof winter gloves. I didn't know if you had any, and you'll need them for phase two."

I quirk an eyebrow at him while I zip up a boot. "Phase two?"

"You'll see," he replies, eyes glimmering.

"I might need them now because I seem to have misplaced my gloves," I say. He *tsks* but hands the gloves over to me.

Brooks helps me slip my arms into my thermal winter coat, and then I follow him outside. The sidewalk and driveway around our cars have been shoveled off already. "How long have you been here?" I ask.

"I didn't need an hour of time before picking you up, but I didn't want to rush your getting-ready process. So I came over and shoveled while I waited," he replies, opening the passenger door for me.

"Okay, I don't know what you had planned, but there's a big hill behind a church in town that not as many people go to. If your car can make it up the steep street, that might be a good place to try," I suggest.

"That's exactly what one of my colleagues recommended," Brooks replies. He tilts the map on his phone toward me. "Is this it?"

"Yep! Let's try it!"

Brooks drives slowly to our destination. Some streets have been cleared well, while others are still covered with snow. When we reach the street that leads up to the church on the hill, it's easy to see it falls into the "hasn't been cleared yet" category.

"I wonder if that was intentional on the city's part," I muse. "That's a bummer."

"I'm not giving up that easily. Let's park here and hike our way up," Brooks says, pulling to the side of the road. "This means we'll have the whole hill to ourselves!"

He opens the trunk to get the sleds out, and we begin hiking up the side of the street. Brooks holds my gloved hand in one of his while pulling the sled ropes with the other. By the time we make it to the church parking lot, we're barely breathing—a combination of the physical exertion and bouts of uncontrollable laughter.

It's early and cold, so we're the first and only people here. Our dedication is rewarded when we reach the back of the church and take in the view of the undisturbed snow. Pine trees are laden with coats of white, snow banks adding dimension to the monochrome blanket. The sun filters through a thin layer of clouds, the resulting sparkle giving the illusion that everything is dancing.

"Oh, this is gorgeous," I whisper, watching the mist from my breath blend into the magic before evaporating.

"*Mmmhmm*," Brooks responds, and I glance over to find him watching me.

"I almost feel bad disturbing it. The snow looks so peaceful," I say.

Brooks pulls out his phone and takes several photos of the view, including one artistic angle of me looking out over the hill. After a couple of selfies, he puts the phone away and hands me a sled. "It's officially been documented. Now, it's time to tear it up!"

I grin and take the sled, plopping down next to him. "Last one to the bottom buys lunch!" I yell, and we launch ourselves simultaneously.

The cold air flies through my hair, blowing off my hood and rushing around my face as I soar down the slope. I hear Brooks' laugh mix with my scream as we sail toward the bottom of the hill, but he abruptly slows behind me. When I reach the bottom, I look back and see marks from where he dug his hands into the snow to slow himself down.

"Hey! You reverse cheated!" I accuse.

"Like I was going to let you buy lunch," Brooks responds. But his smile quickly transforms into a smirk. "But now that that's settled, you're going down, Sneaks."

We spend the next hour climbing up the hill, flying down on our sleds, and climbing back up again. Half the time we're coming up with ridiculous races or challenges, and half the time we're laughing and relishing the adrenaline rush.

A handful of other people have arrived and joined in the sledding extravaganza by the time 10:00 rolls around. At the bottom of the hill, I lay down on my sled, arms spread wide. "That's it. I'm done for. I'll never climb stairs again." Giant puffs of mist appear and disappear above me as I huff out deep breaths. I close my eyes against the bright sun until a shadow falls over me. Squinting one eye open, I see Brooks standing over me, grinning.

He holds his hands out to pull me up. "All right, if you're going to wimp out, we'll have to move on to the next round of snow day fun."

Instead of taking his hands, I grab a handful of snow and playfully throw it in his face. "I'm not a wimp!" I exclaim. Suddenly, I realize my very vulnerable position of lying on the ground. I scramble to stand, but not before Brooks drops a giant armful of snow on me.

"How dare you?!" I shriek, but any real admonition is negated by my laughter. I'm scooping up handfuls of snow as I yell, "I thought you were a gentleman, Brooks Murphy."

"You thought wrong!" he yells back, right before a snowball hits me in the shoulder, disintegrating on impact and spraying snow across my face.

A second wind of energy floods through me as we send snow flying back and forth, heckling each other with zero true malice. Our snowball fight ends when Brooks suddenly pulls me out of the way seconds before a guy on a sled sails through where I had been standing. I'm clutched against Brooks' chest, shielded in his protective arms.

"Sorry about that!" the sledder calls out from a few yards away, waving a hand in our direction.

"No problem!" I call back, breathless from the adrenaline of the close sled collision and current chest collision.

Brooks stares down at me, eyes intense. "You okay?" he asks, and I nod. I'm frozen in his embrace, in his gaze. His eyes drop to my lips, and I know beyond a shadow of a doubt that he's thinking about kissing me. Because I'm thinking about kissing him. And Brooks and I are quite often thinking the exact same thoughts.

Laughter from a nearby group of sledders reminds us of our surroundings, though, and we slowly break apart. "Time to go?" Brooks asks, voice thick.

"Yep!" I say, grabbing my sled and taking the hand Brooks offers.

We're back to laughing by the time we reach the car. Now that I've stopped moving, the coldness in my bones seeps out, making me shiver. Brooks cranks up the heat and turns to me. "Are you ready to get out of the snow? We can totally skip phase two and go change before lunch instead."

"Absolutely not," I state firmly. "I need phase two of snow fun. Let's go!"

His grin lets me know he's delighted that I pushed to continue. He reaches in the back seat and grabs two travel mugs and a thermos. "Hopefully the hot chocolate is still warm. The thermos claims to keep liquids hot for ten hours, so if it's not, I'm sending a strongly-worded letter to the manufacturer."

I chuckle as I hold out the mugs for him to pour the hot chocolate into. It's still steaming, so no complaints required. We sit in the car for a few minutes, thawing out in the warmth of the heater and the hot liquid.

"Will your students be extra crazy tomorrow after a snow day?" I ask.

Brooks snorts. "Oh, they'll be maniacs, for sure. But tomorrow's chaos will be well worth today's pleasure."

I'm no longer shivering from cold, but his words send a different shiver through me. "Tell tomorrow's Mr. Murphy thanks for taking one for Team Breegan."

"Anything for you, Sneaks," he says with a smile. He places his mug in the cup holder and shifts the car into drive.

Ten minutes later, we park on one of the streets surrounding City Park. Brooks reaches into the back seat again to grab a grocery bag, then turns to me with a twinkle in his eye. "It's snowman time."

We exit the car and find a corner of the park that hasn't been overtaken by young kids yet. Luckily, this is a wet snow that packs well, making it easy to get the giant snowball started. Brooks and I laugh as we push the bottom layer of the snowman into place.

Looking around us, I realize that we've already used up most of the snow in the immediate vicinity. "We did not plan that very well. We probably should have started farther away and rolled the first ball this direction."

Brooks stands beside me, surveying the area and considering my words. "You are not wrong."

"I'm never wrong," I airily state.

He *tsks*. "Oh, really? I think you're forgetting the time you claimed that we would 'never in a million years get caught' flamingo-flocking Assistant Principal Jackson's yard."

I punch Brooks in the arm. Between my gloved hand and his thick winter coat, I'm sure he barely felt it. "You had to bring that up, huh? I would think you could have let that memory die."

"A week of detention tends to sear itself into long-term memory," he teases. Principal Jackson was smart and made us serve our detentions on opposite weeks, lengthening the punishment for both of us. I shake my head but smile.

"We'd better roll up the second layer before the pesky kids steal all the good snow," he adds.

We quickly create two more balls of snow but have to carry them over to our base. I'm sweating underneath my layers by the time we're done. Once we've secured the three tiers of the snowman with additional packed snow as glue, Brooks dumps out the bag of supplies.

"Oh my goodness, you really went all out, didn't you?" I say when I see the full array. A bag of carrots, a hat and scarf set, plus a small bag of actual coal wait to be added to our blank snowman.

"Snowman-building is serious business!" Brooks exclaims. "Except you'd never believe that they don't sell corncob pipes anymore, so it can't be Frosty. I suppose we shouldn't be endorsing tobacco products in a kid-friendly park anyway. You start on the face while I find the perfect set of sticks for arms."

I'm giggling to myself as I follow Brooks' instructions. I take off my gloves so I can have the dexterity to position the pieces of charcoal. Choosing the perfect nose-shaped carrot, I complete the face as Brooks returns holding two sticks.

A few minutes later, we stand back to admire our completed snowman. We take several pictures and selfies to memorialize our creation. "It's perfect," I say. "A perfect snowman for a perfect snow day."

"With the perfect snow date," Brooks adds, smiling over at me. He takes my hand in his, and I feel warmth spread through me, despite the fact that both of our hands are like ice. "But I think it's time for an indoor date. I'm frozen solid," he adds.

"No arguments here!"

———

Once we're back in the car, Brooks turns the heat up again. We swing by my duplex and then his apartment so we can change into dry clothes before going to lunch. Brooks comes out wearing light jeans and a deep navy quarter-zip sweater, looking so effortlessly handsome that it's all I can do not to suggest we stay right here in his apartment. But that's *not* the best idea for the current stage of our dating relationship.

His appearance does make me grateful that I took a few extra moments to choose a cranberry-red sweater dress with black tights and boots as my outfit. Or maybe Brooks dressed up because I dressed up. Either way, I have zero complaints about Brooks' attire.

We head to Sandy's for lunch. I forgo my usual sandwich order to get hot soup instead, and Brooks follows my lead. It's almost 3:00 p.m.

by the time we finish our late lunch, and I fear this might be the end of our day together.

"Want to walk over to Bookafe for coffee or pastries?" Brooks asks, his eyes hopeful.

"Yes!" I instantly reply. *At least I'm not the only one who doesn't want our date to end.*

After a brief walk through Center Square, we order decaf specialty coffees and muffins. I purposely guide us to the table in the back, tucked between bookshelves stocked with works by international authors. This is the table where Mateo first declared his interest to Lana. Considering how in love they are now, this table might be blessed with special relationship powers.

Another two hours fly by as we talk about anything and everything. We swap outrageous stories from our jobs and trade funny memories from high school.

"Ugh," Brooks groans. He covers his hands with his face. "I'll never live that down, huh?"

"Brooks, they couldn't get the suds out of the fountain for *weeks*. Of course, you're not living that down!" I laugh.

"It's their own fault for installing a fountain on a high school campus. Whose idea was that?! They were probably fired," Brooks says defensively. But his ornery smile lets me know he's not truly defensive in the slightest. "And what about you, Miss 'Flash Mob During Algebra?' I don't think Mr. Owens appreciated your choreographed interruption."

I gasp with mock outrage. "You cannot prove that I was the mastermind behind that!"

Brooks rolls his eyes. "Please. I recognized all those dance moves." He pinches my side, causing me to both yelp and blush.

"We had a lot of fun times in high school, huh?" I remark.

"We did," Brooks agrees. His brow furrows. "At least, until I—"

I clap my hand over his mouth to stop him from speaking. "No, sir. Forgiveness. Grace. Moving forward."

His gaze softens as he takes my hand and kisses it.

It's dark by the time we leave Bookafe to walk to Brooks' car. Lazy snow has started falling again, softly drifting through the light of the street lamps. The stillness of the night feels touched by winter magic, by every kind of magic. No one else is out at the moment, giving us the illusion of walking through our own private winter wonderland.

"Hold on," Brooks says, tugging my hand to a stop. "There's this snow dancing challenge trending right now. This is the perfect opportunity!"

"The old regency era one?" I ask, knowing exactly what he's referring to. "Yes, let's do it!" Brooks props his phone up on a window sill, and we laugh our way through the choreographed moves. We watch the video together, and I'm left breathless noticing the twin expressions on our faces.

Lighthearted joy coupled with intense yearning. The very essence of what I've always felt with Brooks. Well, *almost* always felt.

"I won't post this until you give me the go-ahead," Brooks says, breaking me out of my contemplative stare. I glance up at him, at the tenderness and sincerity in his eyes.

A smile slowly breaks out across my lips. "Houston, we have a go," I joke with mock seriousness.

Brooks matches my teasing with a stiff salute before pocketing his phone. He takes my hand to twirl me around before pulling me close in his arms. "I'll post it later tonight. But first, a dance just for me," he whispers against my ear.

Imaginary music plays around us as we slowly sway on the silent sidewalk. Snowflakes continue to dance with us on our otherwise private dance floor.

After two or twenty minutes—I can't be sure—I draw back to search Brooks' eyes. Everything familiar about him hangs there in his gaze. The playfulness that was always matched by his intensity about me, about us. The humor coupled with endless curiosity.

But there's newness there too. A maturity to his joviality. His unbound optimism has been tempered by an appreciation for what can be lost. His rose-colored lenses tinted with the desire to make positive changes to reality.

I love this Brooks.

The thought sends fire through my veins. As much as I loved Brooks in high school, with the fullness of whatever capacity a teenager has to love—it's nothing compared to what I'm experiencing now.

I see my thoughts mirrored in Brooks' eyes, even if neither of us speak any words aloud. And once again, I'm suddenly desperate for him to kiss me. Desperately hoping he'll close the few inches of space between our lips.

But a swift assessment of the war in his expression informs me that he's not going to. Given our history, he's not going to be the one to push in this area.

And I love him even more.

"Brooks, I want you to kiss me." It's spoken as a whisper with the weight of a demand.

The spark in his eyes serves as the *Are you sure?* question that his voice doesn't ask. I nod my head. *Yes, I'm sure.*

Brooks draws in a shaky breath, and, in the next second, his head tips down to meet my lips with his.

The kiss is a caress at first—light, gentle, asking. Brooks moves to thread his fingers through my hair, cupping my face against his, and my fingers instinctively clutch at his chest. His kiss is a fire that my soul slowly melts into, rekindling the embers of everything we've felt for each other.

I kissed Brooks plenty of times as teenagers. But kissing him now is like reading a book after watching the movie adaptation. It feels familiar in a comforting way, and yet . . . different. Richer. Fuller. There's a depth—an intricacy of detail—that the movie can never quite capture the way written words do.

And I'm absolutely addicted to this intricacy. I never want to leave the richness of Brooks' lips against mine. Never ever want to lose this again.

My fingers make their way up to the back of Brooks' neck as his mouth angles against mine. The embers of us are ablaze again, a wildfire.

Brooks breaks away from the kiss, touching his forehead to mine, my fingers still wrapped behind his neck. "Teegan," he breathes, brushing a thumb across my cheek. I hadn't realized there were tears trickling there until he wiped them away.

I see the moisture in his eyes as he whispers.

"It's you."

And I know exactly what he means.

It's you*. It's still you. Always you. Was never not you.*

"I know," I softly reply. "It's us. Everything."

CHAPTER TWENTY-SIX

I kissed Brooks tonight

AMAYA

What in the world makes you think a text is an acceptable form of communication for that statement??

LANA

Wait! Mateo and I are driving home from a friend's house. Give me 5 min and I'll be able to video call

AMAYA

I might call without you . . .

LANA

NO

Don't you dare Amaya

Teegs don't you talk to her without me

I sit on my bed, quietly laughing at their exchange.

LANA

Mateo says I can call now and he'll pretend not to listen but I told him no

Amaya's video call comes through, and I laugh harder as I answer. "Lana's gonna kill you."

She waves me off as Lana's face pops onto the screen. "Beef! This is unacceptable," Lana whines. "I just need a couple of minutes!"

"What? I thought we could spend those minutes rehashing the time you called to tell us all about your first kiss with Mateo," Amaya teases. Now my laughter fully erupts.

"Oh, yes. Please do recount that story," Mateo says in the background of Lana's video. I can hear the giant grin in his voice.

Even though Lana's face is dark in the dim light of the car, I can still see the blush forming on her cheeks.

"You were there. You don't need the playback of that story," Lana huffs.

"Yeah, but I don't know the juicy version as heard by the Beefs," his voice teases. Lana jerks suddenly, and I deduce that Mateo must have pinched her side.

"Let's just say it was crystal clear that Lana was *very* into you," I say loudly, grinning.

"Which was news to no one," Amaya adds.

"What? It was an epic kiss!" Lana exclaims. Then she smirks, looking away from the camera. "The first of *many* epic kisses." She leans fully out of the screen now, no doubt to kiss Mateo.

Amaya groans. Lana wags her finger at the camera. "You asked for it, Beef. You're the one who started this."

"She's got ya there, Amaya," Mateo says. "Lucky for you, we just parked, so I'll pretend to get out of the car, but really, I'll secretly sit here eavesdropping." I see Lana playfully punch her fist in Mateo's direction, then hear his deep laugh. His face leans into the screen as he says, "I'll leave you all to your juicy stories." After placing a quick kiss on Lana's temple, his face exits the view, and a car door shuts.

"All right, dish," Lana demands.

I give them the play-by-play of our fun snow day, capped off by our *very* romantic dance and kiss in the snow. I'm fully aware that my eyes are starry and my lips permanently frozen in a dreamy smile as I share the story.

"You really like Brooks, don't you," Amaya says, more as a statement than a question.

"I . . . I think I more than like him," I admit, chewing on my lip.

Amaya's eyebrow quirks. "Already? Two months ago, you were driving to KC to distract yourself from the pressure of deciding whether to even give Brooks another chance. And now you're already thinking the 'L' word?"

Lana's face is more sympathetic. "Maybe the piece of you that loved Brooks so long ago never really died. Maybe that's why the love has been quick to come alive—because it was never quite gone in the first place?"

I nod, appreciative that she seems to understand. "I know it sounds a little crazy. And I haven't said it to him. That might be *a lot* crazy. But my heart just . . . knows. Because it's Brooks. The same, yet better. Like who we were and who we would become were always meant to be. The love of our lives."

Lana looks teary, and although Amaya's eyes still look slightly skeptical, she's smiling.

"I'm so happy for you, Beef," Lana says. "I mean, of course I still want you to be careful with your heart. But my gut has a good feeling about this. I'm glad we got to meet Brooks at your birthday party. I wish we could spend more time with him. When I needed help processing my feelings, it was really helpful that you both knew Mateo from Arrow and had seen us together."

"Long distance friendship sucks," I affirm. "But I'm grateful to still have you both in my life."

"Seriously," Amaya chimes in. "Just think—you may never have reconnected with him if we hadn't pushed you to find some peers at church. Let me know whether to collect the finder's fee from you or Brooks," she finishes with a wink.

I giggle. "I think we'd both gladly chip in."

———

"Sooo, anything new in your life, Teegan?" Sofia asks the question with so much sparkle in her eyes, you'd think she had diamonds in her irises. The rest of the girls turn to me with eager, knowing looks.

We're sitting in my living room after our Bible study, eating brownies and sipping decaf coffee. I narrow my eyes and point my finger around the circle. "You've been scheming together, haven't you?"

Sofia huffs and tosses her hair. "Come on. There's no way you don't like Mr. Murphy. You two made all sorts of googly-eyes at each other when you visited The Hangout. And you've been acting *extra* cheerful lately. We want the tea." She raises her mug at me, but it's filled with coffee, detracting from the punchline.

I mime zipping my lips, earning a groaned "Teegaaan!" from Sofia. The other girls immediately chime in with pestering remarks.

"Fine, fine. I can confirm that Brooks and I have been officially dating for several weeks now." I say it with an exaggerated sigh, but I can't help the enormous smile that spreads across my lips.

"I knew it!" Sofia yells triumphantly. "I'm telling you—I'm a good luck charm for love. Both of my life mentors wound up finding the guy of their dreams. First Lana, now you. I should start charging for my services."

My well-aimed throw pillow smacks Sofia across the face, only causing a new uproar of laughter.

"Show us pictures! Sofia met him, but not all of us have!" one of the girls exclaims. I carefully select a few photos to show them, which they appropriately fawn over. I mean, let's face it—Brooks is a *very* good-looking guy.

They're greedy for more, so I decide to show them the snow dancing video we took, which they all immediately recognize from its viral rounds on social media.

"Oh, you two are the perfect social media couple," Sofia remarks. "He totally matches your energy for the camera, which isn't the case with every guy." Her observation kicks off a long, giggling conversation about which guys from Arrow would engage in trending videos and which ones would never.

As they chatter, Sofia's remark has my mind racing with a growing idea.

CHAPTER TWENTY-SEVEN

"No, you have to jump higher initially if you're going to get both legs up over my arm," Brooks says, breathing hard from laughing.

We've been in my living room for the past two hours, attempting every couples challenge we could find. At least, every one that wouldn't put any of our body parts in awkward places. I may be in love with the man, but I'm not quite ready for my booty to be all up in his face.

We got the upside-down move on our first try, which gave us false confidence. Other challenges took several efforts, but we've managed to nail each one so far.

The challenge we're currently filming looks like a deceptively simple kickover move, but it requires me to raise both feet above our clasped hands before he tips me backward over his other arm, which is around my waist.

Given my dance background, I expected this to be a breeze, but twenty-eight failed attempts later, we're both rolling on the floor laughing rather than making serious progress. Maybe it's the hysterical laughter that's inhibiting our efforts. Not sure which is the chicken and which is the egg.

Regardless, we'll likely have hours of bloopers recorded on my phone by the time we ever get this right.

I'm flat on my back on the floor again, Brooks hunched over me, hyperventilating with laughter for the thirtieth time. "That's . . . it!" I gasp between laughs. "I . . . give up!"

Brooks reaches a hand out to pull me to my feet. "I think we need to play to our strengths better. Let's learn some dances instead."

And thus, another two hours pass with us learning and performing one viral dance after another. We take turns picking the dances, only taking short breaks to refuel with candy. Nothing like a good jolt of sugar to keep the dance moves flowing.

Brooks was right—this is absolutely playing to our strengths. We manage to nail each dance in a fraction of the time it took us to figure out any of the gymnastic challenges. Each time we play back a finished product, I can't help but smile at how good we look dancing together.

Totally in sync. Vibing with each other's energy. Playing up each other's best moves.

Eyeing each other with intense "I want you" expressions.

It's honestly getting a little warm in here, and I'm not sure that has everything to do with the physical exercise.

Brooks swipes a hand through his tousled hair, smoothing it back into place. "All right—we totally slayed, but I'm cooked."

"You and your Gen Alpha slang," I say with a laugh. Brooks grins and holds up his hands in a "whatever" gesture. He flops onto the loveseat, grabbing my hand to pull me down with him. I lean my back against the arm of the loveseat, tenting my knees over Brooks' outstretched legs. He wraps an arm around my knees, hugging them to his chest.

He props his head against his other hand, arm leaning on the back of the loveseat. "So, tell me something about you that would surprise me."

I tilt my head. "Something that would surprise you?"

"Yeah, you know—something I've missed these past years that I wouldn't expect from you," he says.

"*Hmmm.*" My eyes search the ceiling for an idea. "I hated my public speaking class."

Brooks raises his eyebrows. "But why? You're a natural at talking in front of people."

"I don't mind attention or telling stories to groups of people on the fly. There was something about preparing a memorized speech that I couldn't get into. It felt too rehearsed," I say.

He nods thoughtfully. "I guess I could see that. But you know I'd sit and listen to you spout off memorized facts all day."

I nudge his chest playfully with my knees. "Your turn. Something surprising."

Brooks leans forward with an earnest expression. "You would never have guessed this, but I became a teacher."

Now I gently kick his chest with one foot. "I already told you that surprised me, so that doesn't count. Try again."

He taps a finger on his chin. "The summer after my freshman year of college, I traveled with a group to run a basketball camp in Germany."

I shake my head. "While interesting, you wanting to travel internationally is zero percent surprising. Or to play basketball. Try harder, Brooks," I admonish, punching his arm.

"Fine, fine. I like to cook and watch *The Food Network* for fun," he says.

"Really?" I question, eyebrows raised. "You learned to cook? That *is* completely surprising."

"Well, after . . ." He pauses. "I stayed with my dad for a while after my mom . . . I wanted to do something to help my dad. He basically only ate takeout unless someone brought him food. So, I learned to cook for us."

Follow-up questions about how his dad dealt with Angela's death—how *he* dealt with her death—linger on the tip of my tongue, but they hesitate to come out as spoken words.

"Tag. You're it," Brooks says, tapping my shoulder. "Surprise me again."

"I worked at McDonald's one summer," I state.

Brooks' mouth falls open. "I don't believe you."

After briefly laughing, I explain. "At the Summer Projects with Arrow in Florida, we worked during the days and did Bible studies and leadership training in the evenings. Of course, the most popular jobs available were the ones on the beach or in retail at the outlet malls, which I did work the other two summers. But after my sophomore year, I decided to take one of the less-desirable jobs."

Brooks shakes his head slowly, an expression I can't quite read in his eyes. "I bet that McDonald's manager thanked their lucky stars to have you working there for the summer. You were probably the most cheerful McDonald's employee ever," he says.

The warmth in his eyes as he gazes at me makes my heart slowly catch fire. "Your turn," I murmur quietly, not looking away.

"Well, I can tell you one thing that was entirely unsurprising," Brooks says, taking a deep breath. "The way my feelings for you clicked right back into place. Least surprising thing in the world."

I bite my lip, breaking eye contact. Looking back up, I lean my head against my hand, mirroring his position. "When did you know?"

He lets out a breathy laugh. "The second I walked in and saw you, I knew it was a matter of time. At least, assuming that you were single and that you were anything like your old self. My heart saw you and just thought, 'Oh, there you are.' Like I'd been waiting all these years for you, not even realizing I was waiting."

Brooks looks down as his thumb traces circles on the side of my knee. "It's not like I was sitting around pining for you all those years. I don't think I ever consciously thought I'd get another chance with you. But subconsciously, I could never really care deeply for any of the women I tried to date, which is why I barely dated. I wasn't willfully holding out for only you. But once I saw you again, my heart could finally release the breath it had been holding for all those years."

He reaches over to cup my cheek. "When you shut me down from trying to apologize on the car ride back from the silent disco, I was worried that your heart wouldn't ever feel that same exhale of relief. I tried to convince myself that seeing you was merely my chance to *stop* subconsciously living in a holding pattern, to be open to a relationship with someone else in the future."

My voice is barely a whisper. "When did you know?" I repeat, looking for a different answer now.

A thoughtful smile quirks Brooks' lips. "When you were sick. Specifically, when you fell asleep during *Trolls*, and your hand somehow found its way to mine while you were sleeping. That small gesture gave my heart a taste of hope. Even if you weren't knowingly ready to give us another chance, that maybe *your* subconscious wanted it. Wanted me."

His blue eyes look a shade darker now, his stare making my heart race.

"I always wanted you, Brooks. That's why I was scared. I was scared to still want you," I whisper.

We move to each other in one fluid motion, our lips finding each other like complementary magnets. My hands are in his hair while his hands wind around my knees and my waist, pulling me closer. I sigh as he deepens our kiss, but seconds later he breaks away.

"It's time for me to go home, Sneaks," he murmurs, voice raspy. I nod, then quickly swivel my feet to the floor to stand. As much as my lips are screaming at the loss of contact from his, I'm so grateful for the way he's respecting our boundaries. Not just mine, but *ours*.

I walk him to the door, and he presses one last kiss to my lips. His smile turns playful as he says, "You'd better be sending me all the good footage from tonight. And I'm not talking about only the polished moments where we nailed it. I want the moments where you're falling to the floor."

Rolling my eyes, I playfully shove him out the door. "Goodnight, Brooks."

Chapter Twenty-Eight

I find myself feeling jealous of Lana and Mateo more than once over the next couple of weeks. While I'm grateful to be dating Brooks now, after we've had years to grow and mature into adulthood, Lana had some definite perks dating Mateo in college. Like getting to see each other multiple times a week at Arrow events, soccer games, and official dates.

Adulting is for the birds. What I'd really like to do is hang out with Brooks all day every day. Too bad he has to spend his days teaching and evenings studying. Not to mention almost every single one of *my* evenings is taken up with Arrow events and Bible studies. A fact that has never really bothered me before now, considering my extreme extroversion and night owl tendencies.

But now, it means I barely get to see Brooks outside of small group on Wednesdays. Well, okay, and on our weekend date nights. And sitting by each other at church. Maybe lunch after church. And video calling occasionally.

But it's not enough!

Every second I spend with him only makes me crave *more* seconds, *every* second.

Then again, I recognize this as one of the early symptoms of how I let my identity get so wrapped up in him back in high school. And I swore to Logan that I was mature enough not to repeat that behavior.

So, I'm making a concerted effort to deny at least *some* of the times I impulsively want to text him. And not create extra reasons to see him. Instead, I make time to get coffee with Joy and grab lunch with the other girls from small group. I even initiate an evening to relax at home with Gina instead of going our separate ways to campus.

Another idea pops into my head.

> I haven't seen you in a while! Would you want to come to the Arrow meeting tonight for old time's sake?

BAILEY

> omg, that would be so fun. I've thought about coming some Thursday but didn't want to be the awkward old person crashing the meeting.

> Whatever! You should come any time you want to! You still fit right in with the college crowd <wink emoji>

BAILEY

> Ok, I'll meet you there!

The rest of the day is a blur, as Thursdays always are, but I find myself legitimately looking forward to seeing Bailey tonight. It's such an evolution from our college days.

I'm in the lobby of the student union greeting people as they arrive when Bailey walks in. I wave her over, and she gives me a hug and a sincere smile.

"Talk about a blast from the past. I feel like I'm back in college again!" she exclaims. "Does it ever feel like you never left?"

"It kinda does sometimes," I admit. "Which is fun some days and slightly weird others. How's your week been?"

"Good! I really feel like I'm getting a handle on the job," Bailey says. "Of course, I was finally in the swing of things with the soccer team just in time for their season to end. But now we're neck-deep in basketball season, and I'll feel more prepared for the women's soccer team this spring. It's a fun challenge to tailor nutrition based on the athletes' specific needs."

"Bailey? Is that you?" Rachel's voice gets louder as she walks toward us. "It's so great to see you!" she says as she gives Bailey a hug.

"You too!" Bailey replies. "I'm back in town working with the athletic department, and Teegan invited me to come to the old stomping grounds tonight!"

Rachel gives me a surprised but encouraging look. *I guess she was not as oblivious to the tension between Bailey and the Beefs as we thought she was.*

"I'm so glad she did! I should stick you up on stage to emcee announcements for old time's sake," Rachel teases.

"Goodness, no!" Bailey laughs. "Where's the After Party tonight?"

"Heading to Mom's Diner for late-night breakfast food," I reply.

"A classic," Bailey says with a smile.

"Teegan is still the queen of After Party planning," Rachel says. "I seriously don't know what we would do without her."

There's a meaningful tone to her statement that cuts like a knife. And not a painless scalpel. A very dull knife, where you feel every excruciating millisecond of the cut.

My skin starts to feel itchy, my breath too tight.

"Oh, anyone could do it!" I say. I gesture with too-large hand movements. "I love planning social events, but it's not an exclusive talent."

Bailey gives me a weird look. Because I'm acting weird.

"Why don't we go in and find a seat? We can grab a place close to the TriAlphas, if you want," I redirect, pulling Bailey into the meeting room. Away from Rachel and the awkward undercurrents that will drag me under if I don't escape now.

"What was that about?" Bailey asks under her breath.

"What was what? Not sure what you mean!" I whisper as we take seats.

"Uh-huh. Sure," Bailey replies, one eyebrow raised.

I'm saved from responding by the worship band inviting everyone to stand, the loud music canceling out any opportunity to continue the conversation.

My mind wanders throughout the meeting. *I know I should tell Kent and Rachel that I'm considering other options for next year. That I'm possibly leaning toward not returning to Arrow staff. Strongly leaning.*

But they'll be so disappointed in me! They'll think I'm a quitter, that I'm giving up on such an amazing opportunity to have a spiritual impact on students. I don't want them to think less of me. Or to think I'm just getting bored. This isn't a boring job! I don't want them to take it personally, to think I don't like working with them.

Ugh. There are so many potential adverse outcomes to this conversation.

I'm not sure what Kent is sharing in his message because I'm too busy feeling trapped by catastrophic what-ifs. It's becoming increasingly difficult to take full breaths as my thoughts churn around worst-case scenarios.

I close my eyes, letting my body sprout wings and climb above the clouds. I'm flying away, over the ocean, heading toward a beautiful sunset. Drifting away from the discomfort.

How long can I keep flying away?

When the meeting ends, I introduce Bailey to several girls, although she already knows the TriAlphas. I can tell that Bailey's emotional tank is filling up by being here and reliving her college days, and I realize how happy it makes me to see Bailey happy.

We sit with a huge group of sorority girls at Mom's Diner, regaling them with stories from our "good ol' days" in AOPi and TriAlpha. I go out of my way to emphasize how great of a leader Bailey was because, when I set aside our petty, immature rivalry, it's the honest truth. Bailey was a great leader in TriAlpha and in Townsend's Greek system in general.

The crowd thins the later it gets, but Bailey and I linger there, sharing memories and a cinnamon roll. "So, why were you acting so weird earlier when Rachel talked about you being the After Party Queen? It's not like that's news to anyone," Bailey says.

I take a quick mental inventory of my options. Play this off and bypass talking about my unknown future, or be honest about why it made me so uncomfortable.

Sighing, I settle on the honest option and speak in a low tone. "I haven't really talked about this with anyone outside of Lana, Amaya, and Brooks, *especially* not Rachel or Kent. But I'm thinking about not coming back to Arrow staff next year."

Bailey raises one eyebrow but gently nods. "What's making you consider a change?"

I blow out a breath. "It's not that I don't love the job. Because I do. And I know it fits within how God has wired and gifted me." I chew my lip before continuing. "There's this growing sense inside me that this might not be the *only* thing God gifted me for. A curiosity to explore something new. Well, kind of new, kind of old—to go back and give teaching a real chance. But I'm not sure how to make the decision."

Bailey's head is nodding with understanding, not skepticism, which feels encouraging. "You're certainly suited to the full-time college ministry life, but that doesn't mean it's the end-all be-all. Clearly our situations are different, but choosing to make a change and move back to Brooklyn has been exactly what I needed in this season. Maybe it won't be forever, but for right now, I'm enjoying my job. And I've loved connecting with you, Lana, and Amaya—even your other small group friends I met at your birthday party. Brooklyn feels a lot like home for now, and it's been healing in ways I don't think I would have found in Texas or California. So, don't be afraid to make a change if you think that's what God is leading you to do. I'm always here to be a sounding board if you need it."

"Bailey, I'm really glad you came to Arrow tonight. And really glad you moved back to Brooklyn. I'm so grateful to have another chance to be your friend," I tell her. "I can't tell you how encouraging it's been to have you as a listening ear to talk to about life and Arrow stuff. Especially since you understand everything but aren't caught up in the middle of it."

Bailey's smile is warm when she responds. "I'm really glad too, Teegan. While I wish I would have acted differently in college so we could have been better friends then, I'm glad we have the opportunity now."

———

Despite having an enjoyable time with Bailey at the meeting and After Party, my body is buzzing with anxious energy when I get home. The logic of knowing that I should just talk to Kent and Rachel is outweighed by my flight response.

Nope. Don't want to do that.

I decide to text Brooks instead, unsure if he'll be awake at this late hour.

> Hey there! Sorry if I wake you up. Was wondering if I could see you tomorrow after school?

I set my phone down on the nightstand and change into pajamas, trying to keep my hopes of him texting me back appropriately low. Who am I kidding? Even graded on a curve, I'd be getting an "F" in "success at keeping my hopes down." That is, if checking my phone every other second is any indicator.

The longer my phone stays stubbornly silent, the more my heart sinks. I go to the bathroom to brush my teeth and finish getting ready for bed. Tucking myself under my pink comforter, I blow out a long breath. I can feel the deep frown curling my lips down, sulking that Brooks isn't available to break me out of my spiral.

Super mature, Teegan. Better hope Logan doesn't find out.

My phone pings, and my heart lurches at the sound. Propping myself up on my elbows, I eagerly unlock it, expecting a "Yes!" text from Brooks.

BROOKS

> Sorry, tomorrow won't work for me

My lungs slowly deflate, and my heart shrivels.

> ok

Setting the phone down, I plop back on my bed and fight off tears. *Don't cry. Don't cry. Just don't think about it, Teegan. Remember the puppy we saw on campus today? Think about the cute little puppy.*

I'm failing miserably (again) in my attempt to redirect my thoughts when the phone suddenly rings, causing me to jump.

It's Brooks.

"Hello?" I ask.

"Teeg, I'm sorry," Brooks says, voice strained. "That was totally rude, and I'm sorry. Of course I'd like to see you. I just . . . I won't be here tomorrow."

"Oh," I answer, one part reassured and one part perplexed. "What do you mean, you won't be here tomorrow?"

"I, ah, I . . ." Brooks trails off. I'm tempted to interject and lighten the tension, but something tells me to stay quiet.

"I'm driving home to KC tomorrow," Brooks finally says. "It's, um, tomorrow is the anniversary of . . ."

Understanding sinks in, strangling my heart. "Of your mom?" I finish for him, voice quiet.

"Yeah."

We're both silent for a beat, listening only to the sound of each other breathing.

"Can I come with you?" I ask. My voice is small because, realistically, I *do not* want to willingly walk into such a sad situation. Into such a painful memory.

But more than that, I don't want Brooks walking into it alone. Not if I can be there with him.

"You don't have to do that, Sneaks," Brooks says. His voice is tender, appreciative. "I'll be with my dad, with Steven and his wife, Julie. You don't need to be there."

"Brooks, I want to be there. With you. For your family. For your mom," I assert before my voice cracks on the last word. I *do* want to be there, not only for Brooks, but for all of them. For Angela. To show her that I'm back, even in some abstract way.

"Are you sure?" Brooks asks. I know he's trying to give me a way out, a way to avoid the sorrow. But I also hear the hope in his voice.

"Brooks, I'm with you. I want to be there."

He's quiet for a long moment. His voice is tight when he murmurs, "Thank you."

Chapter Twenty-Nine

When my alarm goes off Friday morning, I wake up exhaust-ed. No sleep badges were earned last night. I'd tossed and turned in anticipation of today, torn between avoiding sad emotions and supporting the man I love.

I've alerted Kent that I won't be at staff meeting today and canceled the rest of my commitments. I make an expeditious trip to the grocery store first thing when I get up. Then, after taking a solemn shower and quickly getting dressed, I text Brooks.

> Are you sure you don't want me to drive today? I'd be happy to

BROOKS

> It's ok. I can drive. Be there in 10

I'm waiting on the driveway when Brooks arrives. Quickly toss-ing my small duffel bag and winter coat in the back seat, I open the passenger door before he can get out of the car.

"Hey," I greet, tone even.

"Hey," he responds, tone tipping to the depressed side of even.

I feel out what's needed for the trip as we drive out of town. Brooks has a playlist going, but we're pretty much silent during the fifteen-minute drive to the highway heading to KC. He fidgets in his seat, his hands moving from tapping the steering wheel to rubbing his face to leaning an elbow against the window.

Good thing I came prepared.

"I found this podcast called *Revisionist History* that shares interesting but overlooked stories from history. It sounded like something you might enjoy—would you want to listen to an episode?" I ask. I'm carefully watching Brooks' face to gauge his reaction, in case I need to pull out the *Trolls* soundtrack instead.

"Sure. That does sound interesting," he replies, looking genuinely intrigued. I breathe a sigh of relief at having something to distract our thoughts for the few hours we'll be driving. Brooks hands me his phone, and I pull up the podcast on Spotify, quickly searching for the episode about Hitler's Olympics. There are nine episodes in the series, so we'll have plenty of distraction material if this hooks Brooks' interest.

I'm willing to embrace boring history if it means keeping his mind off of where we're heading.

Luckily, the engaging podcast captures our attention. After the first episode, I reach to the back of the car and pull out my other secret distraction weapon. "Reese's Pieces or Bugles?" I ask.

A hint of a smile crosses Brooks' lips, which feels like I achieved Olympic podium status. "Bugles. I can't do any sugar right now."

I tear open the bag, and Brooks holds out his hand for me to place five Bugles on his fingertips. Just like old times.

Between the podcast and snacks, the drive to Lee's Summit passes by in no time. We pull into the driveway of a house I don't recognize. But, of course, it makes sense that Brooks' dad wouldn't want to stay in the house he shared with Angela. Especially with Brooks and Steven grown and no longer living there.

Still, it breaks my heart a little for all of them. And for all of the memories I have from their old house. Sitting at the kitchen table while Angela blasted Tina Turner and cooked dinner—with Brooks goofing off or flirting with me instead of doing his homework. Movie nights in the living room. Game nights in the basement with the basketball and dance teams. Brooks' parents were always fully stocked with snacks and constantly adding to the collection of gaming tables. They were successful in their mission to entice all the high schoolers to hang out there under the casual supervision of "Papa and Mama Murph."

I think I accidentally entered a vacuum chamber. My body suddenly feels deprived of air. My breathing turns panicked as I try to fight off the cage bars slowly extending around my thoughts.

Don't think about it. You need to be there for Brooks. He's got to be feeling a thousand times worse. Pull it together for him. You're on a beach. You're floating on top of the gentle waves of the sea. You're not trapped in the sadness of Angela's absence. Fly above it.

Brooks' face is tight as he turns the car off and takes a deep breath. He's silent as we exit the vehicle and walk up to the front porch.

His dad, Steven Sr., opens the door at our approach. In the span of a second, his eyes soften at Brooks' expression and then light up looking at me.

"Teegan! Brooks told me y'all were dating, but he didn't say you'd be coming today," he says as he steps toward me. He envelops me in a hug.

"Hi, Mr. Murphy," I greet, hugging him back. "It was last minute, but I insisted on coming."

He lingers in the hug a moment longer, murmuring, "Thank you, sweetheart." Then he draws back to look at me, holding me by the shoulders and taking me in. "It's so great to see you. You're exactly the same—but a grown-up version of the Teegan we knew and loved. Which means you can drop the 'Mr. Murphy' title since you're not a teenager anymore. Call me Steve. Otherwise, Steven will be chiming in all day long," he adds with a grin.

"So, what's this? I bring Teegan along, and suddenly I'm invisible?" Brooks jokes. He's forced lightness into his tone, but this smile doesn't make his eyes light up like his real smile does. Steve shifts to hug Brooks, giving him a tight squeeze as well. Brooks claps him on the back in an obvious move to escape the emotional embrace. Or, obvious to me, at least.

I slip my hand into Brooks'.

"Speaking of Steven, when are he and Julie arriving?" Brooks asks.

"They're meeting us at the lake," Steve responds. "They decided to get an AirBnb out there last night."

"Lake Lotawana?" I ask. Brooks' family always took multiple vacations there. Well, vacation might not be quite the right term, considering it's only about twenty minutes from Lee's Summit. There was a small cabin on the lake they used to rent multiple times a year. I tagged along on one of their summer trips, enjoying the sight of Brooks water skiing while I sunbathed on the rental boat.

Steve smiles. "Good memory, Teegan. Yes—we all agreed that Angela would have loved for the lake to be her final resting place. She enjoyed being there more than the rest of us combined."

Brooks' thumb is manically fidgeting with my fingers, so I reach my other hand over to clasp around his. "That's really special. That's exactly what she would love," I say to Steve as I squeeze Brooks' hand.

"We'd better hit the road over there," Steve says. "Want to ride with me in my car?"

"Nah, I can drive us over in mine," Brooks quickly responds. I know he wants the distraction of driving rather than riding as a passenger.

"You ride up front, Mr. Mur—Steve," I interject. "I'll sit in the back! Could I run in to the bathroom before we leave?"

I take an extra moment in the bathroom to collect my emotions. I wasn't prepared for the onslaught of contrasting reactions I'm experiencing. Sadness I expected. But seeing Brooks' dad again filled me with joy—a nostalgic, coming-home sensation. That feeling only made Angela's absence a deeper, bigger hole. And I feel regret that I never got to say goodbye to her. Bitterness that she died thinking that Brooks and I were over forever. Gratitude that we weren't over forever and that Steve gets to see this full-circle moment.

"How do we handle today?" I ask my reflection in the mirror. My natural inclination is to be the positive, bright spot of the day. To try to cheer everyone up with sunshine and rainbows.

But the grief feels too gray. Once again, I fight off the urge to walk out the door and avoid this altogether. "Don't make Brooks face this alone, Teegan," I whisper to myself. "Get back out there."

As we drive to the lake, I keep up a steady stream of conversation with Steve so Brooks doesn't have to talk. I fill him in on the years of my life he missed, throwing in as many light-hearted stories as possible.

We pull into a parking area by Lake Lotawana where Steven and his wife are waiting for us. When I step out of the car, Steven's eyes widen with recognition. His smile tightens slightly, looking like he's trying not to cry. "Hi, Steven," I say with a small wave.

He steps forward and gives me a quick hug. "Thanks for being here for him," he whispers quickly before drawing back and holding an arm out to his wife. "Teegan, this is my wife, Julie."

"It's great to meet you, Teegan," Julie says before also pulling me into a short hug around the large bouquet of forget-me-not flowers she's holding. "I've heard wonderful things."

"I'm excited to get to know you," I respond. Brooks has come to stand next to me after hugging Steven, so I take his hand again.

Steve leads the way on a path around the lake until we reach a bench with a small tree planted behind it. There's a plaque on the bench that reads: *For Angela Murphy. You were simply the best of us.*

My throat tightens, and I blink rapidly to keep the moisture locked behind my eyes. Brooks blows out a slow, long breath next to me, his grip on my hand tensing. He rocks his weight back and forth between his feet as his dad speaks aloud to Angela.

"Hi there, darling," Steve begins. "We're here today to tell you again how much we miss you. Every day. You're always with us in everything we do, a constant presence in our thoughts and our memories. It's still hard to create new memories without you, but we know you'd want us loving the best of each moment. I finally took that birding tour to Canada that I always dreamed about. Got lucky and saw every species of owls I was hoping for. You would have loved the Snowy Owl. She was a beauty."

Steve continues speaking for a couple more minutes, then trails off. Steven and Julie jump in, sharing highlights from the past year, and I realize this must be their annual tradition. To speak their favorite new memories to Angela's memory. I'm barely holding it together by the time Brooks clears his throat to speak.

"Hey, Mom," he starts, voice strained. "Really wish you could have been here this year. Because Teegan's here with me. Yes, *the* Teegan. Your favorite of all time. I don't know how I got so lucky, but God let me back into her life after I was such an idiot. And I know you'd be so thrilled about that." He pauses, and I look over at him. His eyes are red, his lips twitching against the urge to cry. I let go of his hand so I can slip an arm around his waist, tucking myself to his side. Leaning my head against his chest, I wrap my other arm around his stomach and squeeze.

His arm around my shoulders tightens, almost to the point of being painful. But I won't tell him to loosen his grip when I know this is the lifeline keeping him above water.

"Just really wish you were here," he finishes, voice hardly above a whisper. He sniffs hard and clears his throat again. Steve picks up talking, but I don't comprehend a word he says. I'm trying too hard not to fall to pieces so I can hold Brooks together.

Julie hands out bunches of flowers to each of us, and we take turns placing them against the trunk of the tree. I follow their lead, each person taking a private moment alone with their thoughts. When it's my turn, I crouch down to place my flower stems with the others, thinking rather than speaking my words to Angela.

Hey, Mrs. Murphy. Mama Murph. I really do wish you were here to see the man that Brooks has become. You were the best of us, and he's grown up to be the best of you. Thanks for always being there for me. For being a second mom in so many ways. Losing my relationship with you was one of the many hard things about our breakup. But we've both matured in all the ways we needed to as individuals before we could make us last. I hope you can see that. That you're smiling that satisfied smile you had when everything turned out exactly how you told us it would. I'll miss you being with us for all that's still to come.

Standing to my feet, I wipe the tears from my cheeks before turning to face everyone. Brooks, Steven, and Julie walk the few steps down to the lake's edge, and I move to follow them. Brooks' dad catches my arm to stop me.

"Thanks for coming today, Teegan," he says. His eyes fill with tears as he continues. "This would have meant so much to Angela. To see you. The fact that she knew and loved the girl that Brooks would wind up with . . . I can't explain how much that means to me."

I've officially lost the fight against tears now. He hugs me again before we join the others by the water. By the time I reach Brooks' side, he's already cracking jokes, retelling funny lake stories at Steven's expense.

Julie leans in and speaks with a low voice. "It really means a lot that you came today. He never shows it, but I know this tradition is hard for Brooks. He typically glosses over everything, doesn't really show emotion. That's the closest to genuine grief I've seen him express." Her smile is kind, appreciative as she holds my gaze.

"I'm glad I'm here too," I reply before Brooks calls me over.

"Bet I can still beat you at skipping rocks," he declares, holding up two flat rocks.

"You're on, Murphy," I say, brushing aside the heavy emotions so I can match Brooks' need for playful energy now. Pretty soon, we're all laughing and skipping rock after rock over the water's surface. Steve comes out victorious with a masterful ten skips.

After an early dinner at their favorite lakeside grill, we part ways to drive back to Lee's Summit. I share some of my memories of the lake trip I took with them, mostly teasing Brooks about how much he tried to show off water skiing only to lose every competition to Steven. We stop at Steve's house to drop him off before Brooks will drive me home for the night.

I get out of the car to give Steve a proper hug before moving to the front seat. "Thanks for letting me join you today," I tell him. His tight squeeze is his only response.

"Looking forward to seeing you again soon, Teegan," he tells me before heading into the house. "See you in a little while, Brooks."

Brooks and I get back into the car, and he asks, "Where to? You staying with your mom or dad or Amaya?"

"Dad. I'll put the address into your map," I say, taking his phone from him. I didn't want to have to go home to my mom's house and rehash the day's emotional events with her. My dad is less likely to ask follow-up questions. "I would have stayed with Amaya, but she's in Wichita visiting her mom for the long weekend."

"I'm glad I got to meet her and Lana at your birthday party," Brooks says as he backs out of the driveway. "It's more fun being able to picture their faces and personalities with all your comments about them."

I smile. "I only wish you could have met Mateo too. You would hit it off for sure. Hopefully we can make it happen someday."

Brooks glances over at me. "We should fly out to D.C. and visit them."

"Yes! That would be so fun sometime! I've only been out there to see her once," I say.

"I mean, like, tomorrow," Brooks says, voice picking up fervor. "It's a long weekend for MLK day on Monday. We should fly out there tomorrow and back on Monday!"

"Are you for real?" I ask.

"Totally for real. What else do we have going on? Let's just go!" he replies.

I know that this trip suggestion is probably a way of escaping the weight of this weekend. But I'm all for enabling his escapism if it means seeing my best friend.

"Ahhhh!" I scream. "Let's do it! I'll text Lana."

CHAPTER THIRTY

Teegs, don't you dare mess with me about this or I will disown you as my Beef

I'm dead serious. We really want to fly there tomorrow morning. The flights are pulled up and everything

YES!!!! omg I can't believe I'll get to see you!!

<dancing emoji>

Sleeping arrangements won't be ideal but we'll make it work. We have an air mattress we can put in the small office and one of you can sleep on the couch. Unless you want to get a hotel

Heck no I don't want a hotel. I want every possible minute with you

"I'm assuming the huge grin on your face means Lana said yes?" Brooks asks. We're parked down the street from my dad's house.

"Yes! Their apartment is pretty small, so if you don't want to sleep on a couch or air mattress, then you can look for a hotel. But I'm totally staying with them," I say.

"Like I'm gonna miss out on the fun? I'll sleep on the floor if I have to," Brooks replies, eyes alight.

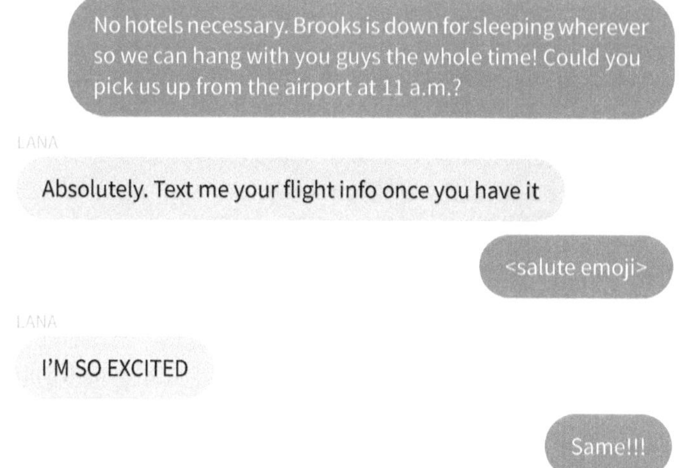

"Tickets are booked," Brooks says, showing me his phone screen. "I'll need to pick you up to head to the airport around six-thirty in the morning. Sure you can pull that off, Aurora?"

He smirks, and I punch him in the arm. He grabs my hand before I can pull back my punch and tugs me toward him. My head comes to rest against his shoulder, and I nuzzle my face into his neck. His fingers reach up to lazily wind their way through my hair.

Brooks nudges my chin with his thumb, tilting my head back to make eye contact.

"Thank you."

The words are quiet and solitary. I know the full weight behind those eight letters, just as much as I know Brooks isn't going to expound further.

I reach my right hand up to trace his jawline, then gently press my finger into the cleft of his chin. There's a layer of stubble there that's a contrast to Brooks' typically clean-shaven face. Further evidence of the emotional toll of this weekend that we aren't speaking aloud. I see it all in his eyes, even in the darkness of the car interior.

Leaning forward, I erase the inches of distance between our lips. The stubble I traced with my fingers now pricks my chin, accentuating the softness of Brooks' lips against mine. His arm wraps around my waist, pulling me as close to him as the car console will allow.

Brooks breaks away from my lips long enough to sear a burning path along my jaw, behind my ear, down my neck. When his lips return to mine, there's an urgency to the press of his mouth. As though this kiss was the balm to heal all the pain of this day.

The pain of *all* the years apart from each other.

I never want it to end. I'll forgo oxygen, sleep, food, water—all of life's supposed necessities—if it means I can stay here in the intoxication of Brooks' kiss.

But we both know it needs to end before it doesn't. We simultaneously pull away from each other. As the car fills with the sound of our heavy breaths, I see Brooks trying and failing to formulate words.

"I better get some sleep if I'm going to make it to our flight in the morning. Sleeping Beauty needed sleep for a reason," I joke. Brooks gives a half smile, then pulls me into a gentle hug. Once again burying my face under his chin, I breathe a kiss onto his neck before sitting up. He puts the car into drive and takes my hand for the short distance to my dad's driveway.

"Six-thirty sharp, Sneaks. Don't make me come in there with a bucket of ice," Brooks threatens, the mischievous spark back in his eyes. I flick his arm before opening the car door.

"Trust me—I'm not going to be late for the chance to see one of my Beefs in person," I say. I move to retrieve my bag from the back seat, but Brooks has somehow beat me to it.

"I'll walk you up to the door and say hi to your dad," he says. "Seems like the gentlemanly thing to do."

As we step into the entryway, I call out, "Dad! I'm here!" Footsteps immediately sound, and my dad rounds the corner, still dressed in jeans and a polo shirt despite the late hour. I'm not sure I've ever seen my dad in sweats, come to think of it.

Dad's smile stays put at the sight of Brooks with me, thanks to my lengthy explanation of our relationship on Christmas Day. I learned my lesson about the men in my life being blind-sided by the reappearance of Brooks.

He extends a hand toward Brooks, who shakes it firmly. "Good to see you, Mr. Jones."

"You too, Brooks. I'm glad about how things have worked out. And call me Morgan," my dad responds.

"I'm not staying, but I wanted to say hello," Brooks tells him before turning to me. "See you tomorrow." He places a swift kiss on my cheek, entirely sweet and chaste in front of my dad. But that doesn't mean my skin doesn't burn afterward.

Dad hugs me and takes my bag after Brooks leaves. "Everything go okay today?"

I follow him to the kitchen because I need a long drink of water after that intense kiss in the car. Following an already-intense day.

"Yeah, as good as it could go, I guess. It was nice to see Brooks' dad and brother and be there with them," I reply, hoping he won't press for more details. Thankfully, he doesn't.

I chug a glass of water.

"So, would Brooks like to join us for lunch or dinner tomorrow?" Dad asks.

Shoot.

"Oh, um, about that," I stammer. I feel my cheeks heating. "We sorta booked flights to D.C. first thing in the morning."

"You what?"

"We decided to fly out and visit Lana and Mateo since it's a long weekend. Kinda spur-of-the-moment. You know me!" The words rush out of my mouth as I take in my dad's disappointed face.

"I do know," Dad mumbles. "I was looking forward to spending a little time with you this weekend."

I didn't even think about how our last-minute adventure would affect my dad. *Gah, Teegan!* "I'm sorry! I promise I'll come back to visit again soon. Brooks needs something fun to distract him this weekend. I think he'd rather not be here in KC the whole time, around all the reminders," I rapidly explain.

Dad raises his eyebrows. "Only Brooks?"

I drum my fingers on the empty water glass I'm still clutching. I shrug.

"It's okay." My dad sighs. "I know you haven't seen Lana in a long time. I'm glad you'll get the chance. I just . . . I would really like to have some time together. Soon."

"I promise," I vow, exaggeratedly nodding my head. "Brooks is picking me up super early though, so I should head to bed for tonight."

"All right. Let me know if you need anything," Dad says. He gives me another hug goodnight. I don't miss the droop of his shoulders as he retreats to his room.

It's okay, Teegan. You can come back in a few weeks. But for now, let's focus on Lana!

And Brooks.

Let's be real—a good chunk of my focus has permanently shifted to Brooks.

———

"BEEF!" Lana's voice squeals, alerting me to her incoming embrace.

"LaLa!" I squeal back, essentially jumping into her arms.

Any and all onlookers are probably avoiding the crazy women jumping, hugging, and screaming on the sidewalk.

"I'm *so* glad you decided to come visit!" Lana exclaims in my ear, still squeezing me in a tight hug. "This is the best spontaneous surprise ever."

I catch sight of Mateo over Lana's shoulder, dimple popping on his right cheek as he grins at our outlandish display of affection. Letting go of Lana, I give Mateo a side hug as I motion Brooks over.

"Brooks, you got to meet Lana at my birthday, but this is her husband, Mateo," I introduce. "Mateo, meet my boyfriend, Brooks."

They shake hands and exchange greetings. "Thanks so much for bringing Teegan to D.C.," Mateo says. "I probably won't have to buy any gifts for Lana for the rest of the year. This will be enough to keep her happy."

Lana rolls her eyes. "Like that would stop you from getting me anything."

"Fair point," Mateo says, winking at Lana.

Just like old times. It's good to see the spark doesn't die.

Brooks is quick to take my small suitcase from me, so I'm free to loop my arm through Lana's as we walk toward the parking garage. "So, what's the plan?"

"Well, that's up to you," Lana says. "We can take you guys to some of the typical D.C. tourist spots, or we can stick closer to the Silver Spring area and show you around our daily life. Your pick."

"Real life, for sure," Brooks chimes in. Given his profession, I'm a little surprised he wouldn't jump at the chance to tour the nation's capital. My heart melts that he would set aside his interest in history to defer to my interest in my best friend's world.

"Yes, I'd much rather hang out with you guys on your real stomping grounds. I'll bring Brooks back some other time to see all the old stone buildings," I say with a teasing grin over my shoulder at Brooks. He catches my eye and gives a wry smile back.

"Okay, we'll have most of the day to hang out, but Mateo is coaching one indoor soccer game a little closer to D.C. later this afternoon. You can come with us, or we can drop you off at a coffee shop or something," Lana says once we're in their car.

"That depends," I muse, leaning up between the front seats. "Mateo, will we get to see fiery Soccer Lana in action?"

Mateo laughs, then pokes Lana's side. "You know it's impossible to keep her from showing up in the stands."

"Then we're in," I state with a grin, sitting back in my seat. Lana huffs and crosses her arms. But she knows she can't contradict us.

Lana and I chatter the whole drive to their apartment, hardly allowing the guys to get a word in edgewise. After dropping off our suitcases at the apartment and briefly freshening up, we walk to a nearby café for lunch.

"So, Brooks, tell us more about yourself," Mateo says once we're seated with our food.

"I could take that answer a variety of directions," Brooks says. "Door number one, two, or three?"

"All the doors," Lana replies before taking a bite of her panini.

Brooks recaps the highlights of his life from high school till now, mostly sharing information I've heard already. Lana interjects with detailed follow-up questions like the lawyer-in-training she is, which leads to me hearing a couple of stories that I haven't heard yet. Like the time Brooks got benched for two games because he got caught sneaking into a building on campus late at night.

"Listen, everyone swore that the old theater in that building was haunted. We were just checking it out!" Brooks says, defending himself. "Students did it all the time—literally every day—but Coach benched us since we were athletes on scholarship."

"What position did you play?" Mateo asks.

"Point guard," Brooks replies. "I was never tall or bulky enough to play center or forward."

"I'm going to confess: I know nothing about basketball," Lana says. She turns to Mateo. "Can you translate to soccer terms?"

"Point guard would be sort of a combination of forward and midfielder," Mateo replies. "Lots of ball handling and passing to keep the offense moving. But still important on defense."

Brooks chimes in, "Yeah, the point guard controls the pace of the game and runs the offense. I would defend against the opposing team's good ball handlers, but I wasn't ever the big guy in the middle rebounding."

Lana nods. "Okay, that makes sense. I can see the midfielder similarities."

The sports talk is pretty much going over my head, but I don't mind. "Well, if anyone needs tips on chaîné turns or switch leaps, I'm your girl." I dramatically flip my hair.

Brooks wraps an arm around my shoulder, pulling me close enough to kiss the top of my head. "Yes, you are." Then he turns back to Mateo. "Bro, I want to hear more about your time playing professionally. What was that like?"

"Oh, it was League Two, not the *pro* pros," Mateo says.

"Don't let his humility fool you," Lana jumps in. "He was amazing. He was on his way up had he not ruptured his Achilles."

Brooks grimaces. "Ouch. That sounds rough."

"Yeah, that wasn't an enjoyable experience," Mateo replies. "But God used it to redirect my focus. I really did love playing professionally and the relationships with my teammates. I'm incredibly grateful that

I got the opportunity to continue playing after college." He pauses to wink at Lana. "But I've been so happy this year being able to devote my full attention to the *Todos Juntos* soccer club and my master's classes." Mateo gives a brief overview of the nonprofit he started, Lana occasionally chiming in with additional details.

"That sounds incredible," Brooks says, looking thoughtful. "So, you coordinate with the local school counselors to identify kids who could benefit from the program?"

Mateo nods. "Yes, we couldn't do it without them. We've leaned a lot on their expertise and personal knowledge of the kids to build some of the character lessons that we teach through *Todos Juntos* in addition to the soccer skills. It's much more impactful to have an integrated approach between their education at school and how we supplement."

I look at the glazed over, starry-eyed look on Brooks' face and realize a bromance has been born today. A giggle escapes before I can stop myself.

They all look at me quizzically.

I wave a hand. "You have no idea the monster you tapped into, Mateo. Brooks is all about building community involvement in the local schools. It's the heartbeat of his professional outlook."

"Speaking of, I'd love to hear more about your experience with The Hangout while you were there, Lana," Brooks says, turning his attention to her. "Teegan told me you were an ELL tutor, and I've gotten to know Sofia a little bit on Tuesdays. Well, even more so once she figured out I was interested in Teegan. She suddenly had frequent reasons to talk to me."

Lana bursts out laughing. "That sounds like the Sofia I know." She begins sharing about her experience with Brooks, and I notice Brooks leans in with a furrowed brow, as focused as I've ever seen him as he grills her with questions. Lana meets his intensity brow for brow, lean for lean.

Mateo smiles and raises his eyebrows at me from across the table. I successfully stifle my laugh this time.

I stifle zero laughs once we get to the soccer game. Even though the team consists of fourth graders, Lana cheers them on (and yells at the refs) as though watching one of Mateo's professional matches. It's exactly how I remember her when I accompanied her to the soccer matches our senior year, after they started dating.

"I understand now," Brooks whispers in my ear, nodding his head in Lana's direction. His exaggerated wide-eye expression forces another burst of giggles out of me. For as much as Lana is losing her mind, Mateo is completely calm and collected, calling out instructions in both English and Spanish to the players on the field. Watching them huddle around him and his white board during half time is about as adorable as you could get.

After Mateo's team wins the match, Lana heads to help pass out post-game snacks. Brooks and I follow her down, and he's soon in the thick of the kids, congratulating them and pointing out all their good moves. The crowd eventually dissipates as the players follow one of the other coaches out of the complex.

"So do you provide transportation to and from the games?" Brooks asks Mateo as we walk out to the car.

"Yep. A lot of these kids wouldn't have a parent or guardian available to get them to and from games and practices. They're working long hours at multiple jobs most of the time," Mateo responds, and Brooks nods thoughtfully.

"We got a grant to provide healthy snacks for the kids too," Lana says. "They get a snack at the beginning of every practice or game and again at the end. Otherwise, too many of them would be trying to exercise on empty stomachs."

"The wraparound support really is phenomenal," Brooks says. He taps his temple. "I'm taking lots of mental notes."

We pick up pizza for dinner, taking it back to the apartment. After eating, Lana suggests we play team Dutch Blitz, a popular card game among Arrow students during college. We fill Brooks in on the rules, and he catches on quickly. We're soon beating Lana and Mateo every hand.

"Ugh," Lana whines. She turns to Mateo. "Babe, stop being so nice! You've got to let your competitive side out. Division playoffs mode—come on!"

Mateo pinches her waist and leans over to kiss her neck. "You're competitive enough for both of us!"

"That's it!" Lana exclaims, playfully pushing Mateo away. "We're playing boys versus girls."

"Yes!" I exclaim, high-fiving Lana.

Brooks fist bumps Mateo and says, "The Beefs versus the Bros."

Of course, Mateo pulls out all the stops now, simply to get a rise out of Lana. We're all shrieking and practically slapping each other's hands as we smack cards down on piles. When all is said and done, the Bros are victorious and the Beefs are stewing.

I'm sulky about the loss, and Lana is straight up glaring daggers at Mateo. Brooks and Mateo are celebrating with dramatic flair, dancing as though completely unbothered by our ire.

Mateo breaks first (no surprise there). He stands behind Lana and wraps his arms around her, burying his face in her hair. "Come on now—don't be a sore loser." Lana's frown remains firmly in place, but Mateo whispers something that causes her to fight a smile. Then he says, "How about we go get slushies? That always makes everything better."

Lana huffs her agreement, and we both drop our angry acts.

Brooks quirks an eyebrow, looking over at me. "Slushies? Why slushies?"

Mateo claps him on the back. "You still have so much to learn. Don't worry—you'll soon be acquainted with all the Beefs lore."

CHAPTER THIRTY-ONE

The next morning, muffled voices in the kitchen alert me that I'm likely the last one to wake up, no surprise. I throw on a sweatshirt and stumble to the bathroom to brush my teeth. And my hair. And to splash cold water on my face.

There's a doctored-up cup of coffee waiting for me when I join Lana, Mateo, and Brooks at the table. "Morning! What's the plan for today?" I ask before taking a long drink of caffeine.

"We thought we'd eat a quick breakfast here, and then Brooks said he wants to see the *Todos Juntos* office," Lana answers.

Mateo cuts in, "Even though I told him it's a boring office in a commercial building. We practice at different parks and facilities around the area that let us use their spaces for free or highly discounted rates."

"Hey, if it's an important part of the daily life of Lana and Mateo, then I want to see the boring building," Brooks says.

I smile over at him, touched by his interest in my friends.

"And then we planned to head to downtown Baltimore. You can see where I take all my classes, and then we can find something fun to do for a while before we come back here for dinner," Lana says.

"Sounds good to me!" I chirp, much more enthusiastic now that I've had coffee.

We follow Lana's plan (as one does if you know what's good for you). We rotate taking showers while eating eggs, bagels, and fruit for breakfast. Once everyone is ready to go, we head out for the day.

When we get to the *Todos Juntos* office, Brooks *ooos* and *ahhs* over everything, despite the truth that it is a plain office. But various team photos line one whole wall, creating a mural of kids' smiling faces.

There are several action shots from games mixed in, and looking at the confident and determined expressions on the players' faces makes me feel sentimental.

"This is just . . . really cool what you're doing here," Brooks says, voice thick with emotion. His gaze sweeps over the photos one last time before we head out to drive to Baltimore.

As Mateo drives, Brooks flips the conversation and drills Lana with questions about her law school experience. "I've been so lucky to be at Maryland Carey Law because I could focus on immigration law and get practical experience through the Chacón Center for Immigrant Justice," she says, turned to face us in the back seat. "Even though I originally wanted to follow in my mom's footsteps and go to UC Davis, I'm so grateful that God redirected me here."

"His plans were always better," Mateo says with a smile, reaching over to tuck a strand of hair behind Lana's ear and running his fingers through the length.

"Yeah, I wonder which amazing best friend of yours encouraged you to loosen up on your original plan?" I tease.

"We're *both* full of good advice for each other, huh?" Lana teases back, glancing knowingly between Brooks and me.

After we see the building that has served as Lana's second home the past few years, we stand around discussing what to do next. The sun is shining brightly, but the air is still chilly.

"I vote for something indoors," I say with a shiver.

"Hey, have you guys ever gone to this glow-in-the-dark splatter paint place?" Brooks asks Lana and Mateo, holding out his phone.

"We haven't, but it looks fun," Mateo replies. "Let's do it."

"Hold on, I'm not dressed for painting," Lana says. "This is my favorite sweater."

"Good point. This is also *my* favorite sweater of Lana's," Mateo says with a grin. He pulls Lana toward him to kiss her.

"No sweaters will be harmed in the making of splatter art—they have full hazmat suits and goggles that you put on," Brooks says, pointing to the description on the TripAdvisor listing.

"Ooo, and you get to choose your own music!" I add, bouncing on the balls of my feet. "Please, Lana, please?"

We reserve a room online, and we make our way there. Brooks chooses a music playlist while we don our protective outfits and take a few "before" photos together.

"We look like we're ready to tackle a pandemic," Brooks says.

"I would absolutely be wearing a mask over my mouth and nose if we were walking into a pandemic," Lana says. "Come to think of it, I'm not sure how much I trust having any part of my face exposed when I'm in the same room with the three of you plus paint."

Mateo waggles his eyebrows at her. "You'll have only yourself to blame for planting the idea in my mind."

The employee shows us to our reserved room and shuts us in. There are four canvases on easels around the room. A central table holds squirt bottles filled with neon paint as well as cups of paint with brushes and syringes inside for more precise splatters. EDM music starts pumping through the speaker, and I'm immediately dancing as I choose my first paint color. The luminescent glow of the black lights adds to the upbeat ambiance as we begin squirting and flicking paint at our canvases.

I'm splashing bright colors at my canvas with abandon, and Brooks is essentially using every viral dance move as a means of throwing color on his. I'm laughing at his Soulja Boy moves when I hear a groan from Lana.

"Ugh, I ruined it. The purple was only supposed to be in this section," Lana says. I can picture her furrowed brow beneath the giant goggles.

"It's splatter paint, LaLa. You're not supposed to have a plan," I chide.

"Let it go, babe," Mateo says as he flicks a giant splotch of purple paint onto Lana's canvas. Her mouth drops open, and she aims a paint-laden paintbrush directly at Mateo, splattering his hazmat suit with neon paint.

His dimple pops as a boyish grin takes over his face, right before he gently splashes a few droplets of paint at Lana's face, speckling her cheeks with glowing purple freckles. Before she can react, he swoops in to kiss her. She drags a paintbrush across his cheek in revenge, but I can see her smiling against Mateo's lips.

"They're so adorable," Brooks stage-whispers in my ear. I boop his nose with neon blue paint before quickly kissing his lips.

"Spin me!" I demand as I pick up two squirt bottles at random. Brooks wastes no time in wrapping his arms around my waist, then rapidly whirls around as I squeeze the bottles. I'm laughing as he sets me back down to assess the effect.

"Well, that didn't really get much paint on the canvas, but still a ten out of ten experience," I say. The version of "Sky Full of Stars" that we listened to in the car on the way to the silent disco starts playing, and I'm suddenly too busy jump-dancing to worry about my painting. Brooks joins in, and Mateo and Lana aren't far behind. It's not long before paint makes an entrance to the dance party.

The music abruptly cuts off and an employee opens the door to let us know our hour is up. We jerk to a standstill as the employee side eyes our paint-covered hazmat suits. He gives us instructions to bring our paintings to the clean-up area before massively rolling his eyes as he leaves.

"I feel like I got sent to the principal's office," Brooks stage-whispers again. He's usually hard to take seriously, but especially with a blue nose and multi-colored cheeks. We all burst out laughing, which causes the poor employee to come back and remind us to follow him. Brooks convinces him to take a few pictures of us first, and then we obediently file to the clean-up room.

"That was sooo fun," I exclaim as we exit the building. "Top five experiences ever."

"Really? Top five?" Mateo asks.

"Teegan's 'top five' is probably more like a list of thirty things," Lana scoffs.

I shrug. "I can't help it if I enjoy life."

"There's too much to enjoy!" Brooks agrees, wrapping an arm around my shoulders as we walk. "This painting will now be the focal point of my apartment decor."

"Which isn't saying much, considering that the walls are currently bare," I tease, poking him in the side.

"I'm starving," Lana says. "All that paint-throwing and dancing around burned through every calorie I've eaten today. Let's grab some dinner here before we head back to the apartment."

"There's a jazz club down the block," Mateo says, looking at the map on his phone. "Want to stow our paintings in the car and walk over there?"

Since it's early evening on a Sunday, the jazz club isn't too packed. We order food and enjoy the music as we chat.

"So, are you hoping to specifically work with kids once you're a licensed therapist?" Brooks asks Mateo.

"That's the plan," Mateo replies with a nod. "Well, I guess more so teenagers than kids. Probably middle or high school age. But I'll wait until I have some supervised clinical experience under my belt before I officially choose a specialty."

"That's awesome, bro," Brooks says. He continues asking more questions, but my attention is pulled away by Lana leaning in to talk in my ear.

"He's really great, Teegs," she says, and I pull back just enough so that she can see my smile. "How are you feeling about things?"

"I feel amazing about it," I whisper back to her. "I know I was hesitant at first—"

"Which was wise," Lana cuts in.

I nod. "Taking it slow was wise. But now, I'm one hundred percent happy. It's like I was watching an incredible movie and enjoying the experience, but then someone came and dropped 3D glasses over my eyes. Brooks makes everything fuller, more immersive. He's like a fun-intensifier, if that was a thing."

Lana rolls her eyes. "Which is exactly what you needed since you tend to never have fun ever."

I playfully push her shoulder, and she grins at me. "I like seeing starry-eyed Teegan," she says seriously, though she's still smiling. The song the band was playing ends, so we sit back to clap. When they slip into a slow melody, Mateo is quick to hold out a hand and ask Lana to dance.

Brooks and I follow them to the small dance floor near our table, and he tugs me close to him. Behind me, Mateo dips a giggling Lana before kissing her, and I see Brooks smile at them before he returns his gaze to mine.

"You have awesome friends, Sneaks," he says, voice low beneath the music.

"I do. And they're your friends now too," I respond as we sway with the beat. "I'm so glad you suggested this trip. I didn't even realize how much it would mean to me for you to get to know Lana and Mateo until we were here."

"I've loved seeing you with Lana and hearing you all talk more about your college years," Brooks says. "It seems like every day I learn more about who you've become and how you got here. And I'm more in awe of you with every new revelation. Compared to who you are, I feel so undeser—"

I cut off his sentence with a kiss. "You're not allowed to say those things anymore, remember?" I remind him with a soft smile. His smile mirrors mine as he presses another gentle kiss to my lips.

Laying my head on his shoulder, I tuck my nose into the crook of his neck. I'm absolutely the type to chase the thrill of exciting experiences. But the sensation of being tucked tightly in the safety of Brooks' arms might just be the best kind of adrenaline rush.

Chapter Thirty-Two

"This went way too fast," I say, clinging to Lana. "I'm not ready to leave!"

She holds me just as tightly. "I wish you didn't have to! But I'll focus on how grateful I am that you came at all."

"Sorry we disrupted your study schedule. I know how you feel about having your plans changed," I tease.

"Ha ha," Lana says, rolling her eyes. "I have all day today to catch up. I'll disrupt plans for you any time, Beef."

Lana hugs Brooks as I hug Mateo goodbye, and then the guys shake hands again. "I had fun getting to know you, Brooks," Mateo says. "I'm really glad I didn't have to fly to Kansas to knock you around."

"I . . . am also glad about that," Brooks states.

"Don't think he wouldn't if needed, though," Lana says, voice serious. Her face turns deadly as she adds, "We both will."

Brooks salutes. "Duly noted. 'Stay on Lana's good side,'" he says, pretending to write on his palm. "Seriously though, thanks for letting us come visit last minute."

"Oh, I'm serious," Lana says, face still *very* serious. I smack her arm with the back of my hand. She instantly switches on a smile. "We had so much fun! Come back any time!"

On the flight home, I regale Brooks with the full-length version of Lana and Mateo's love story. He listens intently, although thoroughly distracting *me* by gently tracing his fingers along mine the entire time.

We leave the Kansas City airport and drive straight back to Brooklyn. Brooks probably does have some prep work to do before going back to work tomorrow, but I'm also pretty sure he doesn't want to see family again this weekend.

"You've heard all about Lana and Amaya. Tell me about some of your close friends," I tell Brooks once we hit the highway to Brooklyn.

"Well, I don't have the same degree of closeness to friends from college like you do. I've kept in touch with my FCA teammates, Brody and Rylen, on social media and texting occasionally, but I feel motivated to talk with them more after seeing what you have with the Beefs," he says. "You know me—I've always had a wide rather than deep circle of friends. Always looking for the best experiences as opposed to having the same people to hang with all the time," he adds with a shrug.

He pauses for a beat before continuing. "Honestly, the people in our small group at church are probably some of my closest friends now. And I've enjoyed getting to know my colleagues at the school in Brooklyn. But it's a little hard knowing that I'll likely be moving on from there again in another year or so."

Brooks glances over at me before clearing his throat. "But, of course, you're my best friend," he says. He's tried to make his tone sound light and breezy, but I hear a layer of apprehension beneath it.

I lean over to kiss his cheek. "Same," I assure him. He reaches down to hold my hand, his thumb brushing the side of my knee where our entwined fingers are propped. "I mean, Lana and Amaya are my Beefs, which is totally separate terminology, so the title of best friend can go to you."

Brooks squeezes my knee where I'm ticklish, causing me to jump and squeal with laughter. With a terrible attempt at a British accent, he says, "Why thank you, your highness, for bequeathing such an important title to one so inconsequential as I."

The playfulness drops from his expression. "All jokes aside, I can't tell you how thankful I am to have you in my life right now. As a girlfriend, obviously, but especially as a friend." He pauses, and it's not till he rubs his eyes that I realize he's fighting back tears.

"I know you were happy to see Lana, but, if I'm honest, this trip to D.C. was really a selfish move on my part. An attempt to get out of town and away from the memories. I've had a hard time really processing everything with my mom," he says. "Well, the more accurate statement would probably be that I haven't processed it at all. I typically distract myself any time reminders of her pop up."

I reach over to gently squeeze his knee. "I understand that reaction."

His lips twitch with a smile. "I know you do. Maybe that's why having you here is making it possible for me to face the memories for once. You get me in a way that not many people do. You knew Mom and loved her, so I can talk about her without having to explain everything. But you're one circle removed from the direct heartbreak. Losing her was a shock—devastation that we were totally unprepared for. The grief has always felt sharp because I've never let myself feel it long enough for the pain to dull into an ache. I know I still have a long way to go, but I guess I'm just saying that you make me feel like I can go there. I can go there because I have you with me."

He huffs a laugh. "Does that make any sense, or are these the ramblings of a lunatic?"

"I wish we weren't driving right now so you could see my eyes," I say. I settle for reaching for his hand instead. "It makes total sense, Brooks. And I'll go there through the grief with you."

After a breath, I murmur, "I'll go anywhere with you." It's such a quiet whisper that he may not have heard me, but his firm squeeze of my hand assures me that he did.

When we reach my duplex, Brooks gets out of the car to carry my duffel bag to the door. Gina's car isn't here, but I linger on the front porch rather than inviting Brooks inside.

He has a fidgety energy about him, so I tip forward to kiss his cheek. He catches me with a hand behind my head, holding me in place close to him.

"Sneaks . . . Teegan. Thanks for going with me this weekend. Everywhere. Everything. Just . . . thank you," Brooks murmurs.

I trace my fingers along his jaw. "You're welcome."

He looks like he wants to say more, so I stand still, holding his gaze.

"I've been wanting to tell you this, but I was trying to wait until it made more sense, until it was the right time for you, but I don't know how to know when that is," he says, his fingers clenching and unclenching in my hair on my neck. "But I know. I've always known."

I hold my breath, anticipating the words he's about to speak. My heart slowly inflates with energy.

"I love you, Teegan," Brooks says, voice confident, no longer a murmur. "I love you."

My heart explodes.

"I love you too, Brooks," I answer, and I fly to his lips. We linger in the kiss, savoring this sacred moment. When Brooks pulls away, he presses his lips, feather-light, to my cheeks, my jaw, my forehead.

I don't want to move on from the magic. How do you say goodbye, even if only for the night, right after you've declared your love? It physically hurts to pry away from him, but we tear ourselves apart.

"Goodnight, Sneaks. I love you," Brooks whispers before he walks back to the car.

I'm only inside for a minute when my phone pings with a text.

LANA

Teegs, you can't obviously lie and expect Amaya to believe it. Just say you missed her SO much and wish she was there

I missed you SO much and wish you were there too

AMAYA

<eye roll emoji>

Overlooking this offense in the name of lifelong friendship

<heart emoji>

AMAYA

But I need to know what Mateo thought of Brooks?

I also need to know. Spill the tea, Lana

LANA

He really liked him! Said Brooks was almost like Teegan in guy form

Lol we've heard that before

LANA

He's fun to be around, but we knew that already. Mateo also said Brooks showed a lot of maturity and passion about what he does in education. And he asked a lot of good questions about our experiences. He respected that a lot

I like that about him too <heart eyes emoji>

LANA

And we both agreed that he's totally obsessed with you, Teegs <winking emoji>

AMAYA

Well that's a good thing

I'm fairly obsessed myself

Chapter Thirty-Three

If our text message thread is any indication, Brooks and I are both riding the high of reintroducing the truth of "I love you" into our relationship. However, I know that despite the rush of our trip to D.C. and our newly-professed feelings, Brooks is still experiencing the lows of grief. I know because *I* am still feeling those "I can't breathe" moments any time I think about our time by his mom's bench at the lake.

I decide to surprise Brooks with lunch at school. Even though he only has thirty minutes, I'm hoping it will be a bright spot to his day.

After scanning my driver's license to check in at the school office, a passing teacher offers to show me to Brooks' classroom on her way back to her own.

"We've heard lots about you around here. I recognized you from the videos that Brooks posts, but it's fun to meet you in person!" she says.

"Oh no, I did not think about a social media reputation preceding me," I respond with a laugh.

"Don't worry. Your preceding reputation is glowing," she replies, a twinkle in her eye.

"What subject do you teach?" I ask as we wind through the building. Thank goodness I have a guide—I absolutely would have spent half of Brooks' lunch period trying to find his classroom.

"Seventh grade science. Never a dull moment!" she says right as the bell rings and students spill into the hallways. "You might want to wait a minute for the students to clear out, but we've reached your destination," she adds, pointing to the room across from us. "It was great to meet you, Teegan. Hope to see you around again."

"Thank you for the help!" I call after her as she walks away. I hear her switch to her "teacher voice" as she scolds a couple of boys who are roughhousing. It reminds me of Brooks' voice when he rescued me at the silent disco, which I can now openly embrace as "sexy."

I need to practice my teacher voice.

The certainty of that thought feels at peace in my heart, and I smile to myself as I walk into Brooks' classroom. There are two students still inside, huddled around a desk as Brooks points to something on a worksheet.

"You need a little more explanation of how the branches of government keep power in check. Tell me a specific example," he says to one student. I linger in the doorway to continue observing without revealing my presence yet.

"Um, like how the President can't pass laws, only Congress can?" she says, uncertainty in her voice.

"Exactly!" Brooks responds. "List out at least one example for each branch on your bullet list so you can use it in your final essay."

"Okay. Thanks, Mr. Murphy," she replies as she stuffs the paper in her backpack. She and her friend turn just as Brooks looks up and notices me. All three of their faces break into smiles.

"Hey!" I say, stepping forward.

"Ooo, who's this?" one of the girls asks.

Brooks grins and declares, "This is my girlfriend, Teegan."

"Nice to meet you, girls!" I greet with a wave as I reach them.

"You're so pretty!" one of them remarks, and I remember how much I loved the unfiltered conversations I had with students during student teaching.

"Gorgeous is the word I think you're looking for," Brooks chimes in, his smile impish.

The girls look as though they've been handed a pot full of tea ready to spill at lunch. "Nice to meet you, Ms. Teegan. See you tomorrow, Mr. Murphy," they say as they exit the room.

Once they're gone, Brooks pulls me to him and quickly kisses me. "Mr. Murphy, how extremely unprofessional of you," I tease.

"They can fire me if necessary," he teases back before planting a longer kiss on my lips. "Now, what are you doing here?"

I hold up the Taco Lucha bag in my hand. "I brought lunch!"

"I love you forever," Brooks says with mock solemnity.

"All it took was tacos." I sigh with an exaggerated eye roll.

Brooks pulls me closer to him, hand on the small of my back. "All it took was you," he murmurs, then gently kisses me.

As tempted as I am to give in to his kiss and lose all sense of reality, there is the very *real* reality of our current surroundings. I pull back and poke him in the chest. "Behave yourself," I chide, smiling.

We quickly devour the tacos as he fills me in on The Hangout happenings from last night. With ten minutes before his lunch break ends, he offers to lead me back to the front office.

"I'm going to need a map so I can find your room on my own next time I come to visit," I say as we make our way through the hallways.

"I'll happily draw a map myself if it means you'll keep coming back," he replies with a grin. I'm so tempted to reach over to hold his hand, but I restrain myself.

When we reach the front entrance, Brooks turns to me. "This was the best surprise, Sneaks. Thanks for coming to see me."

"I had to see your classroom for myself," I say. There aren't any students around, so I quirk an eyebrow and add, "How else can I picture sexy Mr. Murphy in his element?"

Brooks groans. "That was a low blow, making a comment like that when I can't kiss you." The intensity in his gaze sends a tremor through my body. His eyes just did a perfectly sufficient job of kissing me from two feet away.

My voice is breathy as I say, "See you at small group tonight."

Brooks glances at his watch, then meets my eyes again. "Only 344 minutes."

"How are things going with Brooks?" Catherine asks conspiratorially.

My mouth is filled to the brim with one of Sarah's oatmeal cookies. I could be convinced to eat oatmeal for breakfast if it was in the form of one of her cookies.

It's the end of the small group meeting, and the girls are all standing in the kitchen. I can hear the guys laughing in the living room at whatever story Brooks is entertaining them with.

I hold my hand in front of my still-chewing mouth. "It's going great!" Swallowing hard, I take a sip of water to wash down the cookie crumbs. "In some ways, it feels brand new, and in other ways, it feels like we clicked right back into place. Like gears that got misaligned and then put back in the right spot."

"Well, you seem happy," Natalie observes. "You have that glow that moms have after giving birth."

"Whoa, no need to talk about babies yet," Catherine says.

"I'm not saying they're going to have babies right now! I just see it every day—it's a good comparison!" Natalie defends. "Although, you guys would absolutely have the most beautiful babies. Just saying."

"Let's back the conversation right up!" I exclaim, cheeks red. "Back to the 'Brooks and I are having fun dating' stage."

Thankfully, the conversation ends as the guys file into the kitchen, carrying their glasses and coffee mugs to the sink.

"Would anyone be up for a concert Friday night?" Brooks asks the group.

"Who's playing?" Will asks.

"I dunno. Some indie band is playing at the concert venue in Center Square. I heard some colleagues talking about it," Brooks replies with a shrug.

"You're gonna go to a concert without even knowing who the band is?" Brian asks, incredulous.

"Sure! It will be a good time, even if the band is no good," Brooks says.

"I'll go!" I respond with enthusiasm.

"Zero surprise there," Sarah teases. "But I'll come too! You two are pushing me to be a little more fun."

"What? So now we're not fun if we don't go?" Will asks with mock offense. I see a smile pass between him and Sarah, and I'd bet money they'll be the next to fall in Joy's plans to pair us all up.

CHAPTER THIRTY-FOUR

I laugh out loud when I read Joy's text.

A few hours later, I ring the doorbell at Joy's house. She answers almost immediately, pulling me into a hug before gesturing inside.

"You're a lifesaver, Teegan. I left the office a little early today, but I would have spent the extra time stressing about what to wear instead of productively getting ready!"

I *tsk* at Joy. "You are not that old! You're what—thirty?"

"Thirty-one," Joy replies.

"Same, same," I say as I follow her back to her bedroom.

"Still, I don't think that my accounting cubicle wardrobe screams 'hip concert attendee' in any universe," she jokes.

I pat her on the shoulder before stepping into her closet. "We're going to find you something amazing."

As I begin thumbing through her shirt hangers, Joy dives right in to conversation.

"Seems like things are going really well with Brooks," she sing-songs. "I'm not saying 'I told you so,' because I technically didn't tell you that you *should* date him. I'll settle for 'I totally called it.'"

I chuckle as I hold up a white shirt on a hanger before placing it back on the rod. "Things are definitely going well. Super well. All kinds of extremely well," I say, not even attempting to hide my goofy grin.

"It was a risk that paid off," Joy observes. "I'm glad you lived bravely."

"Yeah . . . about that," I mumble, turning to her. "There's another risk I've been calculating. Or attempting to calculate. You know, on my chocolate bar calculator."

Joy huffs a laugh and smiles, encouraging me to continue talking.

"I've been considering the idea of moving on from my staff position with Arrow to give teaching a try," I admit, twirling a finger through my hair. "But every time I think I've officially decided, I can't bring myself to take action. I talk myself out of bringing it up with my bosses every time."

"What are you telling yourself when you talk yourself out of it?" Joy asks.

My mind circulates through possible explanations at breakneck speed. Something about Joy's role in my life makes me feel safe enough to vocalize the inner turmoil that I haven't really expressed to anyone. That I've barely acknowledged, even to myself.

"That I'll be a disappointment. Not only to Kent and Rachel, but to the rest of the staff team. All the students." I pause again before speaking the hardest part. "Maybe even a disappointment to God."

Joy's eyebrows shoot up. "What makes you think you would be disappointing God?"

"Because the Arrow job description is basically all of my personality traits and natural gifts rolled into one bullet-point list. I'm great at it. I get to make such a deep impact on so many girls who are trying to grow spiritually in college. I'm literally making a spiritual impact *as my full-time job.* A position I thrive in. Is it . . . wrong to not want to do that anymore?" I ask, chewing my lip.

Joy places her hands on my shoulders. "Oh, Teegan. Think about it this way. Is it wrong for me to work as an accountant at a tax firm instead of being on staff at our church?"

"Of course not! That's totally not what I meant!" I exclaim.

"I know you don't mean that for *me,* but do you mean that for *you?*" Joy asks. I'm silent, so she continues. "Why would what's true for me be different for you? What if this desire you're feeling is God giving you a chance to impact people through a different avenue? God will use you no matter what your vocation is, Teegan. Whether that's with college students here, or elementary students in Kansas City, or . . . architects in Alabama," she says with a wave of her hand. "As long as your heart is his, God's going to use your life to encourage others."

I remain quiet, allowing her words to sink down into my soul. When I still don't respond, she shakes my shoulders slightly. "You hear me?"

I nod. "Yes, ma'am."

Joy scoffs and rolls her eyes. "You just promised me I'm not old and then go around calling me 'ma'am.' The audacity."

I throw my arms around Joy, hugging her tightly. "Thank you."

"You're welcome. Now find me something to wear before you have to go home and get yourself ready to see your man tonight." She's grinning when I pull back to make eye contact.

I return my attention to her half of the closet, eventually choosing a black blouse with a lace mock turtleneck, pairing it with her best pair of jeans. Once I've selected a pair of black ankle boots to complete the look, I stand back to assess.

"Perfection. Caleb might be tempted to skip out on the concert when he gets home and sees you," I tease with a wink.

"No way. I'm not missing the chance to feel young tonight. Or to watch Brooks shamelessly flirt with you. Not to mention—I have a feeling there are some other romances blooming," she says with a sly smile.

"If it means other people will be as happy as I am with Brooks, I hope you're right."

Everyone except Brian and Candace is meeting outside of the concert venue. Brooks bought group tickets, so we'll all walk inside together.

When Brooks picked me up from my house, we discovered that we unintentionally matched again. I'm wearing a black midi dress with a denim jacket, and Brooks has on a black t-shirt and gray jeans.

"Aww, you two are too cute," Joy says when she sees us outside the venue entrance. "Let me snap a picture of you."

"I take back my claim that you aren't old if you're going to use phrases like 'snap a picture,' Joy," I tease. She swats at me but takes my phone. I wrap my arms around Brooks' waist for one photo, then pop my foot and kiss his cheek for another.

"You adorable lovebirds and your PDA," Catherine teases, joining the group. Brooks grins and takes the comment as a challenge to press a quick kiss to my lips, heating my cheeks in the process.

Once we've all assembled, we head inside before the band takes the stage. They turn out to have decent talent, the lead singer's voice reminding me a lot of Benson Boone. Brooks and I lead the charge in getting the group to dance and sing along once we catch on to the song refrains.

For their final song, the band fully leans into the Benson Boone similarity and plays "Beautiful Things." The entire crowd scream-sings along. My arms are in the air as I sway my hips to the beat when I feel Brooks' arms circle my waist from behind me.

He sings the lyrics in my ear, and I pivot my torso so I can see his face. We're suddenly the only two in the room as the dancing crowd fades to gray. Brooks' smiling eyes darken as they drop to my lips when I mouth, "I love you." A second later, he eases his lips down to mine. The kiss is firm yet delicate. Yearning yet satisfying.

It's perfect. We're perfect. My Brooks and me.

I'm so happy.

"Ow ow!" Natalie's voice cat calls, followed by Will's enthusiastic *whoop*.

I just grin as Brooks chides them for being more immature than his middle schoolers. I'm too deliriously happy to be embarrassed.

CHAPTER THIRTY-FIVE

With each day that passes, Brooks takes up more and more of my mental space. It's both good and bad—bad because I have a harder time focusing on all that pesky adulting I have to do. Fantastic, because it provides an easy escape from my ongoing anxiety about talking to Kent and Rachel about my future.

At this point, I'm 95 percent sure that I want to pursue teaching next year. But I'm 100 percent sure that I don't want to have that uncomfortable conversation with them.

So, I focus on the delirious happiness that is my relationship with Brooks.

On the second Sunday of February, I'm getting ready for a date with Brooks. He's cooking me dinner to show off his new culinary skills. "Beautiful Things" has been playing on loop while I apply makeup, but the music is interrupted by a calendar reminder.

Call Dad.

Ack. I'm supposed to be at Brooks' apartment in half an hour. I don't have a lot of time, but I know I'll forget altogether if I don't call him now. Hence the calendar reminders.

I dial my dad on speaker phone, thinking we'll keep our conversation brief.

"Hey, Dad!" I greet when he answers. "How are you?"

"Hi, hon," he replies. "I'm doing great. What about you?"

I give a short but sincere response, including an assurance that Brooks and I are doing well.

"I'm glad you called because there's something I've been wanting to talk with you about," Dad says, voice slightly tense. "Would you be able to come to Kansas City next weekend?"

"Ummm, I'll need to look at my calendar to know for sure. Why?" I ask, setting down the tube of mascara in my hand.

"I had hoped to talk with you in person when you were here a couple of weeks ago, but, um, there's someone I want you to meet." The tone in his voice has my blood coagulating. I take the phone off speaker and sit on the edge of my bed.

"What do you mean?" I ask, trying to keep my voice even, though I know it's a higher pitch than what could be considered "even."

"Teegan, honey, I've met someone. Her name is Sonya," Dad begins. My blood stops flowing altogether. "We met several months ago, and we've been seeing each other since then. Things are getting pretty serious—serious enough that I think it's time for you and Logan to meet her. I want you both to know her well before I'd think about proposing."

Silence.

"Teegan?"

Silence.

"Teegan, did you hear me?"

My frantic energy finally shatters the silence. "You can't be serious!" I exclaim, standing up to pace the room. "You and Mom have always been so friendly with each other, even after the divorce. Neither of you have dated anyone all these years. We'll never be a whole family again if you get married to someone else!"

Silence.

I pace, my breath shallow and my vision blurring at the edges.

"Honey, your mom and I were never going to get back together. We loved each other once, and we still respect each other, but our time is over. Why would you think that we were going to get back together?" Dad asks, voice strained.

"I don't know! I don't know! I just thought it was possible—it could happen! You've never dated, she's never dated, you always get along so well, and you were so complimentary to her at Thanksgiving. I thought it was possible to be one family again!" My voice is shrill, words pouring out of my mouth faster than I can truly comprehend what I'm saying.

"I don't want to meet her. I can't meet her. I'm not ready for that, Dad," I huff out, fighting tears. I *know* I'm being completely selfish. I *know* I'm being so hurtful to my dad. I *know* I'm being immature to think they were ever going to get back together, to act this way about it now.

I *know* those things. But my brain is incapable of stemming the hemorrhage of emotion bleeding out.

"Teegan—" Dad's voice is cut off when I hang up.

Pacing the room, I try to imagine myself above the ocean. I try to fly my mind away on the sea breeze, the pink sunset, but my ankle is tied by reality, holding me captive. Trapping me as bar after bar snaps into place.

Disbelief. Bitterness. Betrayal. Fear.

Snap. Snap. Snap. Snap.

Hands shaking, I open my texts with Brooks.

> Sorry I need to cancel tonight

I can't. I can't.

BROOKS

> Are you ok? Did something happen?

> I'm fine, just can't come tonight. I'm sorry about the food

I pace, then sit on the edge of the bed, then slide to the floor. My head drops to my knees.

It hurts. I can't. The pain. What if . . . I can't.

"Teegan?" Brooks voice snaps me back to the present. "What's wrong?"

"How'd you get in here?" I ask, ignoring his question and jumping to my feet.

"The door was unlocked," Brooks says, eyes assessing me. "What's wrong, Sneaks?"

"Nope, don't, please don't call me that right now," I say, frantic. The pacing starts again. "I don't think . . . I can't think."

"Teegan, tell me what happened," Brooks says, voice calm.

"My dad, he . . ." I trail off. Brooks' eyes widen with panic, and I realize the fear my half-formed thought induced in him. "No, he's fine. He called to ask me . . . he's been dating someone. He wants me to meet her. He wants to propose to her someday, maybe."

Brooks looks visibly relieved but also confused. I *know* I'm being confusing. Ridiculous. But *knowing* isn't stopping it.

"If he marries someone else, he can't be with my mom," I state.

I hear my own absurdity. The childishness.

"I know it's dumb to think they were going to get back together. I'm not ten years old. But still, I . . . I wished for it. When neither of them ever dated or moved on all these years. When they stayed friends. They used to be so in love. I remember it. And I wished for it again. But there's no second chance."

Brooks' face is blurry now, thick tears welling up in my eyes but not spilling over. He strides toward me and reaches to take my hand in his. I snatch it back.

"I don't think . . . I think this may not be a good idea," I say, voice wobbly. "We rushed into this, fell into each other again because it was so familiar. But I didn't really think through what this would mean, what it could mean, being together. I don't think we—"

"No, Teegan," Brooks cuts me off, voice commanding. He takes both of my hands, not allowing me to pull away. "No. Stop it. We're not doing that."

He takes my face in his hands. His firm touch grounds me, but I still struggle to breathe.

"You forget that I *know* you, Teegan. That we're practically the same person. I know what you're doing because it's exactly what my first instinct would be," he says, voice gathering strength. "You're trying to avoid the potential pain of us not working out, of me someday leaving. You're trying to avoid it by pushing me away now. But you're not doing that. *We're not doing that.*"

I gasp for air as the tears finally spill out. Brooks' thumbs gently brush both of my cheeks. He continues, "We're going to face whatever future pain may come. You were there with me in the thick of my grief remembering my mom, and your presence made me realize I didn't have to face it alone. That I *could* face it since I wasn't alone. So, we're going to face all the pain together. Because we were *always* meant to be together, Sneaks. I'm not going to let either one of us run away from each other out of fear of heartache. It's us against the pain, together. Forever."

His words breathe oxygen back into my lungs. His confidence slows my runaway heartbeat. His assuring eyes pull me back to what's true.

Us against the pain. It's us. It's everything.

I lean into Brooks and let myself cry. My mind stops trying to escape, stops the attempts to flee. I stand in his arms and let myself feel it. All of it—every bad emotion I've been suppressing the past few months floods over me.

The dejection from my dad's news, as immature as it may be. The deflating reality that their relationship is concretely, forever over. The terror of the unknowns. The possibility that I could be hurt like that by Brooks someday. The fear of being honest and experiencing Kent and Rachel's disappointment in me. The unease that it could be a mistake to leave Arrow staff to pursue teaching, that their disapproval would prove merited.

And it *hurts*.

But also . . . Brooks' firm embrace around me prevents my knees from buckling under the weight of the pain. The gentle scratch of his fingers on my back reminds me that I have things in my life that feel good. His kisses on the top of my head and whispered "I love you's" scream at me that I'm not alone in this.

Us against the pain.

———

"Here, drink this," Brooks says, handing me a glass of water. In his other hand, he's holding a mug of decaf coffee that he brewed and doctored with creamer. I try to reach for that.

"No, water first," he says firmly, pulling the mug away. "Hydrate."

After I finally stopped crying (duration unknown), we moved to the living room. Brooks sat me on the couch and cocooned me in fuzzy

246

blankets while he made coffee, which he hands over after I gulp down half the glass of water. He sits down next to me, pulling me close to his side.

"I need to call my dad back," I mumble. I feel Brooks nod against my head, which is tucked under his chin. I switch to a falsely deep voice, mimicking Brooks. "No, Teegan, you don't have to do that right now."

Brooks chuckles, but he doesn't speak up. I sigh. "I know, I know."

I reach for my phone right as a call from Logan lights up the screen.

"Ugh," I groan. Brooks reaches over to tap the answer button, not letting me out of this. I bring the phone to my ear.

"I know what you're going to say, Logan," I answer.

"Well, I sure hope you know that you need to call and apologize to Dad," his voice huffs. "You try to tell me that you've matured enough to be in a different kind of relationship with Brooks, and then you have the most immature reaction possible to Dad."

"I said I know, Logan! Lay off!" Now I huff. "Honestly, I've been bottling up a lot of emotions recently, and it all exploded on Dad. I swear I was just picking up my phone to call him back. Brooks helped me work through everything, and now I'm going to make amends."

"Murph is there?" Logan asks.

"Yes. He talked me down off the ledge of insanity. That's why I was about to call Dad back," I tell him.

Logan grunts some manner of approval.

"By the way—you don't seem very shocked by this news. How long have you known?" I ask.

"Dad told me several weeks ago. Although I already had my suspicions even before he said anything. I'm driving to KC from St. Louis next weekend to meet her. It's supposed to be all of us together. Had you not jaunted off to D.C., Dad would have talked with you about this a couple of weeks ago too," Logan says.

I sigh. "He did say that. But how was I supposed to know he had life-altering news to share with me? He didn't give any kind of hint! How the heck did you suspect already?!"

The eye roll is practically audible in Logan's voice. "Why do you think he changed Thanksgiving dinner to lunch, Teegan? Because he was having dinner with Sonya's family. And he was so distracted at Christmas—it wasn't hard to put the pieces together."

It does make sense now that he's spelled it out for me, but I never would have faced the possibility long enough to piece the clues together on my own.

"I'm hanging up now so you can call Dad. Tell Murph I said thanks for bringing you to your senses," Logan says. "And hey—I love you, sis."

"Love you too," I murmur, then hang up.

Sitting still on the couch isn't an option for my conversation with my dad. I pace between the living room and the kitchen as I apologize and listen to his perspective. Brooks stands in support at one of my pivot points, offering smiles of encouragement every time I meet his eyes.

Although I'm sure my dad still feels the sting of my initial reaction, I've mended the bridge as well as I can. Hanging up, I collapse on the couch. Brooks sits down on the floor next to me, pressing his forehead to mine, lacing his fingers through my hair.

"Well, I'm meeting Sonya next weekend," I state.

"*We're* meeting Sonya next weekend," Brooks corrects.

I half-smile. "You don't have to do that. I'll be okay."

He shakes his head, forehead still against mine, then leans back to meet my eyes.

"The good and the bad, the exciting and the devastating—I'm facing it all with you, Sneaks," he says. He leans forward to brush a kiss to my lips, then whispers, "Us. Everything. Always."

Chapter Thirty-Six

I'm in the middle of possibly the longest prayer walk of my life. Just when I think I've said all there is to say to God, more words come bubbling up, and my feet continue moving. Brooks will be picking me up to drive to KC in a couple of hours, so I really should head home and shower. But instead, I keep walking and talking.

"I feel so many things about today. A lot of things that I'd prefer to brush to the side and pretend don't exist. But I know that's not a viable long-term solution. I love my dad. I want him to know how much I love him. So, please help me keep my reactions in check today. Please help me to get to know Sonya with an open mind."

I pause, mind churning.

"Thank you for putting Brooks in my life to be the voice of reason last week, to understand what I was thinking and how I was reacting, and to stop me from doing something rash. Well, to stop me from doing something *else* rash after I initially shut my dad down. To encourage me to apologize and face things. I'm so grateful that you guided our paths back to each other. It's a gift I didn't know I could ever ask you for. Thank you for giving me what I didn't realize I needed, even if it meant starting with the pain of our first breakup. We needed those years apart to grow into the people we are today."

I think about what Mateo said when he was teasing Lana about changing her plan. It brings a smile to my face and peace to my heart. I think about God's plan for Brooks and me. His plan for my dad, even if it's different than what I envisioned. His plan for my future.

"Your plan is always better."

———

"Ready?" Brooks asks.

I stare at the doorknob, unblinking.

"Not really," I admit. Brooks lets go of my hand so he can put his arm around my shoulders, nestling me against him.

"Together," he says quietly. I nod and reach forward to open the door.

"Knock, knock!" I call out as we step into the foyer of my dad's house. We hang our coats on the rack as Dad comes around the corner to greet us. He pulls me into a tight hug.

"Thank you for coming, hon," Dad says quietly. I hug him tighter.

"You're welcome. I'm sorry again for how I first reacted," I respond, voice barely above a whisper.

Dad pulls back to look at me, hands still on my shoulders. "You know I forgive you. I know it caught you off guard. I'm sorry I didn't somehow prepare you better."

"Let's just move forward," I say, forcing a smile. "Is Sonya here already?"

"Yep. She's in the kitchen talking with Logan." Dad walks that way, and Brooks laces his fingers through mine as we follow.

Entering the kitchen, I see Logan talking with a woman with salt-and-pepper chin-length hair. She's wearing black-rimmed glasses, flowy black pants, and a red floral blouse. As my dad announces our presence, she turns to me with a wide smile.

"Teegan, I've heard so many glowing things about you. I'm delighted to meet you," Sonya says, reaching out to shake my hand.

Brooks gives my hand a small squeeze before letting go, which gives me the strength to lean all the way in and hug Sonya. I don't miss my dad's grateful smile over her shoulder.

"I'm glad to meet you too, Sonya," I say. "And this is my boyfriend, Brooks."

We make small talk for a few minutes before sitting down to eat the chicken, potatoes, and roasted Brussels sprouts they'd prepared.

Sonya asks each of us lots of questions about our lives, listening intently and smiling encouragingly.

"Tell us more about you, Sonya," I say after sharing about my job at Townsend. "I'd love to know more about what's important to your life."

"Well, I'm a few years older than your father, so my two children are both married, and I have two grandchildren," Sonya begins. "Of course, they're the most important thing in my life. They all live here in the metro area, so I get to see them frequently."

"Wait till you meet little Lottie—she's two years old and the cutest little thing," my dad says. He must see the spark of shock in my eyes because his soften as he adds, "I met them at Thanksgiving, but it was my decision to wait longer to tell you and Logan."

Sonya picks up the explanation. "I wanted to introduce Morgan to my family and see how they responded before things got too serious between us. This is the first time I've dated since my husband passed away four years ago, so it was a big step for my kids to meet some-one." She pauses to smile at my dad, warmth and affection filling her eyes. "Of course, they agreed with me that he's extraordinary."

My knee begins bouncing under the table to the increasing tempo of my heartbeat. *My dad is extraordinary. But so is my mom. But so is Sonya. I'm so happy that he's found someone who is so kind and looks at him like he hung the moon. But I still remember when Mom looked at him that way. Why do I have to feel so conflicted about this? Why can't I just grow up and be like Sonya's kids?*

I hate the confusing swirl of negative thoughts in my head. The air in my lungs doesn't feel like the right amount of oxygen. My mind automatically cues up my default coping mechanism. *Fly away, Teegan. Ocean. Breeze. Sunset. Anything.*

My mind comes back to the present moment when I feel one of Brooks' hands squeeze my knee under the table, his other arm draping around my shoulder. He pulls me close enough to press a kiss to my temple before covertly whispering in my ear, "We got this."

Sonya is explaining her job as an insurance agent to Logan, so I pull my attention back to listen. Conversation continues to flow naturally, especially once Brooks steps in to entertain with teaching stories. The genuine laughter serves to temper my flight instinct, and by the end of two hours, I can truthfully say I enjoyed getting to know Sonya.

We say our goodbyes to Sonya, promising to meet again soon. After she leaves, Brooks wraps me in an extra-long hug before announcing that he should head home to his dad's house. Dad thanks him for coming, and Logan gives him a bro hug with a slap on the back.

Logan claps Brooks on the shoulder an extra time as he says, "I'm glad you were here, Murph. I was wrong at Christmas. I want you to know that I'm glad you're back."

"Thanks, man," Brooks responds, giving Logan a second bro hug.

I follow Brooks onto the front porch and bury myself in his embrace. Breathing in his scent to ground my emotions, I sigh into his chest. "Thank you. Us against everything, right?"

I feel his nod before he kisses my cheek. "Always."

"What time do you want me to pick you up to head back to Brooklyn tomorrow?" Brooks asks, pulling back to look at me. He keeps one hand on my waist and brushes the hair out of my face with his other.

I bite my lip, thinking. Brooks skims his thumb across my bottom lip, pulling my eyes to his. "No doing that right now," he says wryly. "I'm trying to be strong for you emotionally, not make out with you on your dad's doorstep."

Laughing, I playfully slap his chest. The distraction from my tangled thoughts has made them clear.

"I think I need to go talk with my mom tomorrow morning, by myself. I'm sure my dad will let me borrow his car," I say. "Could you pick me up after lunch, maybe?"

"Sounds like a plan," Brooks responds. His expression tightens thoughtfully. "I may go talk with my mom tomorrow morning too."

I reach my hand up to cup his cheek. "We can do it. Together, even if we aren't together."

Brooks leans in to kiss me like he can't resist any longer. I let all my anxious thoughts melt away as I focus on the tenderness of his lips against mine.

"I love you, Sneaks."

———————

"You knew at Thanksgiving but didn't say anything?"

My mom and I sit on barstools in her kitchen, mugs of hot coffee in hand. I take a sip from mine to wait for her answer.

"It wasn't my news to tell you, Teegan. Your dad said he was going to talk to you and Logan if things continued between them after he met Sonya's family," Mom says. She places her hand over mine. "But I was okay with it, sweetheart."

I sigh and bury my face in my hands. "Why am I such a child? Why did I expect you guys to get back together like some naive little kid?"

Mom gently rubs my back. "It's not childish to want your parents to be together, Teegan. And I understand how you could have perceived that possibility when Morgan and I have worked so hard to maintain a good relationship after the divorce. I don't know why it took him so long to date someone, but, for me, I've been too focused on finding who I am again aside from being a wife and mother. I didn't have any available head space to date. But I never thought I'd get back together with your dad, so his relationship isn't hurting me."

I blink back tears. "You promise?"

My mom smiles compassionately. "Promise. I really am happy for them. And it won't hurt my feelings if you love Sonya too, okay? If she and your dad are together long term, I want you to love her too."

Leaning forward to embrace my mom, I manage to choke out, "Thanks, Mom. I love you."

We continue talking, but when my mom leaves the room to switch the laundry, I pull my phone out to text Brooks.

> Good convo with my mom. I feel more at peace with the situation at least. How's your morning been?

Less than thirty seconds later, his response comes through.

BROOKS

Good. Hard? Yeah, hard, but good. Just sat and talked a lot about the past few months. The past few years, really. Sort of filling her in on everything. Which makes it painful to think about how much she's missed. But I'm still glad I came

Thankfully no one was around to hear me talking out loud alone like some psycho

<clown emoji> Glad we both had hard but good talks with our moms. Also glad I'll get to have a few hours driving home with you after so many uncomfortable conversations. I'm ready for a car dancing Trolls sing-along. I love you <heart emoji>

BROOKS

Totally agree. Cue it up, Poppy. I'll be at your house in about an hour

Love you always

Chapter Thirty-Seven

B rooks and I return home from KC right in time for my weekly video chat with Lana and Amaya.

"Boy, do I have a lot to fill you in on," I declare as soon as we're all present on the screen.

I launch into a long monologue about everything that transpired over the past week, hardly pausing to take a breath.

"Okay, wow," Amaya responds when I finally finish.

"Well, that was a lot," Lana says. "And you're feeling . . . how, now?"

"I think I'm feeling okay. Objectively speaking, Sonya really was nice. Like, *really* kind. I can see why my dad likes her. She's actually a couple of years older than him, so it's not some weird situation where he's dating someone half his age in some sort of midlife crisis."

I pause to gather my thoughts. "And from my mom's perspective, she's happy for them. She's completely moved on in life, so all of my delusions about them getting back together someday were very much only *my* delusions. Still, that didn't make it *not* hard to see my dad with a woman other than my mom. But having Brooks and Logan there with me this weekend kept me grounded in the moment," I answer.

Amaya snorts. "More like prevented you from running away."

I can't help but smile. "Not entirely inaccurate."

"Can we please pause to recognize the fact that you very nearly ended things with Brooks when you got scared, so you can stop giving me so much grief about temporarily breaking up with Mateo?" Lana huffs.

"She listened to his voice of reason a lot more quickly than you did, though, Lana," Amaya teases. "A certain someone stubbornly took multiple weeks—and multiple people—challenging her to think differently before she made amends."

Lana rolls her eyes, and I burst out laughing. I reassure her. "Okay, okay, I'll commiserate a little bit, Beef. I do understand the knee-jerk reaction."

"Thank you," she says, fighting a smile.

"Oh, and P.S., I'm officially leaving Arrow staff and getting my teaching license next year," I say as an afterthought.

"You are?!" Lana exclaims as Amaya yelps, "What?!"

"May as well just get all the big life developments out there," I say. "But you're the first two to know. I haven't told anyone else yet."

They both hum with understanding. "Keep us posted on how that goes. You know we're in your corner, 'kay?" Lana affirms.

You can do it, Teegan. You have so many people behind you. You're not facing the scary things alone. Stop avoiding.

———

"I've decided I'm not coming back to Arrow staff next year," I say.

My knee is bouncing manically under the table as Kent and Rachel sit across from me. I asked them to meet me before staff meeting, and thankfully a neighbor was able to watch the twins so they could both be present. I downed half of my latte from Raelynn's in thirty seconds. My esophagus might have second-degree burns, but my bloodstream was fully caffeinated and sugared before making this declaration.

Their expressions are a mix of shock and sadness. As tempted as I am to mentally fly away from their reactions, I take a deep breath and brace myself to face their response.

"What are you going to do next?" Rachel asks. Her eyes look sad, but her voice sounds genuinely interested.

"I'm going to get my teaching license and apply for special education positions," I say, forcing confidence into my answer. Because I *feel* entirely confident about this decision—just terrified to speak it out loud to the people sitting in front of me.

"You're going to be an amazing teacher," Rachel responds, eyes soft.

"I . . . I am?" I ask, caught off guard by her affirmation.

Rachel gives a small laugh. "Of course you are!"

"You'll be incredible at anything you decide to do," Kent adds. "And anyone who has any involvement in your life will be blessed for it."

I sit in stunned silence, which is far from my usual self, at least in their experience.

Kent speaks again. "Don't misunderstand us—we're sad to have you leave staff because you're a joy to work with. You've made all of us better the past few years, and the impact you've had on students could never be measured."

"Yes, of course, we're devastated that you won't be back next year," Rachel jumps back in. "To be totally honest, I'll probably go home and cry this afternoon. But that's only because we love you, Teegan. We've loved having you here, and we'll miss you so much. But I trust your discernment to follow where God is leading you. Even if that's away from here."

"So, you're not disappointed in me for pursuing something different?" I timidly ask.

"Goodness, no!" Rachel exclaims. "We know you're going to change lives for the better regardless of your vocation. And we'll be cheering you on, but please keep in touch, okay?"

I blow out a long, relieved breath. "You guys are the best. Thanks for being supportive and for inviting me on staff in the first place. I've learned so much from you over the years. Not to mention, I've personally grown in ways I never would have otherwise."

"Do you want to tell the rest of the staff team today, or would you like to wait a while?" Kent asks.

"Let's rip the Band-Aid off," I reply, and we all laugh. It feels good to laugh when I came into this conversation prepared to . . . well, not laugh.

Gina, Lucas, and Connor are equally as supportive and sentimental when I share my plans at staff meeting. I know that telling all the students in my small groups will be more difficult conversations, but the reassuring responses thus far are boosting my confidence.

"So, who's going to plan social events and After Parties now?" Connor asks.

Gina and Lucas simultaneously yell, "Not it!"

They point to Connor, who groans dramatically.

———

After my Bible study with the AOPis that night, I drive to Brooks' apartment. I didn't tell the girls about my looming departure because I've had enough Band-Aid ripping pain for one day.

It's time for a little balm.

I knock firmly on the door, but there's no answer. Glancing down in the parking lot, I see Brooks' car, so he must be here—unless someone picked him up to go somewhere. Even though it's 9:00 p.m., that seems a little early for him to be in bed.

Knock knock

Seconds later, I hear footsteps inside, and the door opens. It's casual, tousled Brooks answering, and I resist the urge to immediately kiss him.

"Sorry, I had ear buds in while I was grading tests. Helps me stay in the zone," he says. Brooks does *not* resist the urge to immediately kiss me, pulling me to him.

I'm milliseconds away from losing myself in his lips and forgetting my whole purpose for coming. I abruptly jerk away, earning a disappointed whine from Brooks.

"Wait, I came here because I need your help with something," I say with a laugh. He motions me inside and closes the door behind me. I hold up my diploma and add, "I brought this."

Brooks quirks an eyebrow. "Okay? Did you think I didn't believe that you legitimately graduated from Townsend?"

"I brought it in case I need it to apply for my teaching license," I explain with a smirk.

He stills at my words. "You decided? For sure?"

I nod, and Brooks picks me up to twirl me around. "Sneaks, this is incredible. You're going to be incredible. I mean, I know you already were incredible on staff here. And I still would have been excited for you if you had decided that's where you were still supposed to be. But, you know, this is also incredible."

After laughing at his overuse of the word "incredible," I bite my lip to make myself be serious again. "For the record, I'm not deciding this because of you. Well, seeing your passion for your students and being reminded of the impact educators have on kids was a factor. But I'm not choosing this because you want to go back to KCMO someday. After all the praying and thinking and working through that guided journal, the tug toward teaching feels so strong that I know it has to be where God is leading me. And I'm excited to pursue it."

Throughout my speech, Brooks' smile has slowly grown. He's still grinning when his lips meet mine again, but the playfulness quickly vanishes. I break apart and push against his chest, his back hitting the wall. Holding up my diploma again, I say, "Stop distracting me with your lips and help me start this application."

Brooks chuckles and takes my hand to pull me over to the kitchen table. "Okay, but you're not going to need your physical diploma for that. We'll need to order a digital copy of your transcripts."

As he waits for the laptop to power on, he asks, "So, have you told your Arrow leaders about your decision?"

I nod. "I told them over coffee this morning. And the rest of the staff at our meeting."

Brooks whistles. "Wow, less than twenty-four hours after returning from facing your dad, and you're plowing right through another difficult conversation. I'm impressed."

I know he's not being facetious because he, of all people, understands how truly monumental it is for me to tackle these conversations. How much easier it would be to keep avoiding, keep escaping by any means possible.

Brooks looks up from the laptop to meet my eyes when I reach over to lace my fingers through his.

"Us against the pain, right?" I murmur.

He pulls my hand up to meet his lips, pressing a kiss to my knuckles, never breaking eye contact. Brooks leans forward to rest his forehead against mine, then whispers a kiss on my cheek.

"Us. Everything. Always."

Epilogue

Twelve weeks later . . .

Spring sunshine warms my face. A gentle breeze carries the chill from the lake's surface over my skin. My teal dress ruffles with the breath of wind, and I press closer to Brooks' side as we walk hand in hand.

"Are you cold?" he asks, concern lacing his tone. "I can find a jacket for you somewhere. I want you to be comfortable and not cold."

I narrow my eyes at him. He's always considerate, but there's a panic to his question that seems disproportionate to the issue of me being slightly chilly. "I'm fine!" I assure him. He falls silent as we continue walking toward his mom's bench.

He's acting weird, but I suppose that's to be expected, given our destination. Brooks has come a long way in being able to openly talk about his mom without running away from the pain of the memories. We've *both* come a long way in not running away. Having someone else running into the pain with you really does make all the difference.

When we reach the bench and tree, we're quiet for a few seconds.

"Is there something significant about today in your memories with your mom?" I ask, squeezing Brooks' hand in encouragement.

He pivots to face me. "There isn't a significant *past* memory, but I want her here in some way for a *new* significant memory." The breeze blows a strand of hair across my face, and Brooks reaches up to tuck it behind my ear. His fingers linger on my skin, warming me despite the chill. He pulls me down to sit on the bench with him, but angles his body to face me rather than the lake.

Taking my hands in his, he fidgets with my fingers as he speaks. "Teegan, I've told you before, but I'm going to tell you again. You're my best friend. You've made me better in more ways than I could ever count. Just being here today, sitting on this bench—you've helped me get here. And I want you with me for every 'here' I need to get to. I want to be with you for every 'there' you need to reach."

Understanding starts to dawn on me, and my breath comes faster with each word he says.

"I didn't deserve to ever have another chance to be with you, Sneaks. But God was gracious and kind, and he brought me back into your life. And you were gracious and kind, and you allowed me to stay. I'd like to stay forever, if you'll have me."

Brooks slips down to one knee in front of me, tears and intensity mixing with the joy in his eyes. He lets go of my hands to reach into his pocket, and my hands immediately fly to press against my heart.

"I love you. Every version of me has loved every version of you, *will* love every version of you. I never, ever want to be apart from you again, Teegan Jones. Will you marry me?" His voice trembles along with his hands as he holds up a velvet box. The rose gold ring inside glitters with an intricate pattern of diamonds. The glittery effect is probably amplified by the tears blurring my vision.

"Yes! Yes! Yes!" I exclaim, throwing myself at Brooks. My exuberance catches him off balance, and he tips backward on the ground. Both laughing, he steadies me on his leg and crashes his lips to mine. The heat of this kiss is like a soldering iron, melding us together. Never to come apart again.

Until Brooks pulls away from the kiss. I attempt to chase his lips, but he pushes me back with a laugh. "Hold on a second," he says, guiding me back to the bench. Then he slips the ring onto my shaking finger. "I gotta make this official," he adds with a sly grin.

"And I have one more thing," he says, pulling a paper bag out from under the bench. "Thank goodness no one came along and stole this."

He pulls a shoe box out of the bag and opens it, just like the ring box. Inside is the pair of white Dunk Lows with the pink swoosh he had sent me for my birthday.

"I was hoping you might wear these to walk down the aisle, Sneaks," he says, grinning widely. "I'm hoping we might rekindle some old traditions along with the new ones."

I reach forward to cup his face in my hands. "Everything with you. I love you, Brooks Murphy."

———

"Congratulations!" a crowd of voices screams as we walk through the door of my mom's house. There's a huge "You're Engaged!" banner hanging on the wall and people filling every available inch of space.

I scream and bounce up and down with excitement, jumping back into Brooks' arms. "You planned a party?!" I yell at him over the cheering voices.

"We're talking Team Breegan here—of course, there's a party!" he replies with a grin.

My mom rushes to wrap her arms around me. After squeezing her back, I clap my hands and grin as I scan the faces. Our families are here, including Sonya's kids and grandchildren. Everyone from our church small group stands together holding "Team Breegan" signs (except for Will's "Teeks" sign). I see Rylen and Brody, Brooks' teammates from college, as well as some of his teaching colleagues. I take in a smiling Bailey, all of the Arrow staff, and several students from my Bible studies. My elation turns to tears of joy when I see Lana and Mateo standing by Amaya.

Throwing my arms around my Beefs, I give in to the swell of emotions. "Lana! What are you doing here?! You have your graduation in one week! You don't have time to be here!"

"Yeah, right, like I was going to miss my best friend's engagement party over some silly graduation ceremony," Lana says in my ear, still crushing me in a group hug along with Amaya. "Besides, Mateo has been dying to see Brooks again," she adds in a teasing tone.

I see Mateo giving Brooks a bro hug when I finally pull back. A happy giggle escapes at the sight.

"Beefs for life," Amaya says, squeezing my arm. "For *all* of life."

After another long hug, I make the rounds to talk (and happily squeal) with everyone who came to celebrate with us. I show off the ring, and Brooks and I take turns sharing the proposal story. I don't think there's a dry eye in the room when Brooks explains why he chose the location of the proposal. But he doesn't shy away from the emotion, bittersweet as it is. I wrap my arms around him, holding space for grief together, even amid the elation of today.

Because this is just one of many moments when our happiness will be tinged with sorrow. When joy will be shaded with heartache. When hope will be stained with doubt. When disappointment will be streaked with levity.

It's us against everything, together.

Always.

BONUS

Want to read about Teegan and Brooks' wedding?
Check out the bonus epilogue:

Click here
Or scan here:

Enjoy the conclusion to The Beefs' journey by reading Amaya's story next in *Love and Other Distractions.*
Click here or scan the code:

ACKNOWLEDGMENTS

Dear Reader, you're the first person I want to acknowledge and thank. Because you're here reading these words, I'm living out a dream I was afraid to admit that I had in my heart. "Thank you" is not enough . . . but, thank you.

Kyle, get used to being in my acknowledgments. Every book I write is a piece of me, which means it's also a piece of you. Thank you for your insight early in my outlining process that helped me make this story not only better, but even more restorative. My heart feels more whole after writing this book, so thank you for pushing me to write it in this specific way. Thank you for pushing me to write, period.

Hannah, my alpha forever (*awoooo*). Your perspective helps my writing process more than you probably understand, and bb Teegan and Brooks thank you for it. But even more than that, I'm so thankful for your friendship, which is now not only in the digital form of endless voice memos and GIFs, but also for real life. Sassy Hannah and Tracy forever.

Krystal, thank you for not only being an amazing beta reader but also the PA I did not know I needed. All of the spreadsheet-y organized things you do blow my mind and make me look better as an author. You're giving me more time to focus on writing, which is what I truly love. Five stars to you.

Paris, I'm grateful to have your perspective as a beta reader AND as a Bookstagram sounding board. And design expert. And all-around amazing book friend. This has nothing to do with *Love and Other Chances*, but THANK YOU for the gorgeous character art of Clark and Clara for *Saved by Noel*. You're so talented and generous and wonderful in all the ways.

Jen, my dear friend, thank you for letting me pick your Enneagram 7 brain. You helped me really dive deep into how Teegan's mind and heart would function on the inside, not just the outward displayed behaviors. You make life more fun for everyone, but more importantly, you make us all feel so LOVED. I'm so blessed to get to be part of your circle.

Laura Williams—hugs. You'll know why you're here.

To my line editor, Olivia at Winston Editorial, and my proofreader, Diana at Paper Plane Prose—thank you for polishing up my manuscript to get everything flowing nicely.

Parker, thanks for taking all my lofty cover visions and turning them into real art. I'm amazed at how you take my rambling ideas and create something solid and beautiful each time!

A huge thank you to Christin at Monarch Books & Gifts for championing me as an author and hosting my first two book launch events (and planning the next!). Your support means so much, and I'm beyond grateful for your friendship (and your cozy bookstore!!).

To my BEEFS group—thanks for being so much more than a hype squad or street team. I really, truly, honestly love connecting with you. You've made my author journey so fun and fulfilling. I still have a hard time accepting that there are "strangers on the internet" who would love my books so much or care about me enough to want to spend their time hyping me up. You fill my cup.

Jesus, in my acknowledgments for *Love and Other Goals*, I said that I was embracing the fullness of how You had wired me by writing these books. I didn't even understand at the time how You were using these books to show me *Your* love. To heal. To open new doors. Thank You for always having deeper, fuller, better plans than mine.

Also by Tracy Baack

Love and Other . . . Series:

Love and Other Goals
Love and Other Chances
Love and Other Distractions

Christmas in Noel Series:

Saved by Noel
Joy to Noel

Kansas City Crowns Series:

Home Safe
Run Home

Find them here:

Click here or scan the QR code:

About the Author

Tracy Baack connects with readers through relatable romance. She enjoys writing character-driven contemporary romance novels with so much character depth and development, you just might think they're real people. Her books are always closed-door but full of heart-melting swoon, and they end happily ever after (after a little dose of angst).

Tracy lives with her husband and four children in the suburbs of Kansas City, Kansas, where she loves supporting indie bookstores. Her primary love language is sending the perfect GIF for any moment.

Tracy is the author of *Love and Other Goals, Love and Other Chances, Love and Other Distractions, Home Safe, Run Home, Saved by Noel,* and *Joy to Noel* (with more on the way because she just might be a writing addict).

Connect with Tracy on Instagram at @authortracybaack or through her website www.tracybaack.com.